THE WORMWORLD SAGA

The Shelter of Hope

Daniel Lieske

CARACAL™

ISBN: 978-1-5493-0294-7

Library of Congress Control Number: 2018941617

www.lionforge.com

The Wormworld Saga, Volume 2, The Shelter of Hope, published 2018 by The Lion Forge, LLC. © 2018
Daniel Lieske/TOKYOPOP GmbH. All rights reserved. LION FORGE™, CARACAL™ and the associated
distinctive designs are trademarks of The Lion Forge, LLC. No similarity between any of the names,
characters, persons, and/or institutions in this book with those of any living or dead person or institution
is intended and any such similarity which may exist is purely coincidental. Printed in China.

10 9 8 7 6 5 4 3 2 1

Contents

Chapter 1
The Shelter of Hope

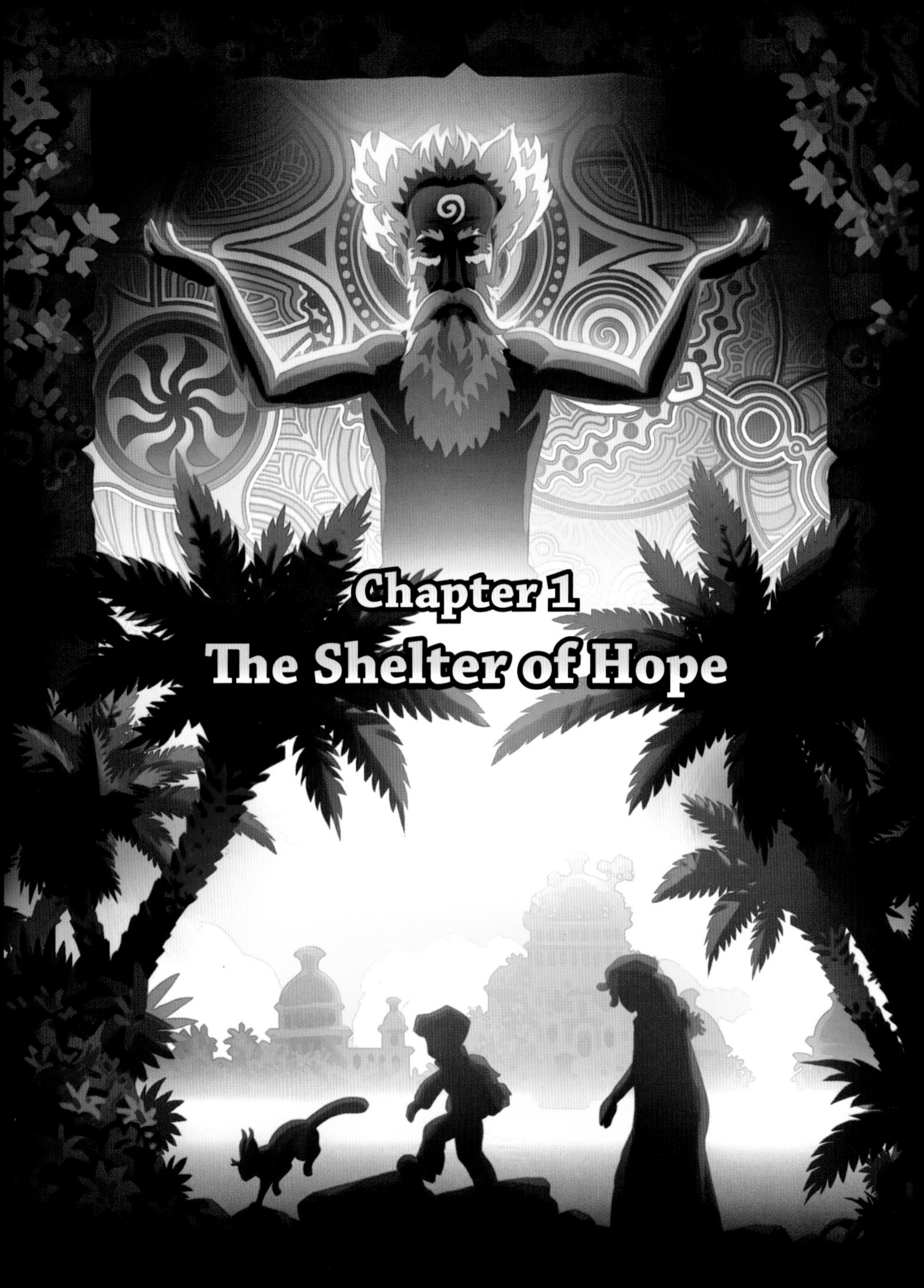

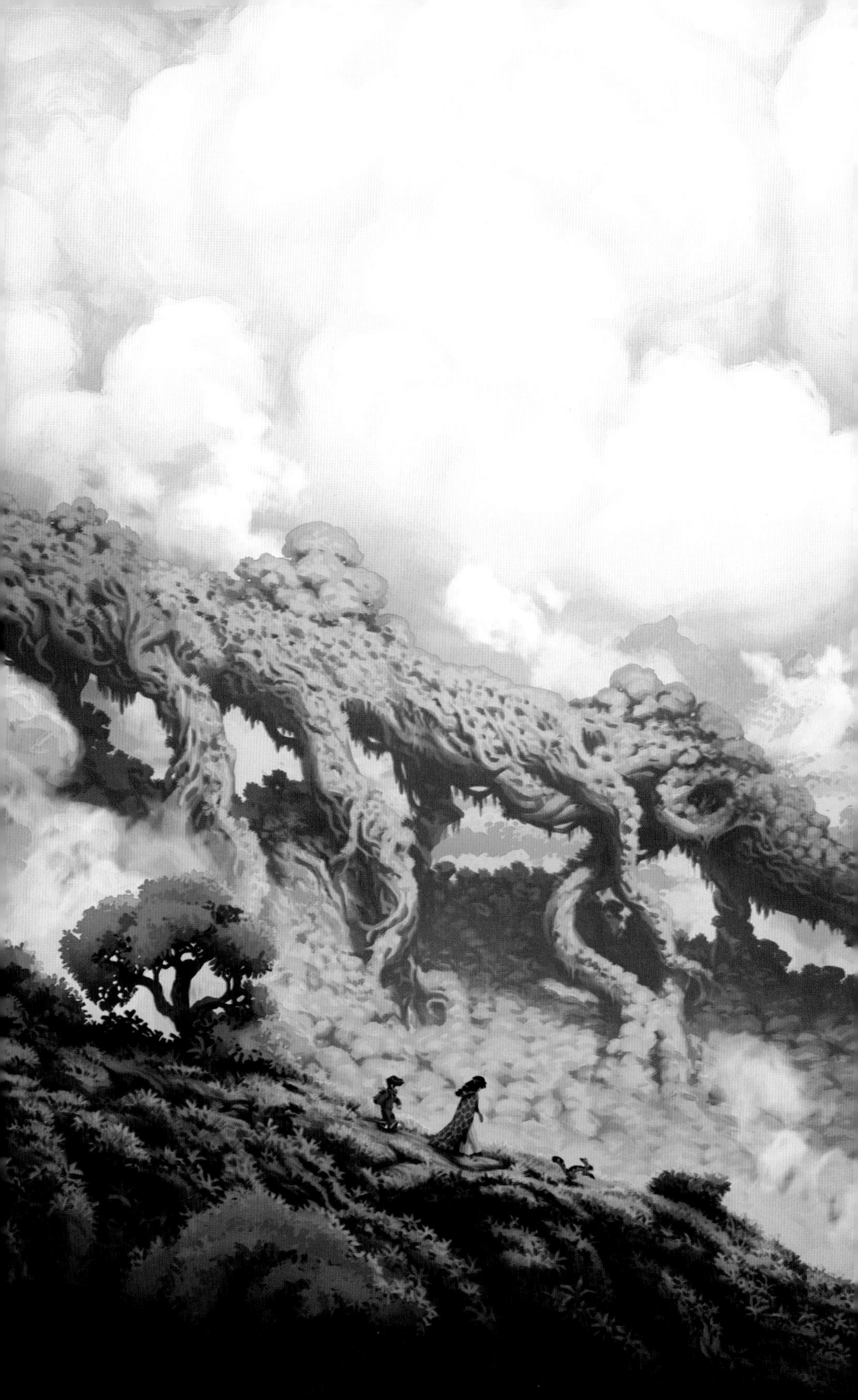

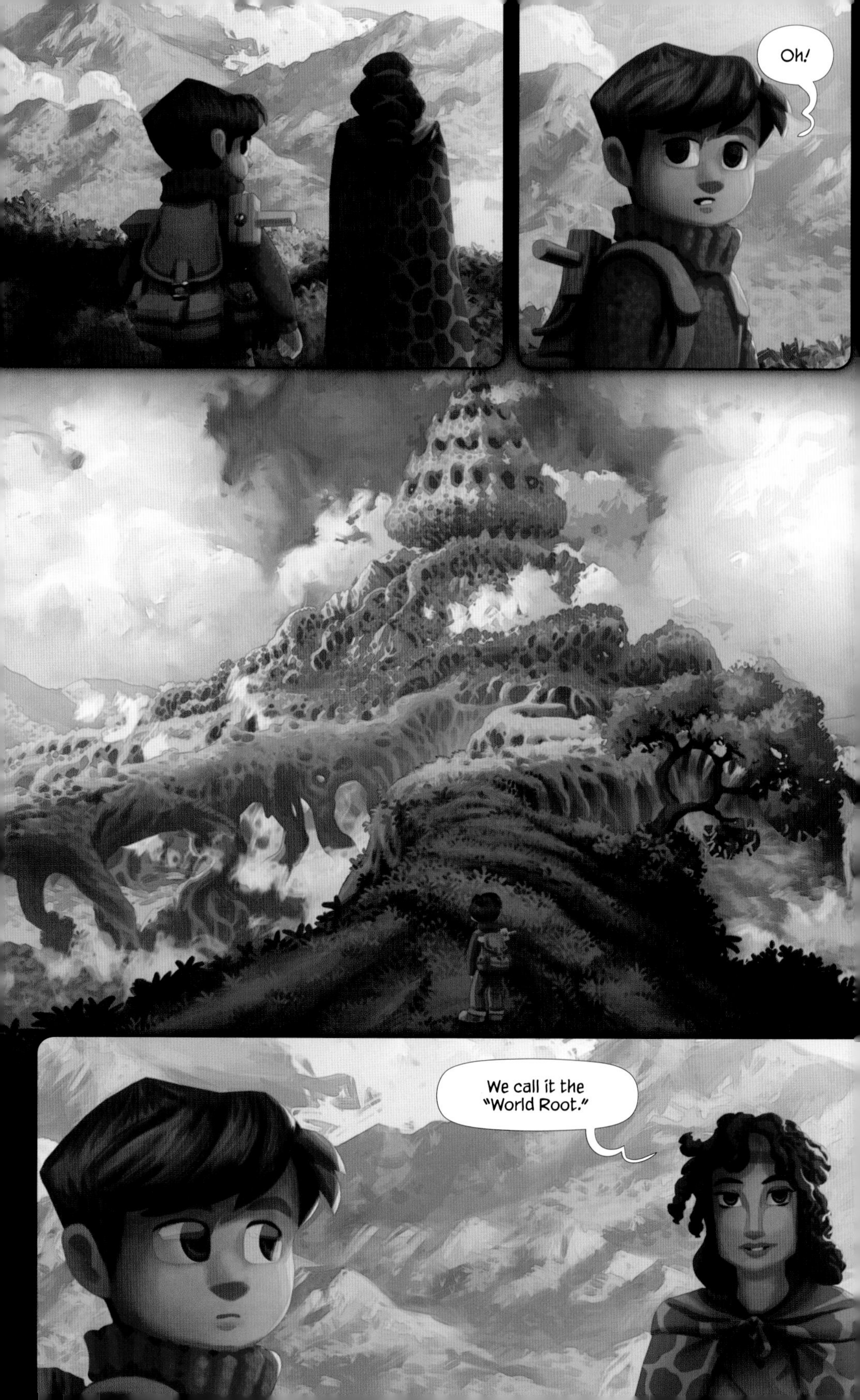
Oh!
We call it the "World Root."

It's our most sacred place. The shrine that the god Jiiva erected himself.
It's the source of all the gifts he bestows upon us.
The place where he provides us our most valuable crystals...
...and where the River of Life originates.
And, of course, it's where I found **you**.
...and where it's teeming with monsters...
Come! We're nearly there!

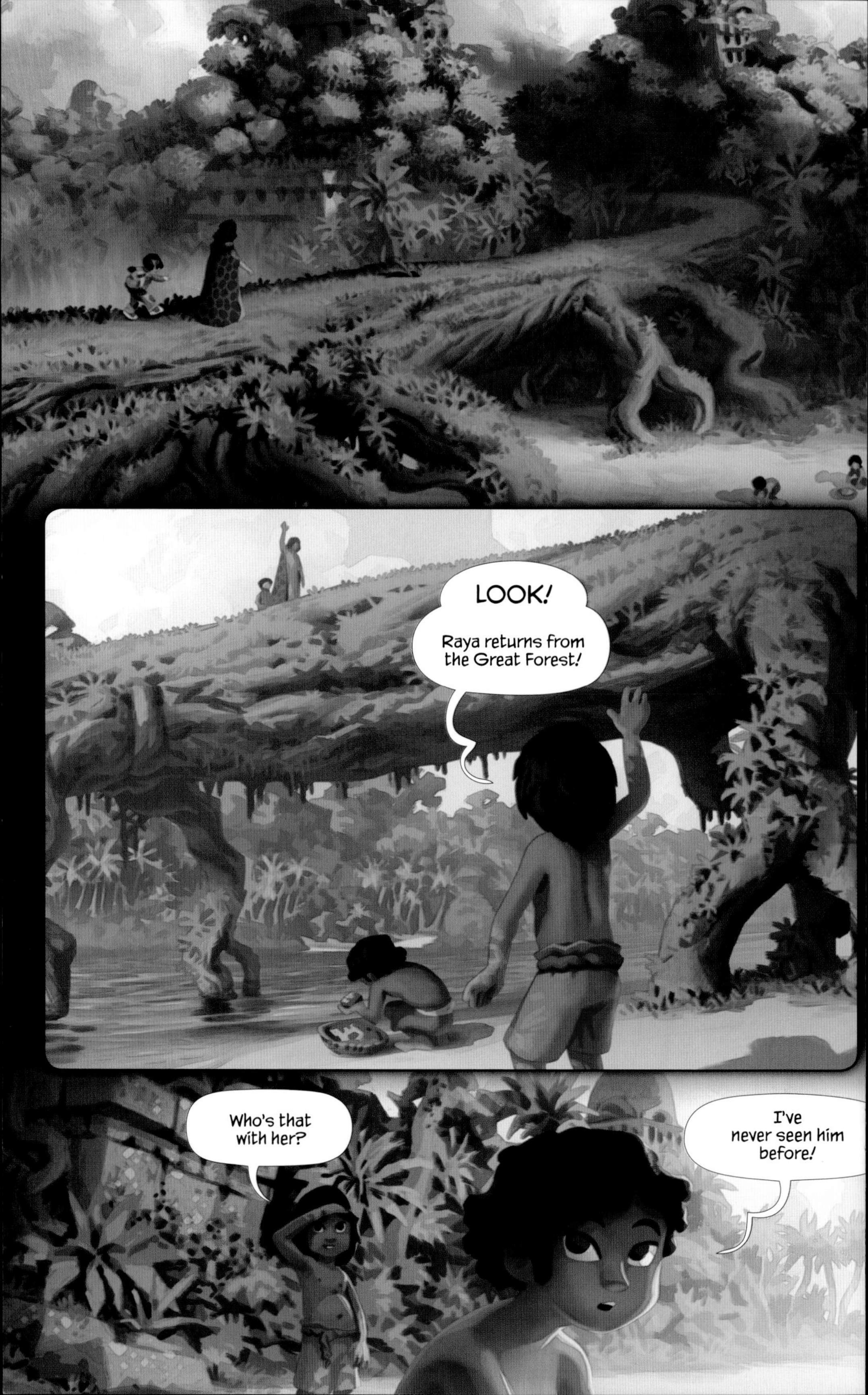
LOOK!
Raya returns from the Great Forest!
Who's that with her?
I've never seen him before!

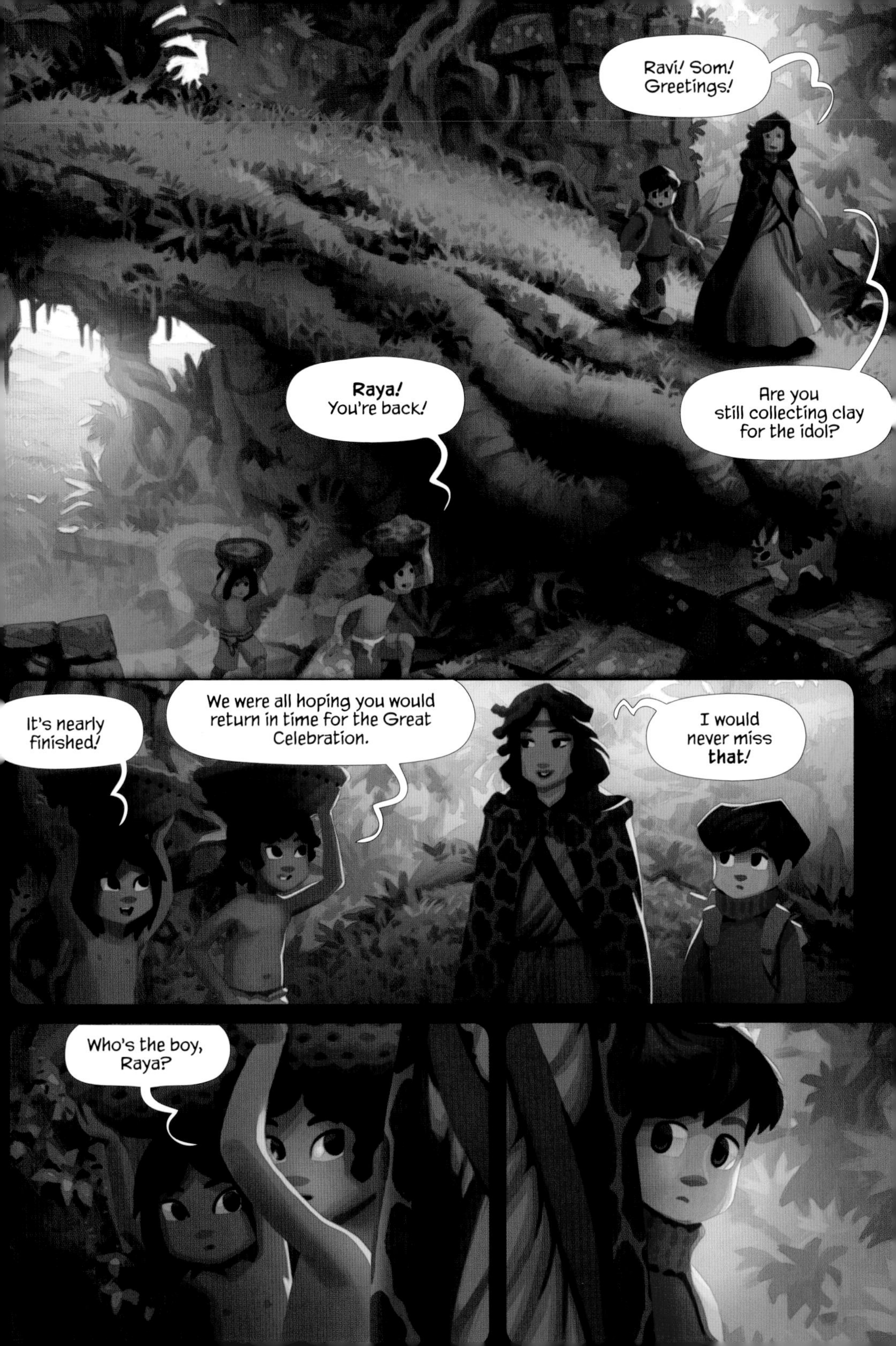
Ravi! Som!
Greetings!
Raya!
You're back!
Are you still collecting clay for the idol?
It's nearly finished!
We were all hoping you would return in time for the Great Celebration.
I would never miss **that**!
Who's the boy, Raya?

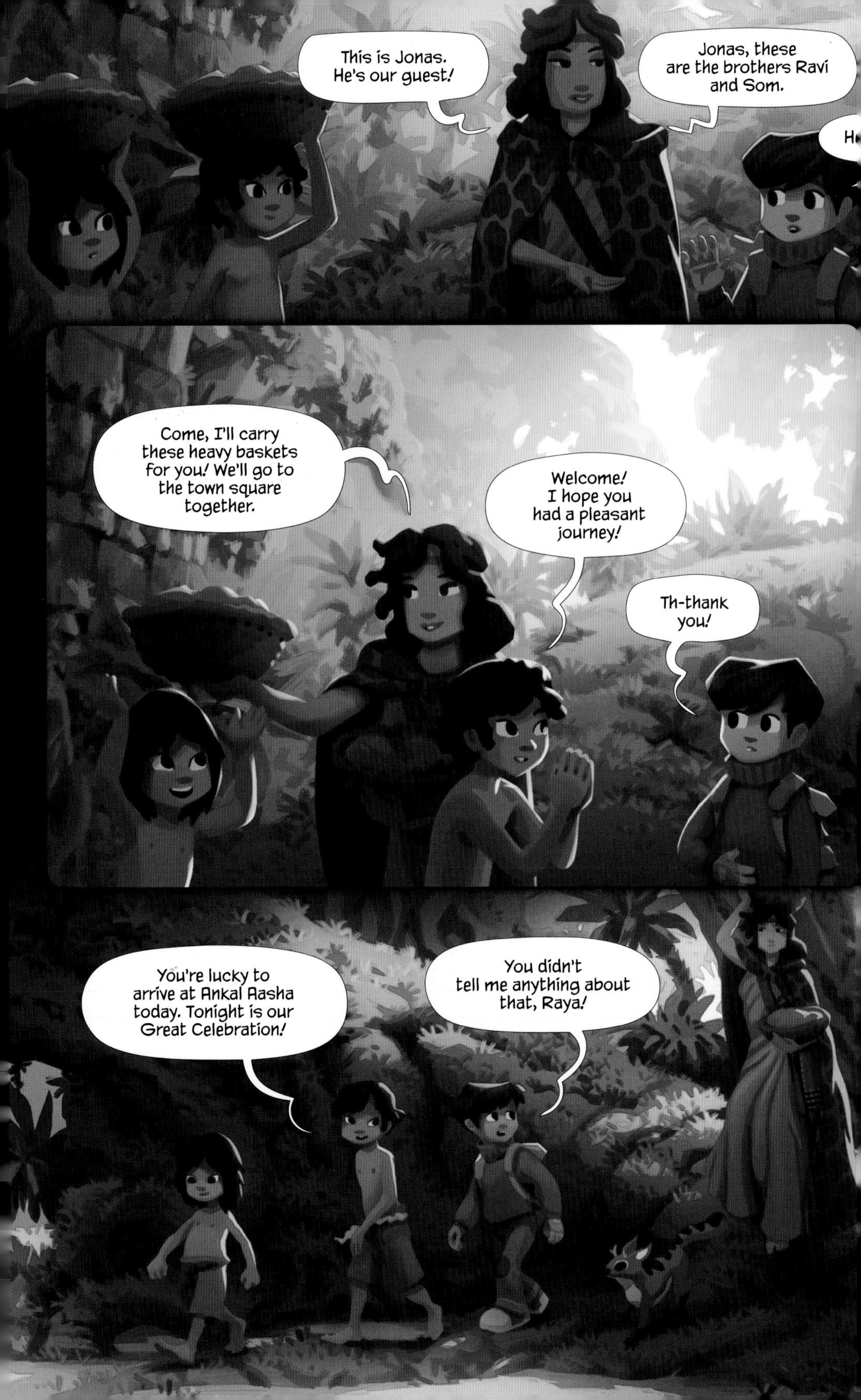
This is Jonas. He's our guest!
Jonas, these are the brothers Ravi and Som.
Come, I'll carry these heavy baskets for you! We'll go to the town square together.
Welcome! I hope you had a pleasant journey!
Th-thank you!
You're lucky to arrive at Ankal Aasha today. Tonight is our Great Celebration!
You didn't tell me anything about that, Raya!

Go ahead! Tell Jonas what it's all about, Som.
With the Great Celebration, we thank Jiiva for giving us a new home and providing for us.
A new home?
We used to live in Kingspeak, but...bad things happened there. So our family came here.
Life has been better here. **Much** better.
Did you have to flee from home, too?
Well...
Sort of...
Hey! Is that a **sword**?
Can I **hold** it for a moment?

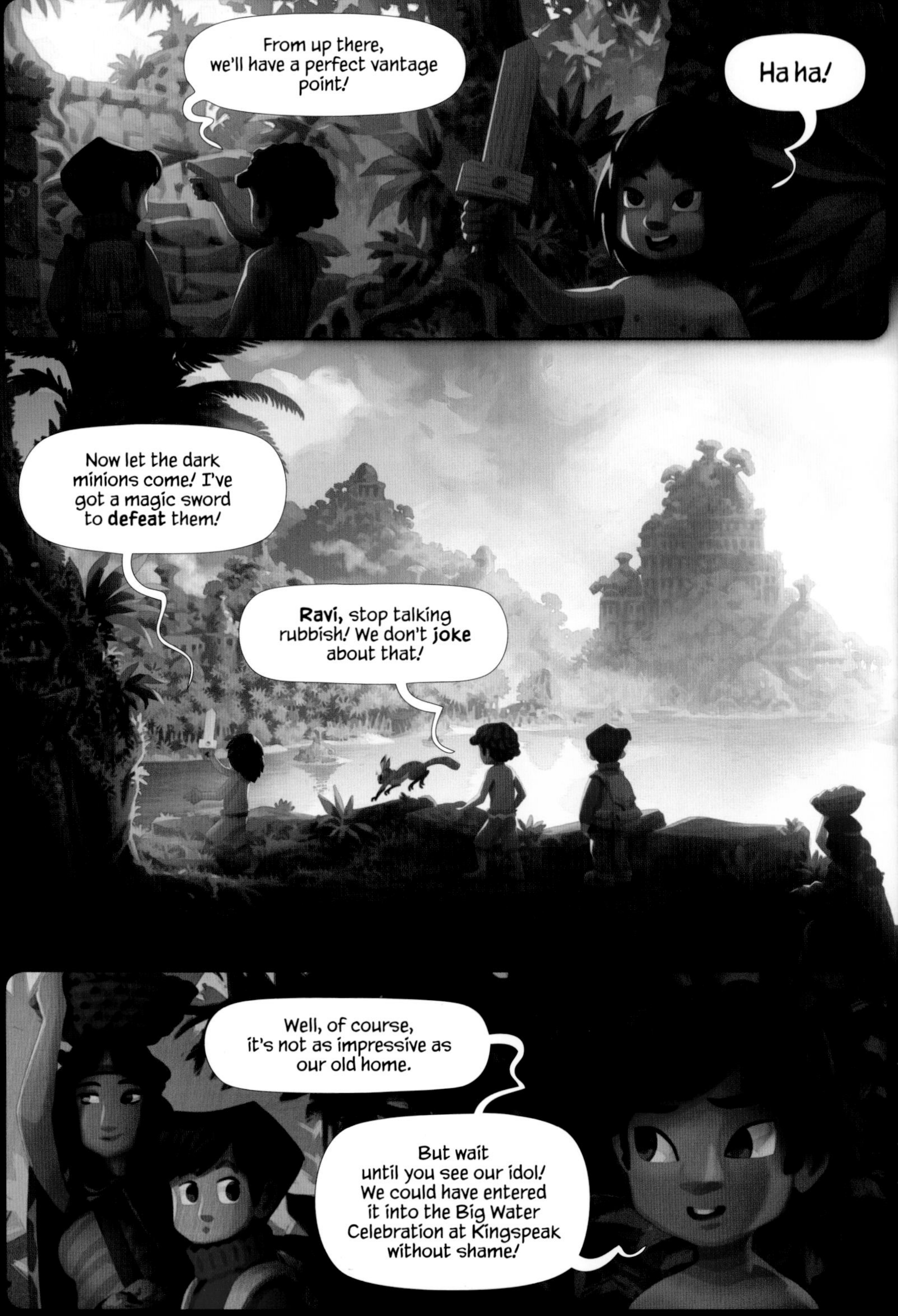
From up there, we'll have a perfect vantage point!
Ha ha!
Now let the dark minions come! I've got a magic sword to **defeat** them!
Ravi, stop talking rubbish! We don't **joke** about that!
Well, of course, it's not as impressive as our old home.
But wait until you see our idol! We could have entered it into the Big Water Celebration at Kingspeak without shame!

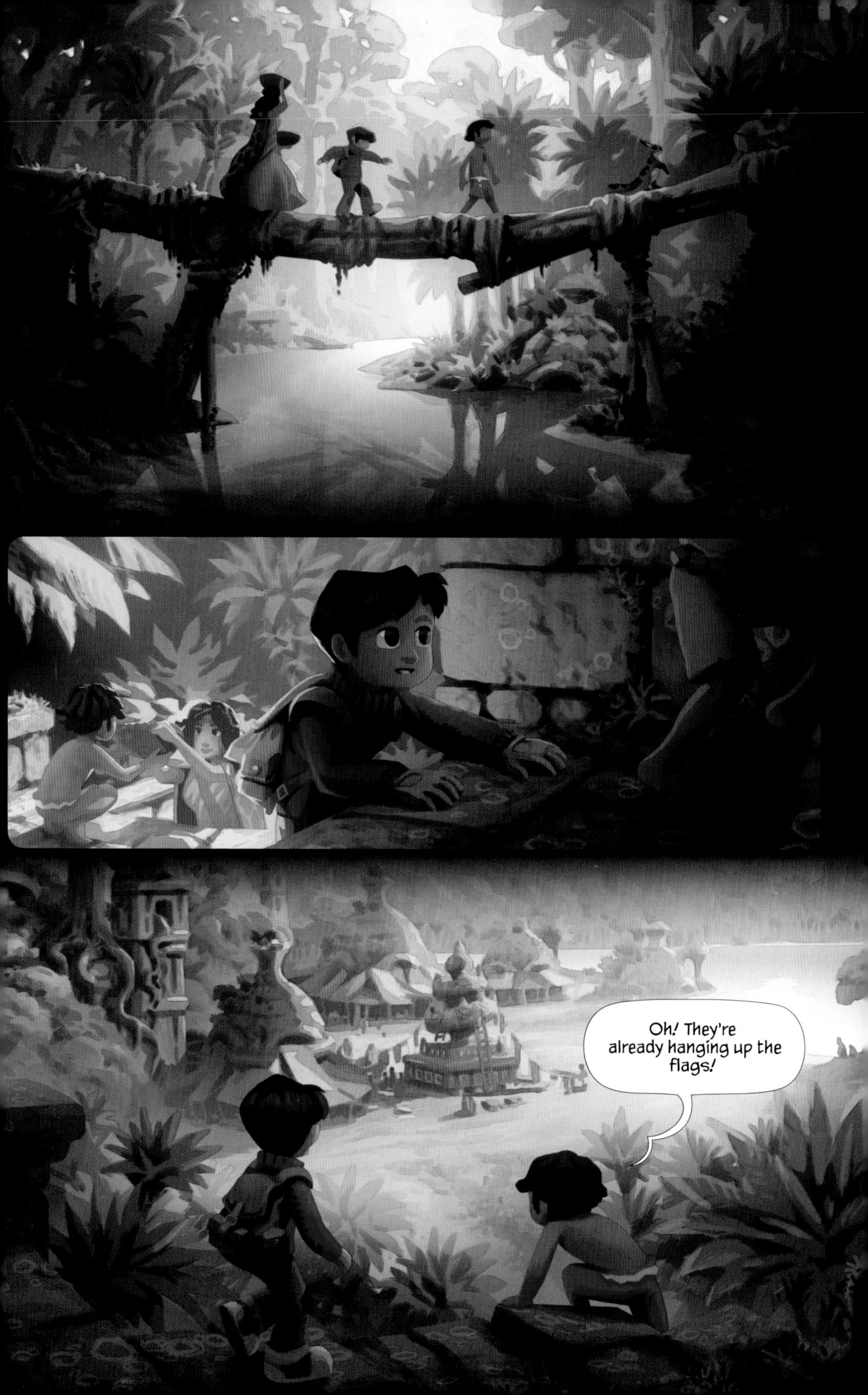
Oh! They're already hanging up the flags!

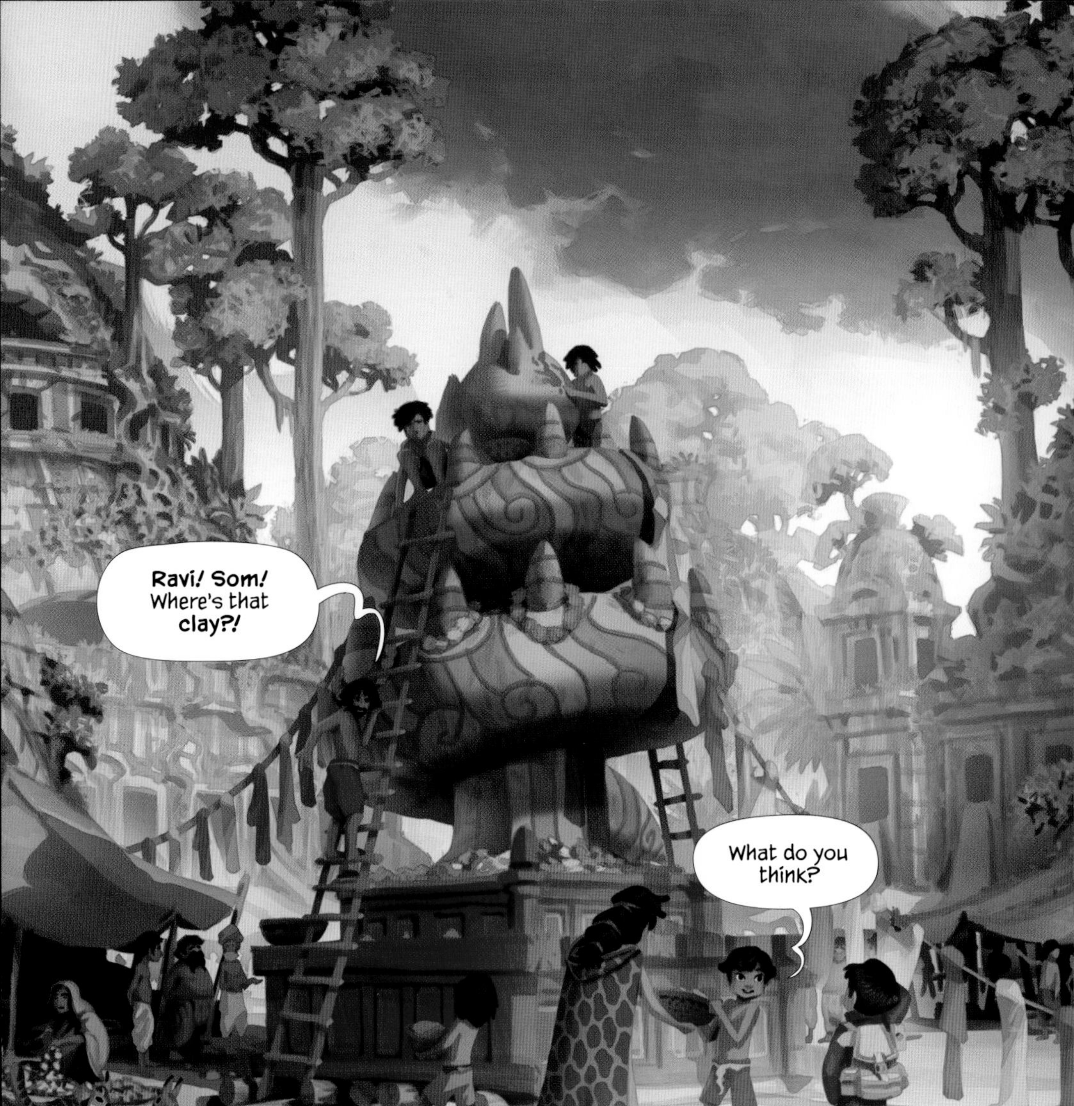
Ravi! Som! Where's that clay?!
What do you think?

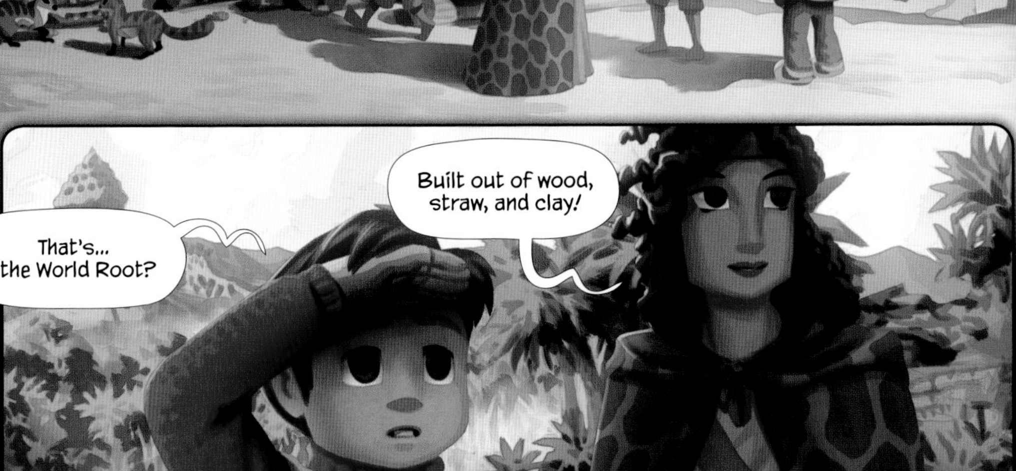
That's... the World Root?
Built out of wood, straw, and clay!

We hold the Great Celebration at the end of each cycle. The idol is built from scratch each and every time. Everyone contributes to it.
During the ceremony tonight, we will sacrifice the idol to the River of Life.
Through this, we thank Jiiva for all that he gives us.
It's odd that your god looks like some sort of **mushroom**.
We believe that this is only his temporary form.
Jiiva lies in a deep sleep.
The form in which he will reincarnate is debated.

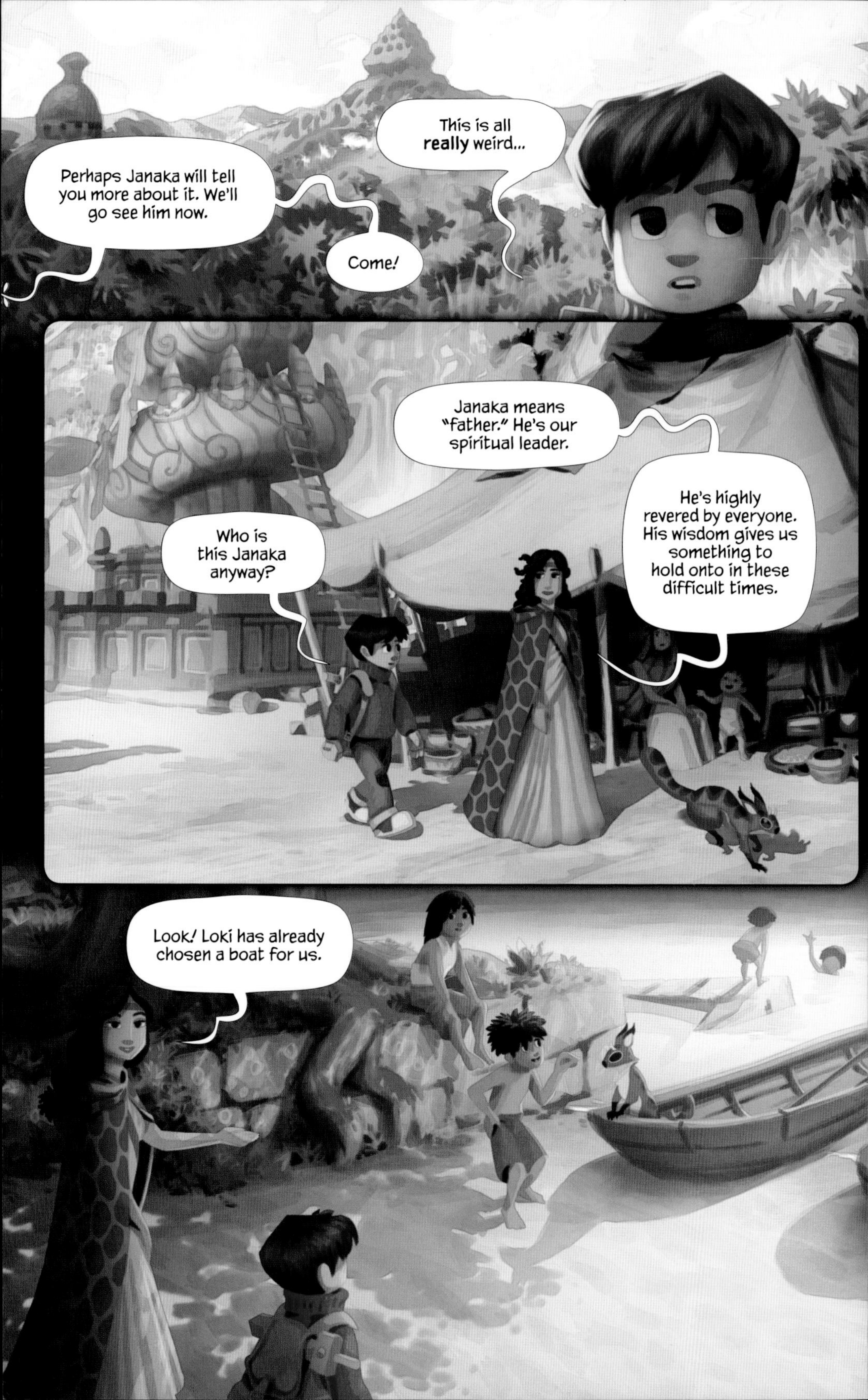

Perhaps Janaka will tell you more about it. We'll go see him now.
Come!
This is all **really** weird...
Who is this Janaka anyway?
Janaka means "father." He's our spiritual leader.
He's highly revered by everyone. His wisdom gives us something to hold onto in these difficult times.
Look! Loki has already chosen a boat for us.

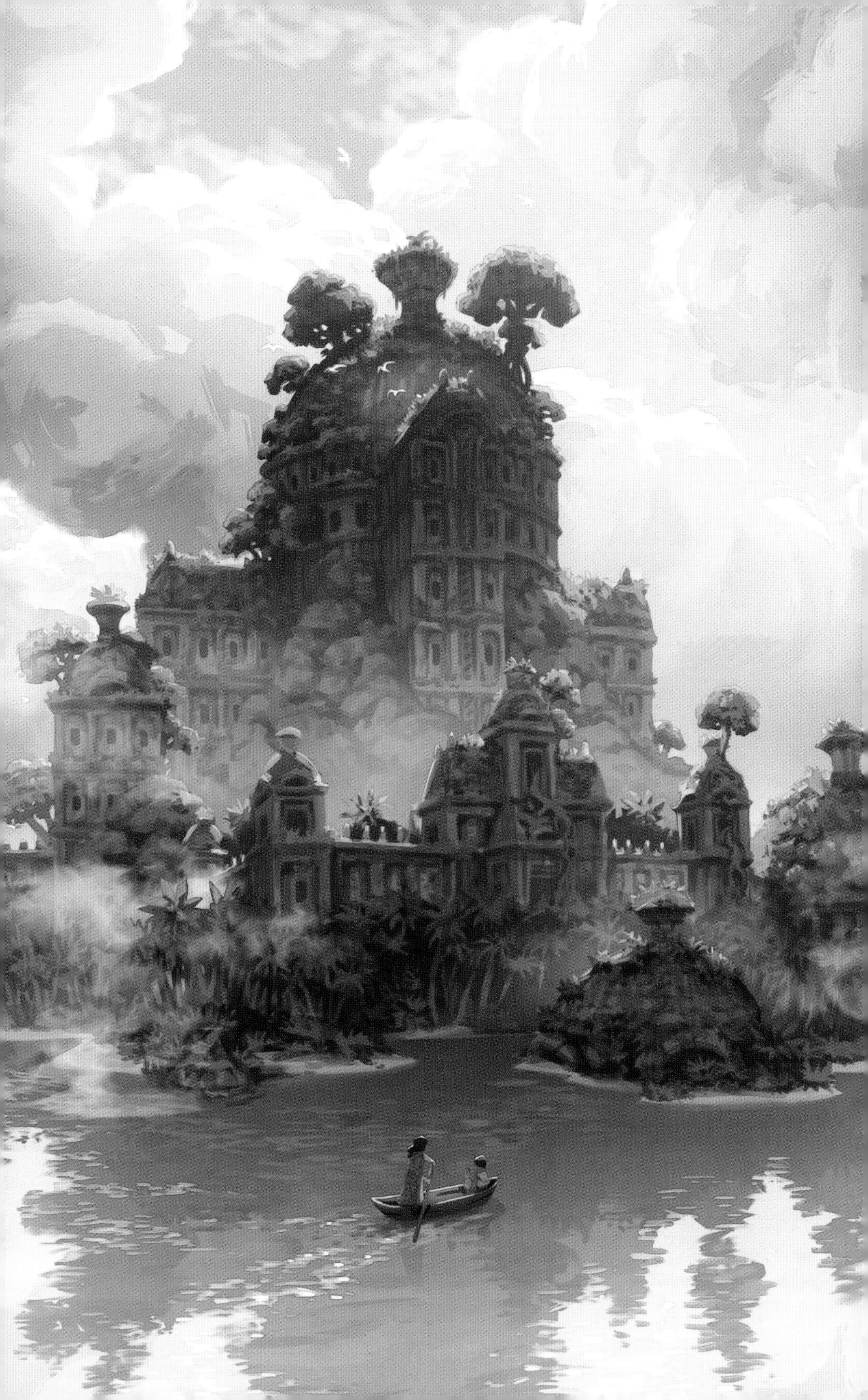

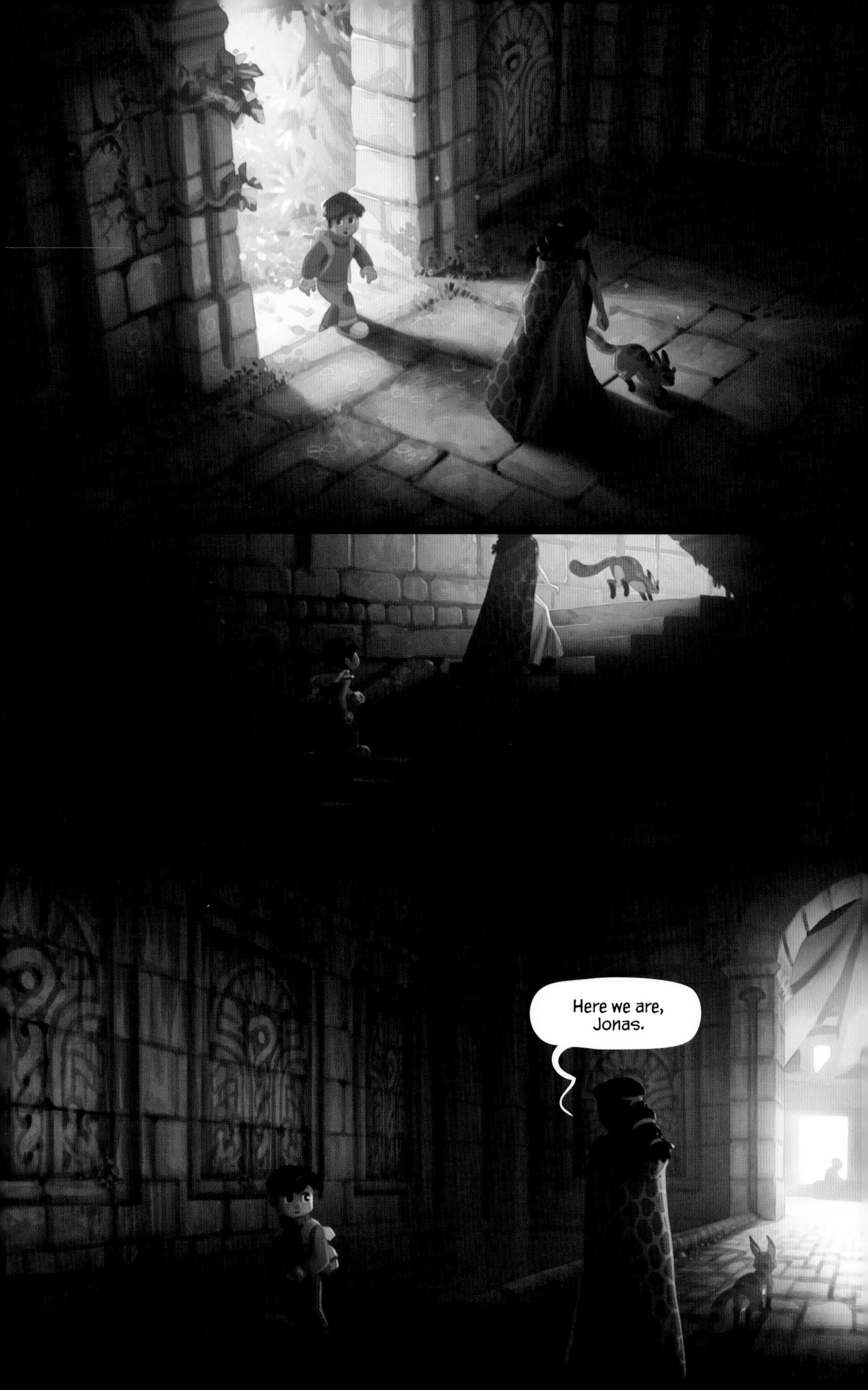
Here we are, Jonas.

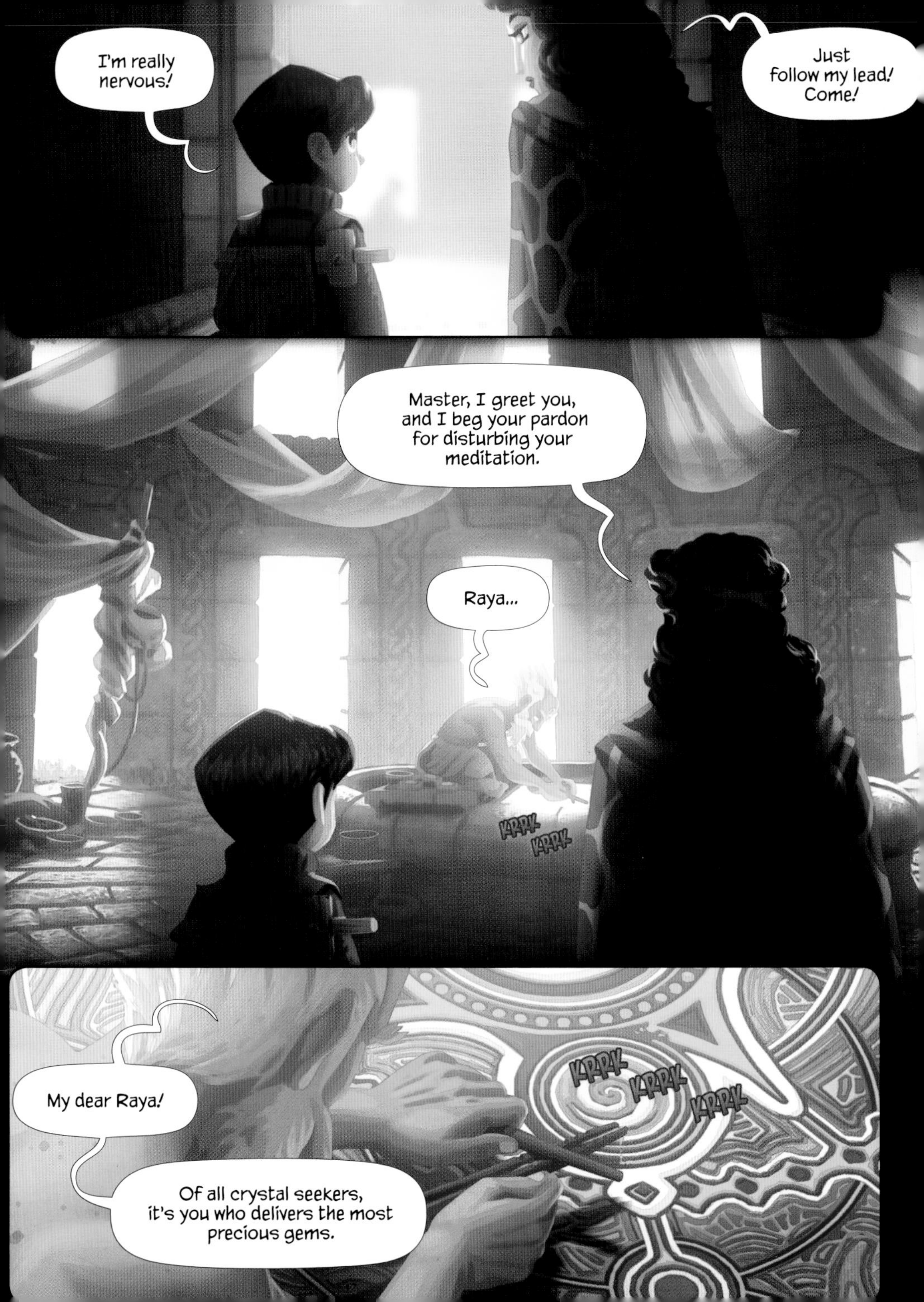
I'm really nervous!
Just follow my lead! Come!
Master, I greet you, and I beg your pardon for disturbing your meditation.
Raya...
KRRK
KRRK
My dear Raya!
Of all crystal seekers, it's you who delivers the most precious gems.
KRRK
KRRK
KRRK

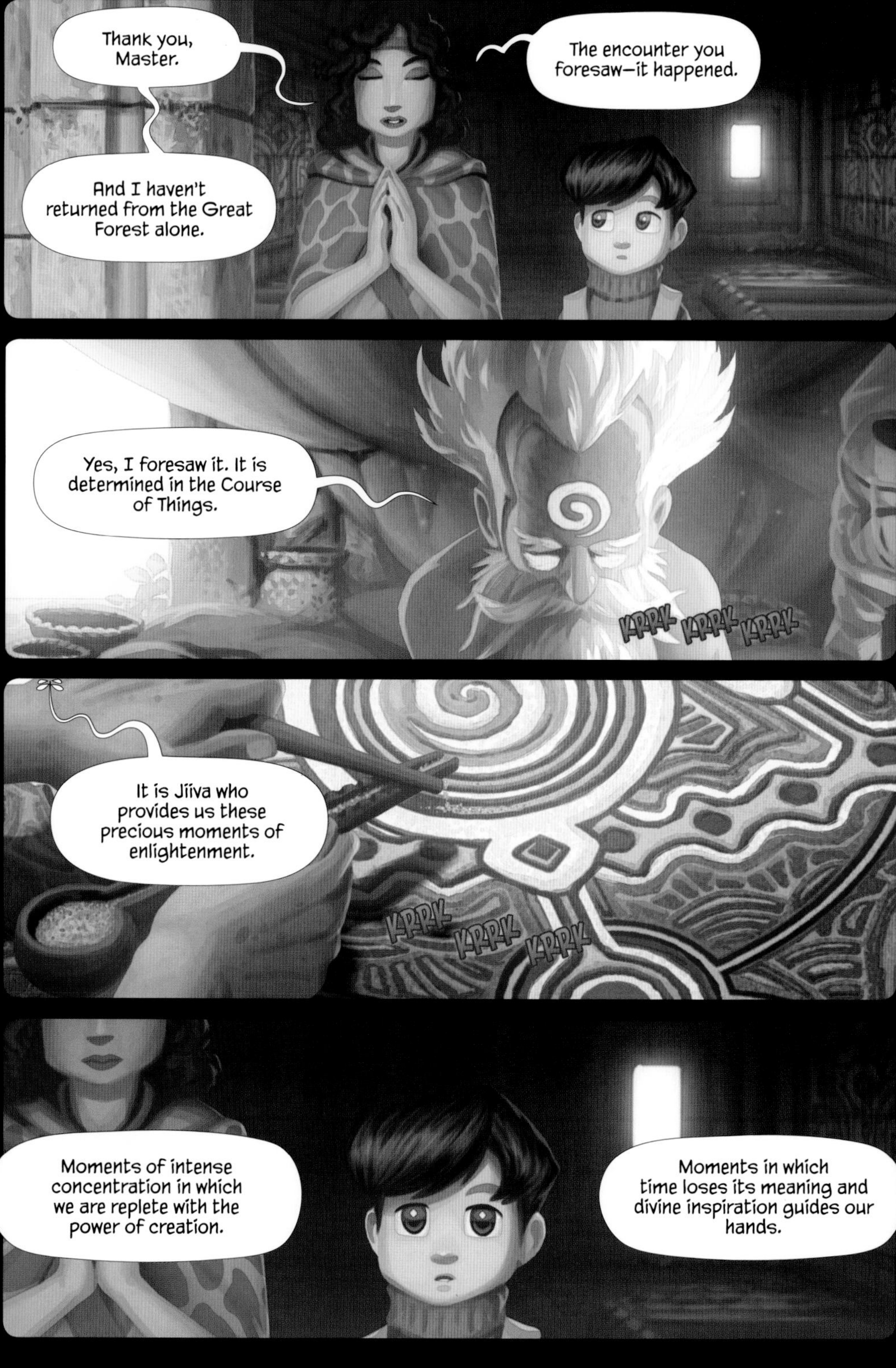

Thank you, Master.
The encounter you foresaw—it happened.
And I haven't returned from the Great Forest alone.
Yes, I foresaw it. It is determined in the Course of Things.
KRRK KRRK KRRK
It is Jiiva who provides us these precious moments of enlightenment.
KRRK KRRK KRRK
Moments of intense concentration in which we are replete with the power of creation.
Moments in which time loses its meaning and divine inspiration guides our hands.

It is in these moments that I see the Course of Things before me.
I see it as clearly as you see this mandala. It is a message of **hope**. For all of us.
It is a message hat says, "The day of esurrection is almost upon us."
CLACK

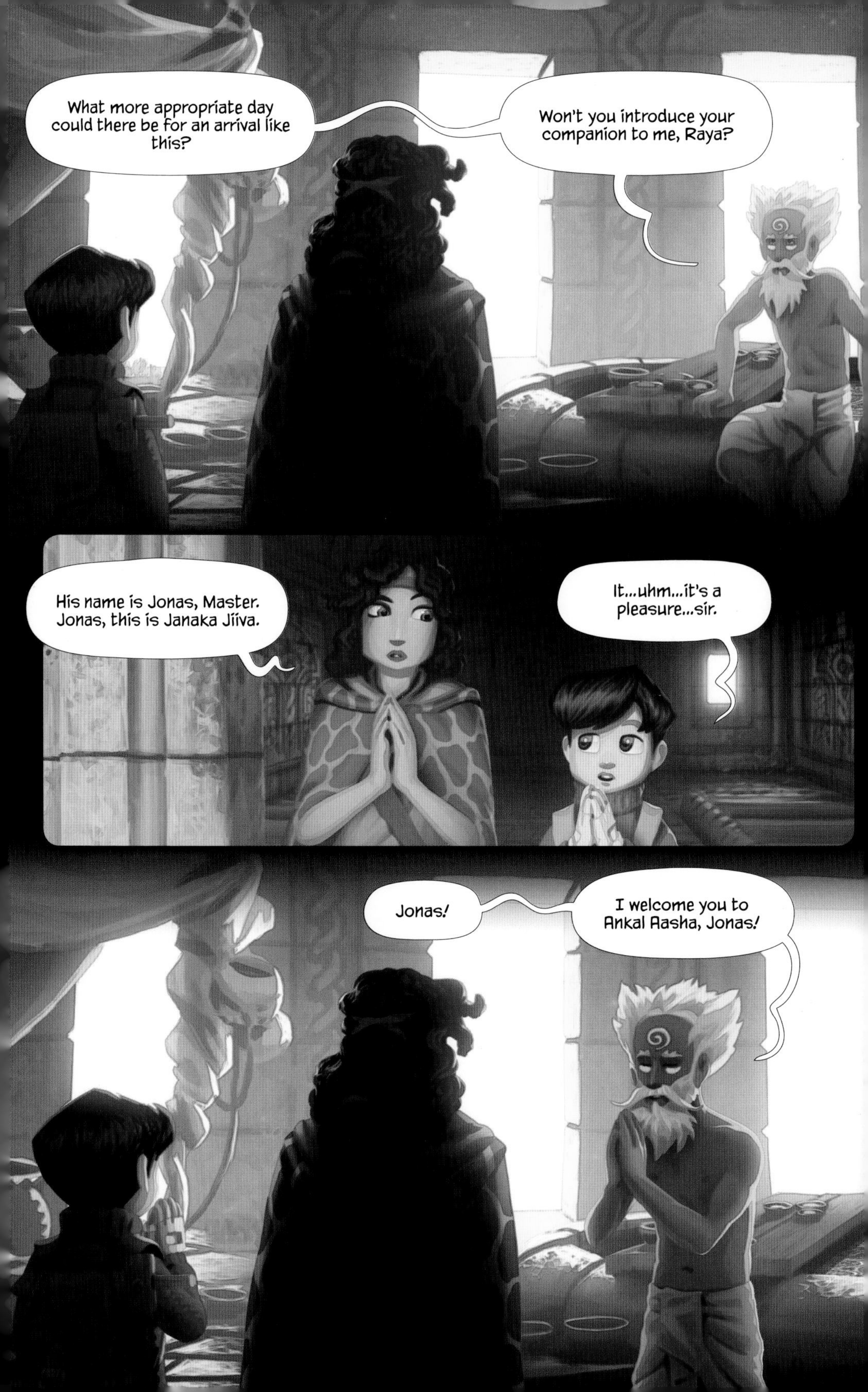
What more appropriate day could there be for an arrival like this?
Won't you introduce your companion to me, Raya?
His name is Jonas, Master. Jonas, this is Janaka Jiíva.
It...uhm...it's a pleasure...sir.
Jonas!
I welcome you to Ankal Aasha, Jonas!

My vision only told me of your arrival. I saw that Jiiva himself would guide you to us.
Now that you are standing before me, I see that you carry many questions. That your own path lies in darkness for you.
Yes, well...Raya told me... actually she **promised** that you would be able to tell me how I can get home.
Returning home. Yes. That's your most fervent wish.
But this is about **infinitely** more than going home, Jonas.
I want to tell you something about this place.
It hasn't always been a shelter of hope, you know.

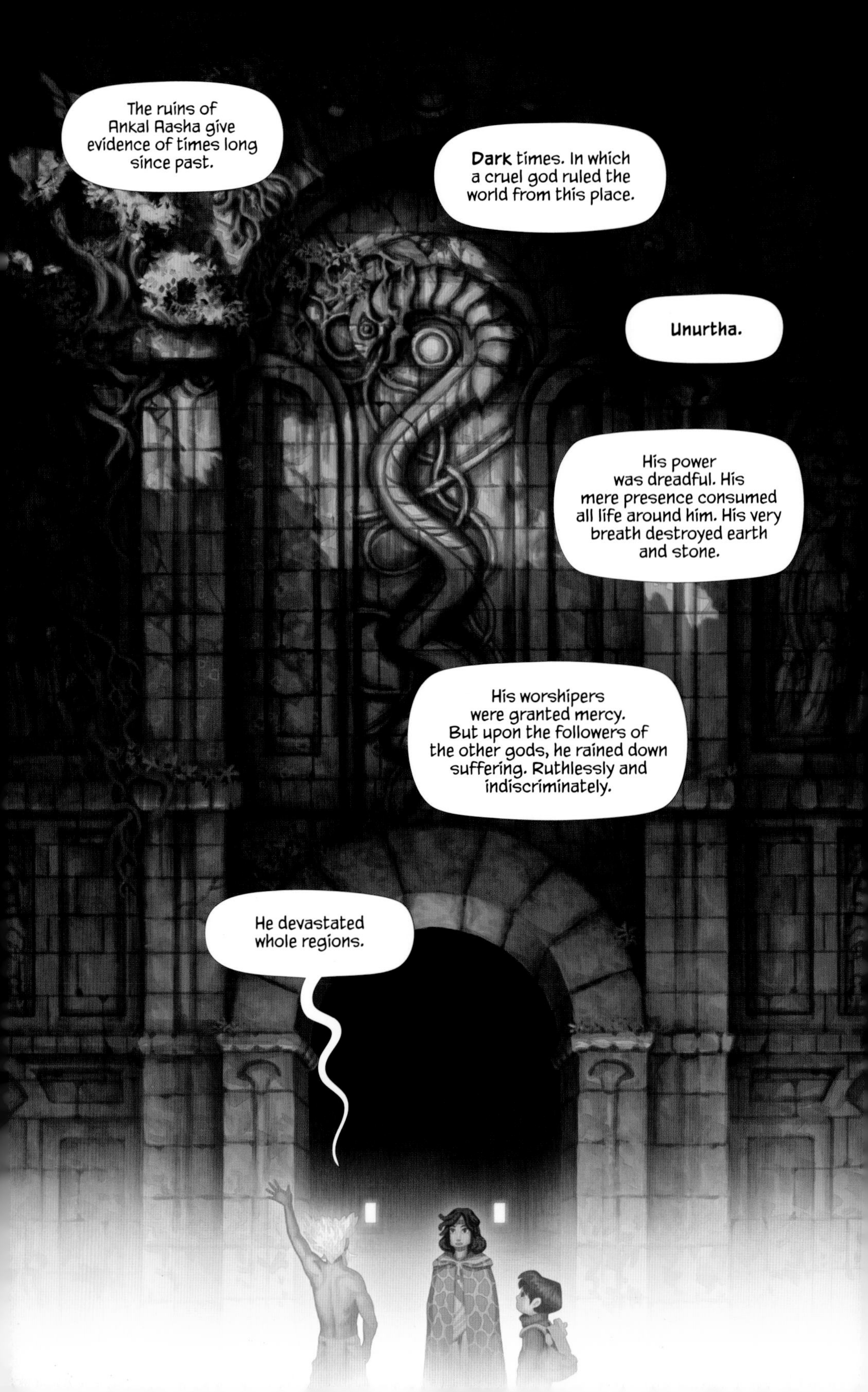
The ruins of Ankal Aasha give evidence of times long since past.
Dark times. In which a cruel god ruled the world from this place.
Unurtha.
His power was dreadful. His mere presence consumed all life around him. His very breath destroyed earth and stone.
His worshipers were granted mercy. But upon the followers of the other gods, he rained down suffering. Ruthlessly and indiscriminately.
He devastated whole regions.

The description of Unurtha's reign of terror in the Ancient Truths is long and detailed.
But they also tell about its end.
Jiíva, the god of life, couldn't stand the barbarity any longer and wished to end it.
But he couldn't oppose Unurtha alone.
Thus, he summoned the gods of the elements—air, water, and earth—to unite with him, and by their combined powers endeavour to **break** the might of Unurtha.
They agreed.
The gods of the three elements challenged Unurtha and smote him upon the ground, and upon him they erected a prison of rock that Jiíva endued with a magical seal, so that Unurtha would be banned forever.
And so Unurtha's dark power disappeared from the world.

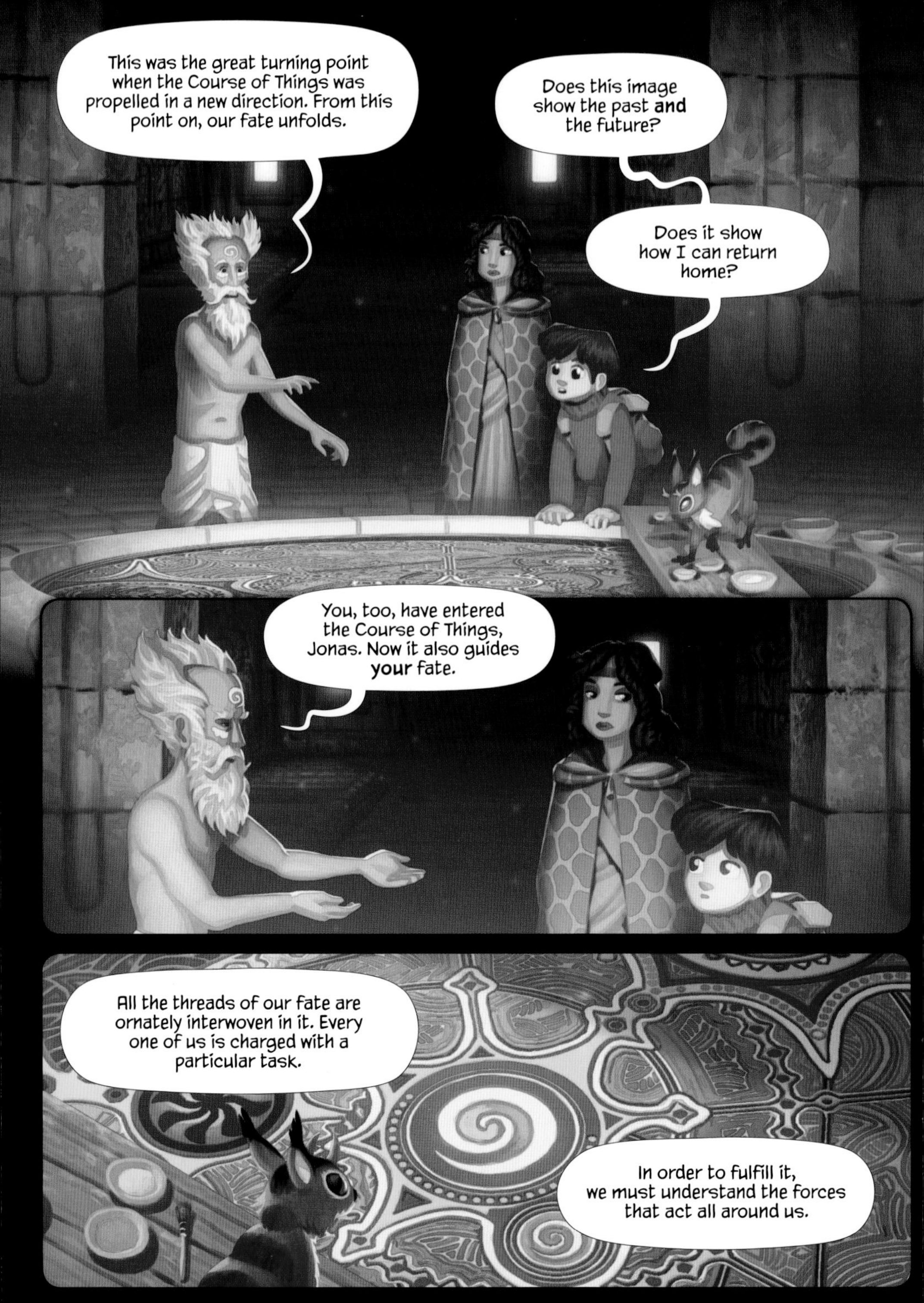
This was the great turning point when the Course of Things was propelled in a new direction. From this point on, our fate unfolds.
Does this image show the past **and** the future?
Does it show how I can return home?
You, too, have entered the Course of Things, Jonas. Now it also guides **your** fate.
All the threads of our fate are ornately interwoven in it. Every one of us is charged with a particular task.
In order to fulfill it, we must understand the forces that act all around us.

They often appear to be at odds with what we hope for.
After Unurtha was defeated, an era of peace should have dawned.
But the struggle with Unurtha had so exhausted the gods that they retreated to rest.
They left the fate of the world to the mortals for a time. And thus a disaster found its course.
Without the guidance of the gods, the people's arrogance grew, until their proclivities ran rampant. They declared themselves masters over life and death and fought wars against each other.
And the inevitable happened: Fifteen cycles ago, when the war between the King of the Center and the Desert Prince reached its climax, Jiíva's seal was **damaged!**

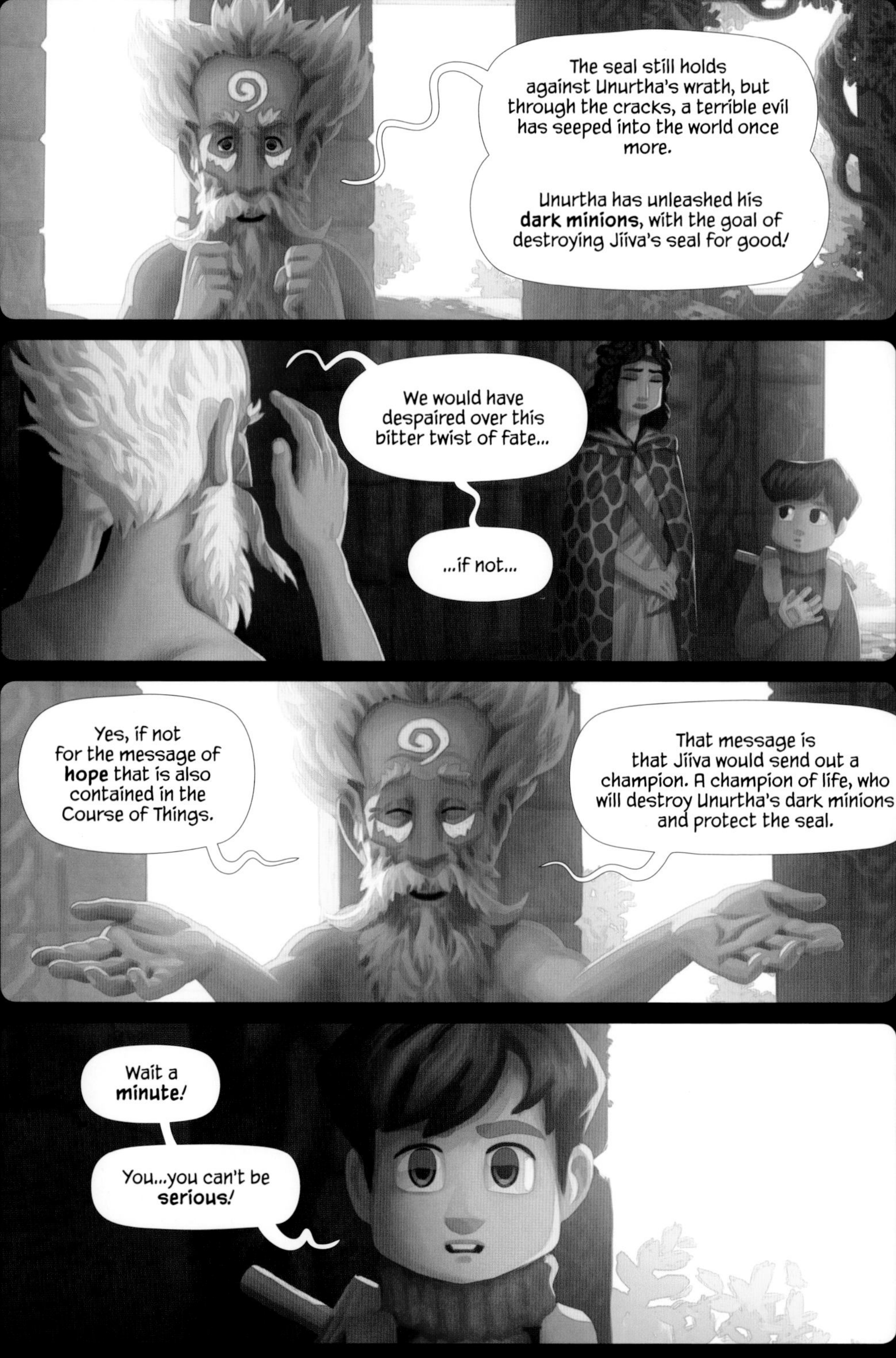
The seal still holds against Unurtha's wrath, but through the cracks, a terrible evil has seeped into the world once more.
Unurtha has unleashed his **dark minions**, with the goal of destroying Jiiva's seal for good!
We would have despaired over this bitter twist of fate...
...if not...
Yes, if not for the message of **hope** that is also contained in the Course of Things.
That message is that Jiiva would send out a champion. A champion of life, who will destroy Unurtha's dark minions and protect the seal.
Wait a **minute!**
You...you can't be **serious!**

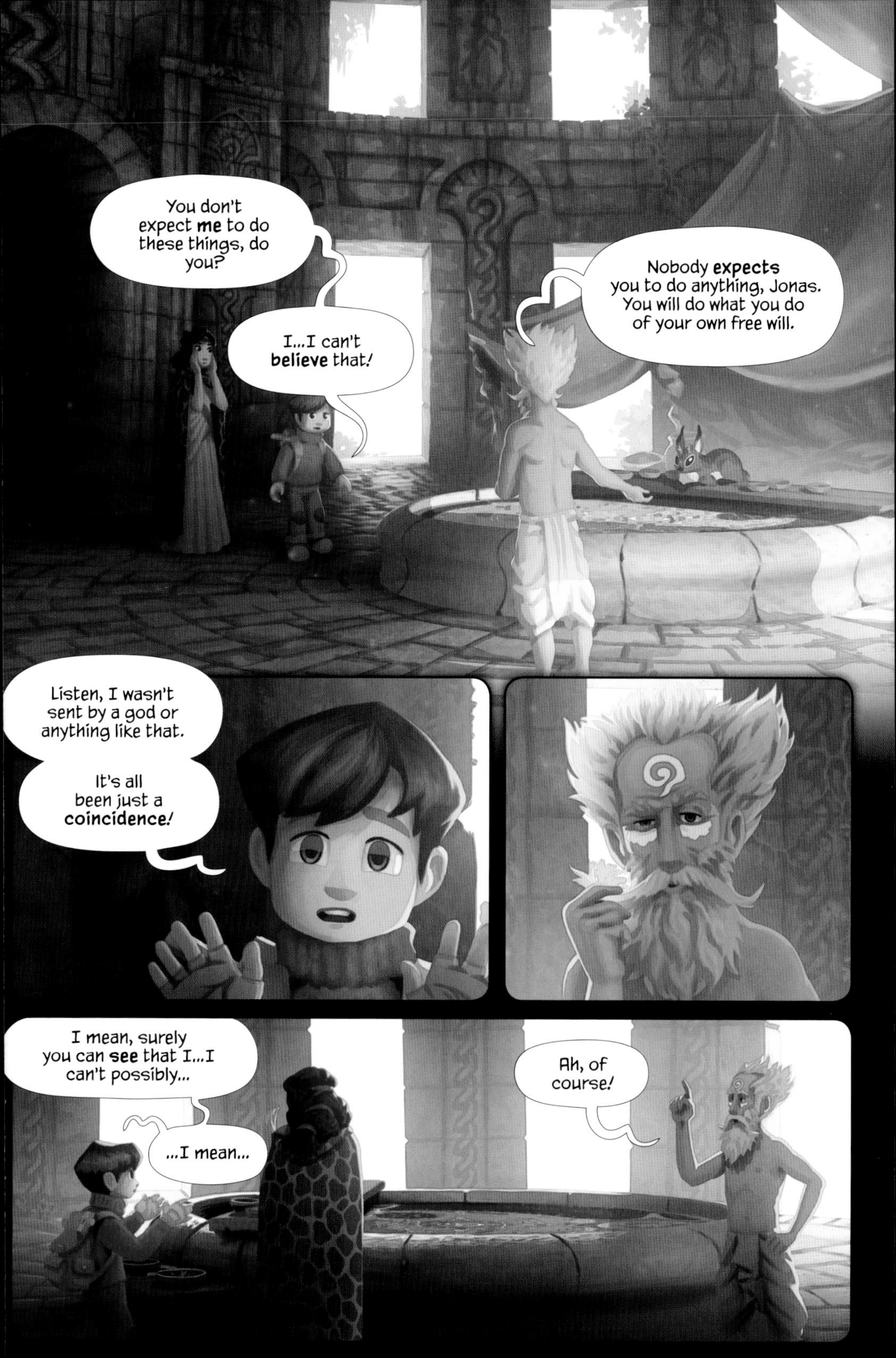
You don't expect **me** to do these things, do you?
I...I can't **believe** that!
Nobody **expects** you to do anything, Jonas. You will do what you do of your own free will.
Listen, I wasn't sent by a god or anything like that.
It's all been just a **coincidence**!
I mean, surely you can **see** that I...I can't possibly...
...I mean...
Ah, of course!

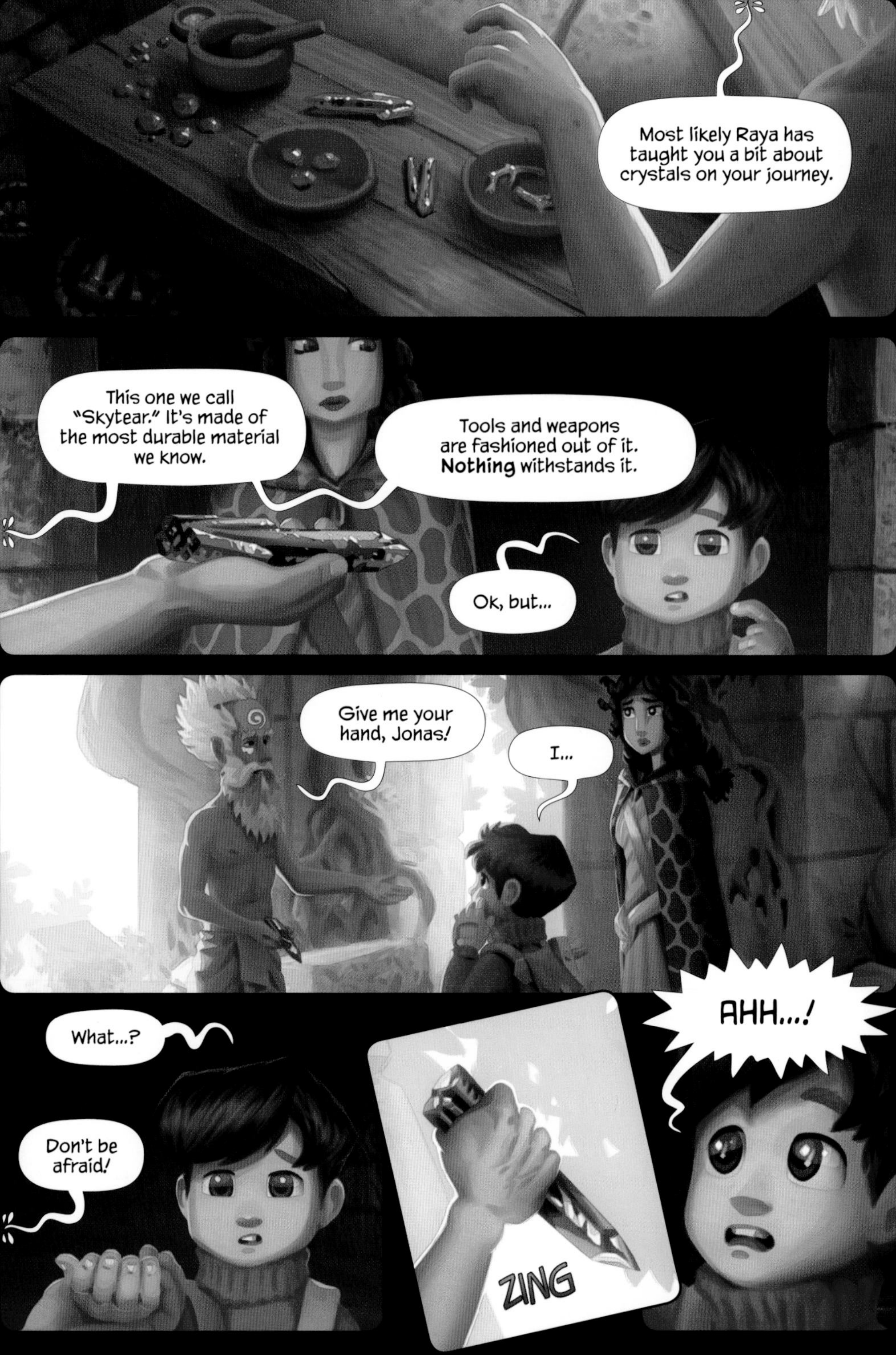
Most likely Raya has taught you a bit about crystals on your journey.
This one we call "Skytear." It's made of the most durable material we know.
Tools and weapons are fashioned out of it. **Nothing** withstands it.
Ok, but...
Give me your hand, Jonas!
I...
What...?
Don't be afraid!
ZING
AHH...!

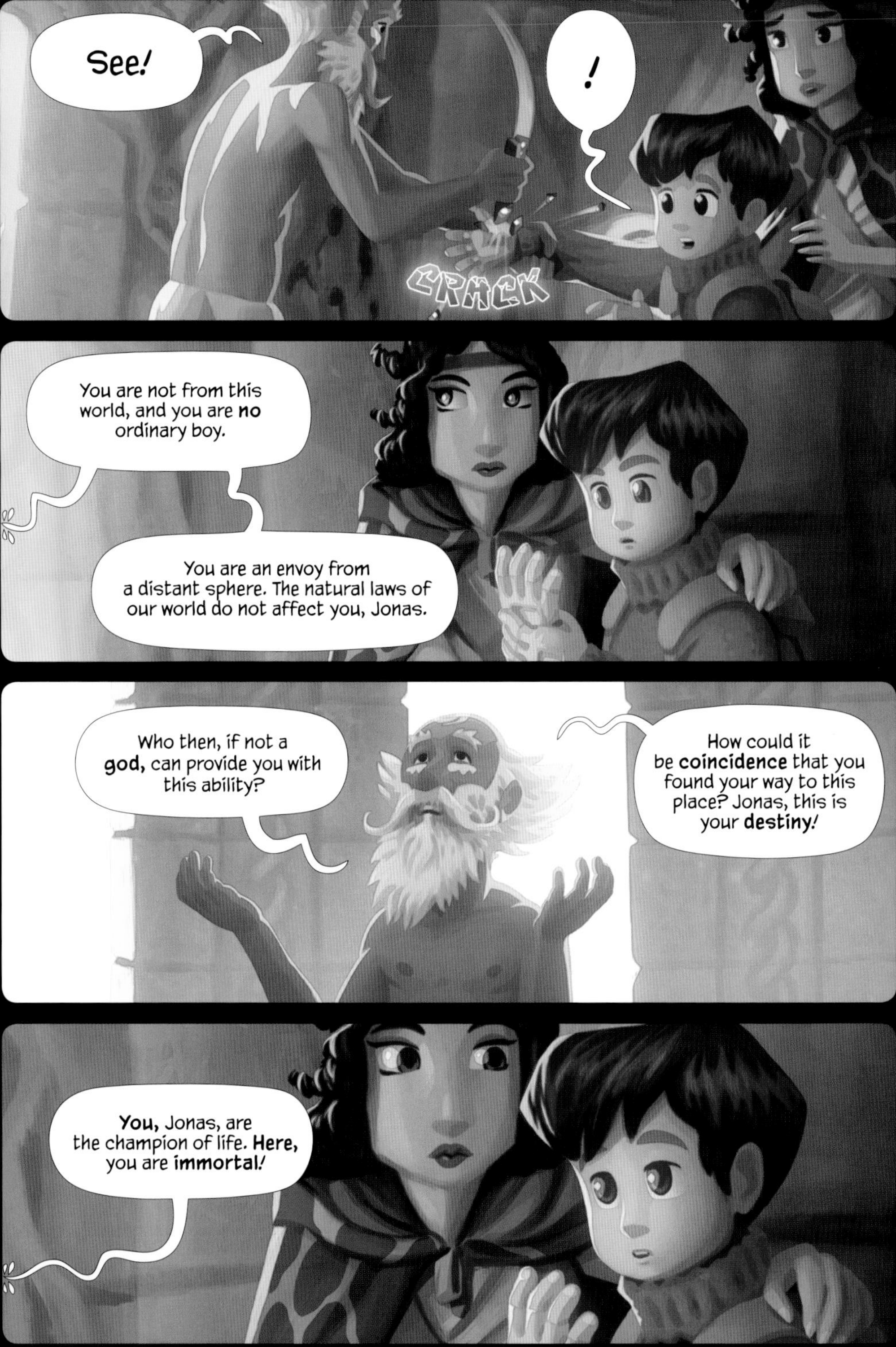
See!
!
CRACK
You are not from this world, and you are **no** ordinary boy.
You are an envoy from a distant sphere. The natural laws of our world do not affect you, Jonas.
Who then, if not a **god,** can provide you with this ability?
How could it be **coincidence** that you found your way to this place? Jonas, this is your **destiny!**
You, Jonas, are the champion of life. **Here,** you are **immortal!**

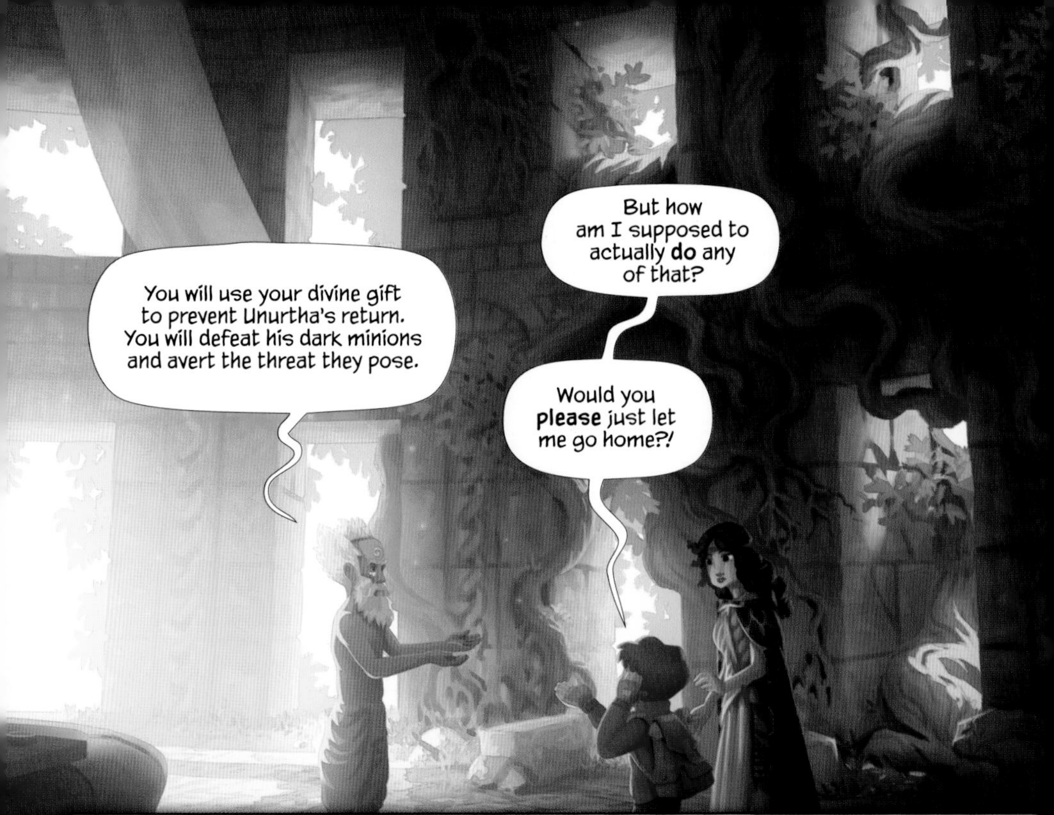
You will use your divine gift to prevent Unurtha's return. You will defeat his dark minions and avert the threat they pose.
But how am I supposed to actually **do** any of that?
Would you **please** just let me go home?!

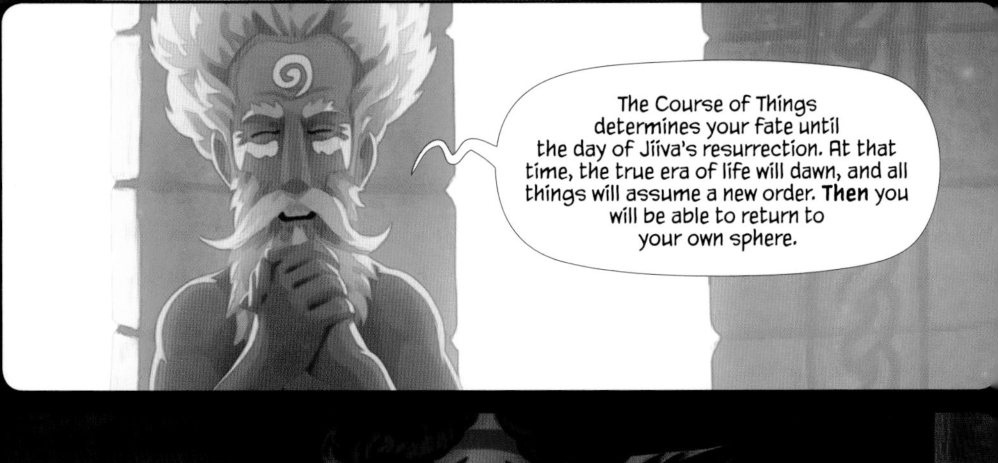
The Course of Things determines your fate until the day of Jiiva's resurrection. At that time, the true era of life will dawn, and all things will assume a new order. **Then** you will be able to return to your own sphere.

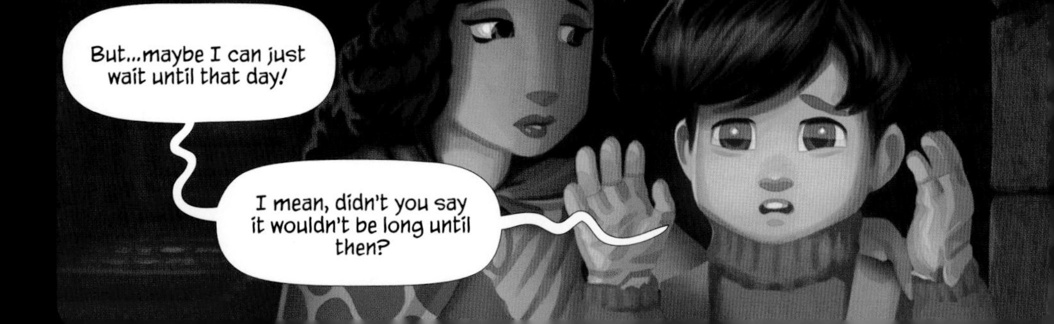
But...maybe I can just wait until that day!
I mean, didn't you say it wouldn't be long until then?

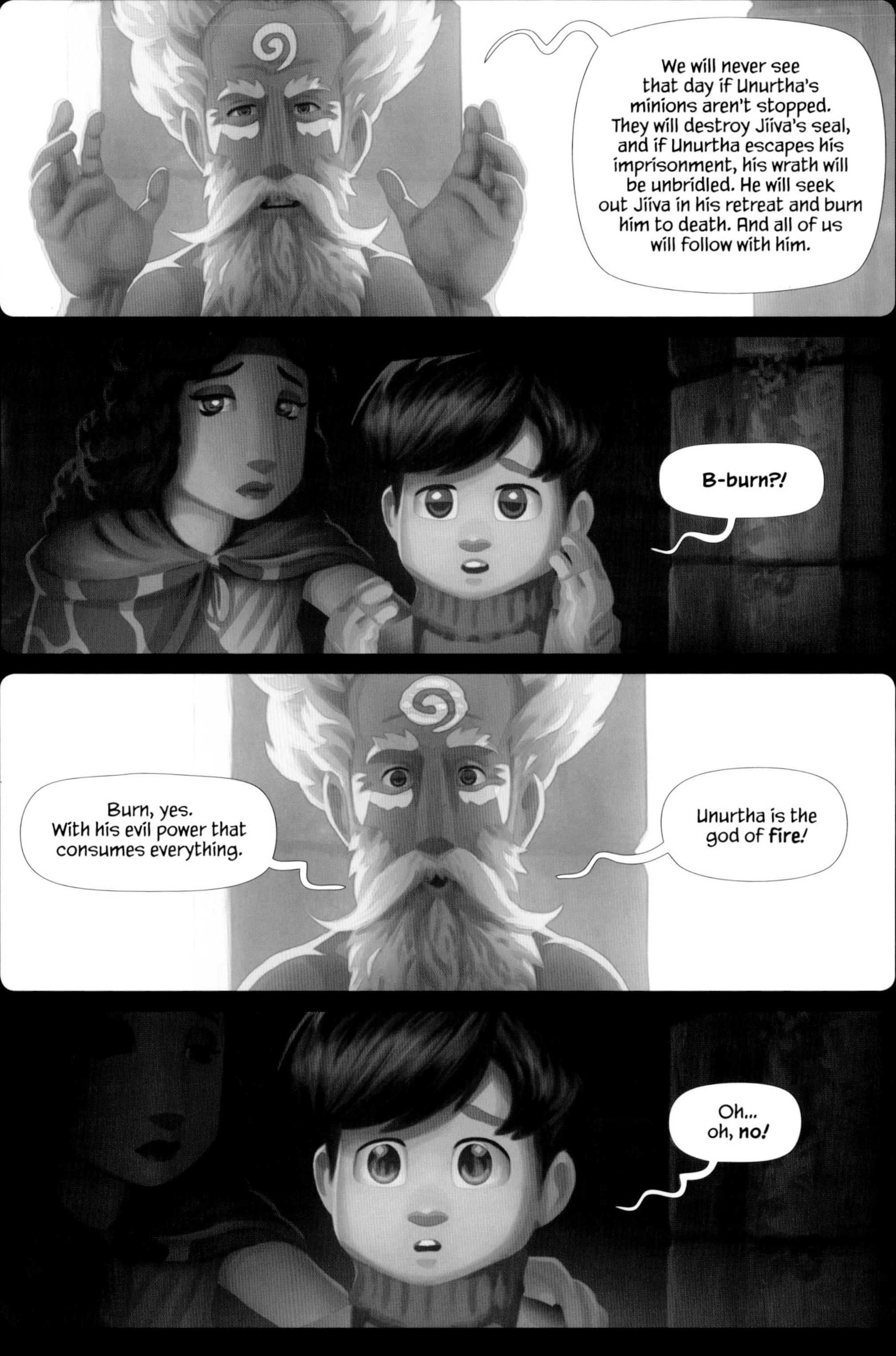
We will never see that day if Unurtha's minions aren't stopped. They will destroy Jiíva's seal, and if Unurtha escapes his imprisonment, his wrath will be unbridled. He will seek out Jiíva in his retreat and burn him to death. And all of us will follow with him.
B-burn?!
Burn, yes. With his evil power that consumes everything.
Unurtha is the god of **fire!**
Oh... oh, **no!**

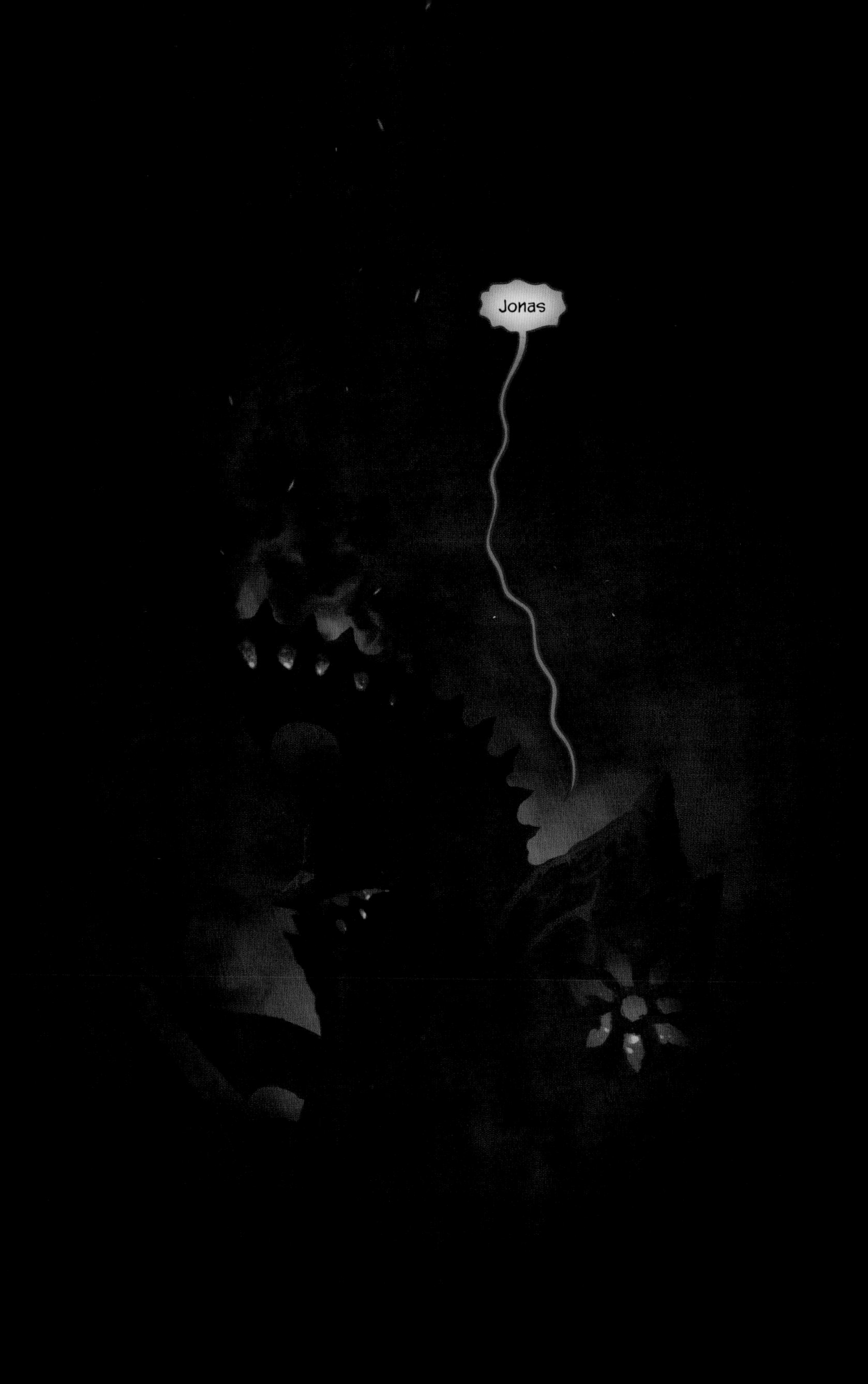
Jonas

Chapter 2
Call of the Worm Mountain

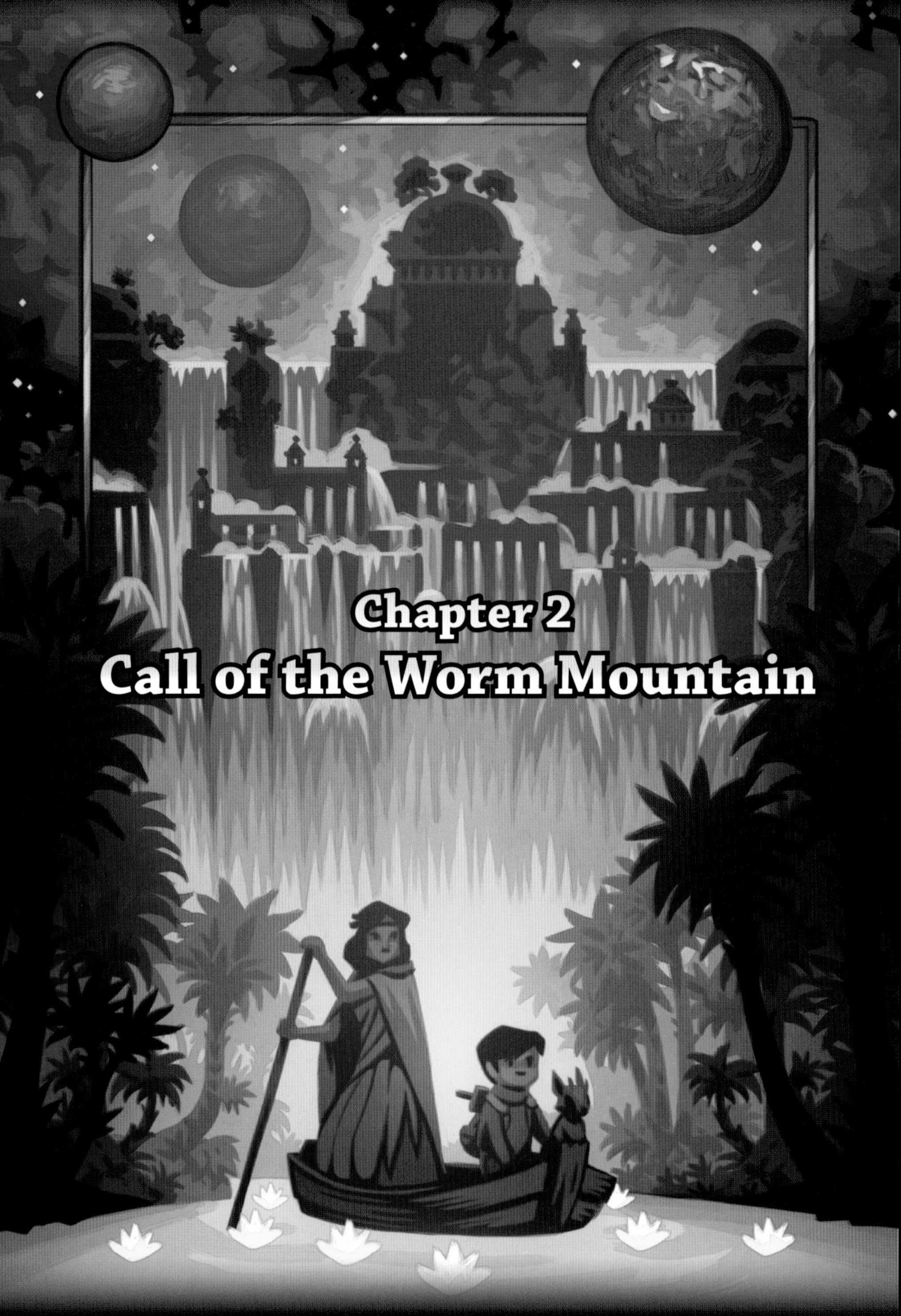

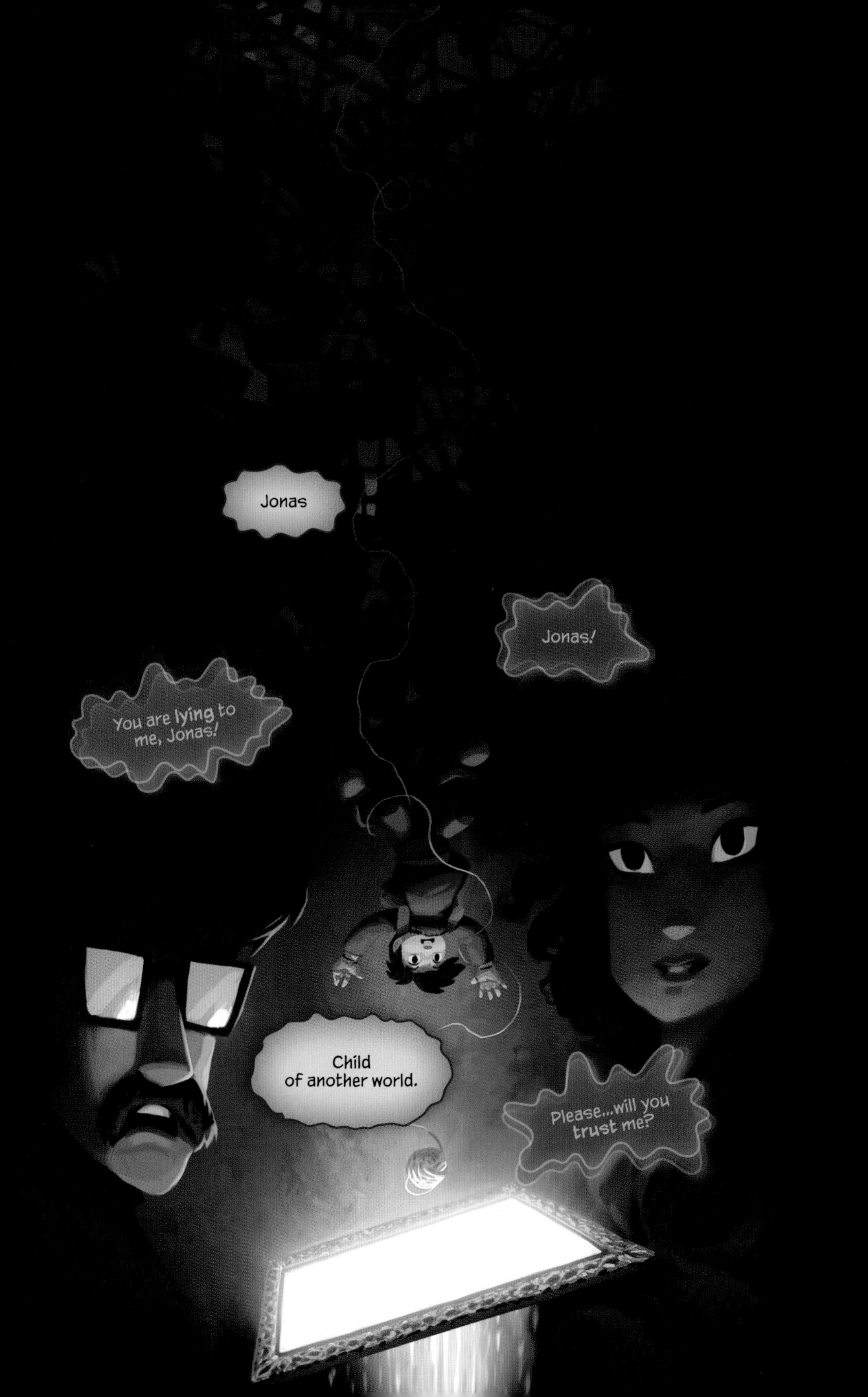
Jonas
Jonas!
You are lying to me, Jonas!
Child of another world.
Please...will you trust me?

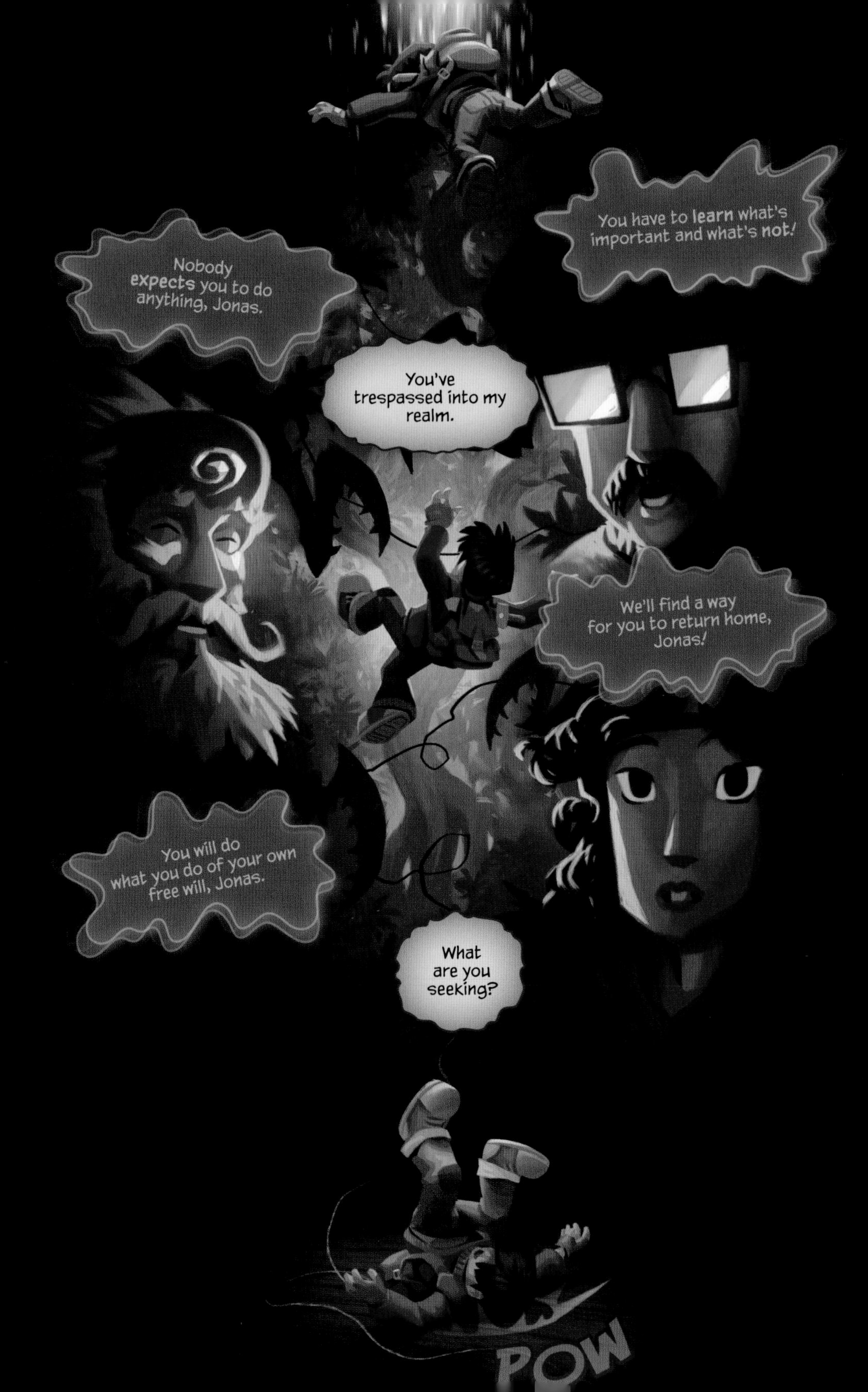
You have to **learn** what's important and what's **not**!
Nobody **expects** you to do anything, Jonas.
You've trespassed into my realm.
We'll find a way for you to return home, Jonas!
You will do what you do of your own free will, Jonas.
What are you seeking?
POW

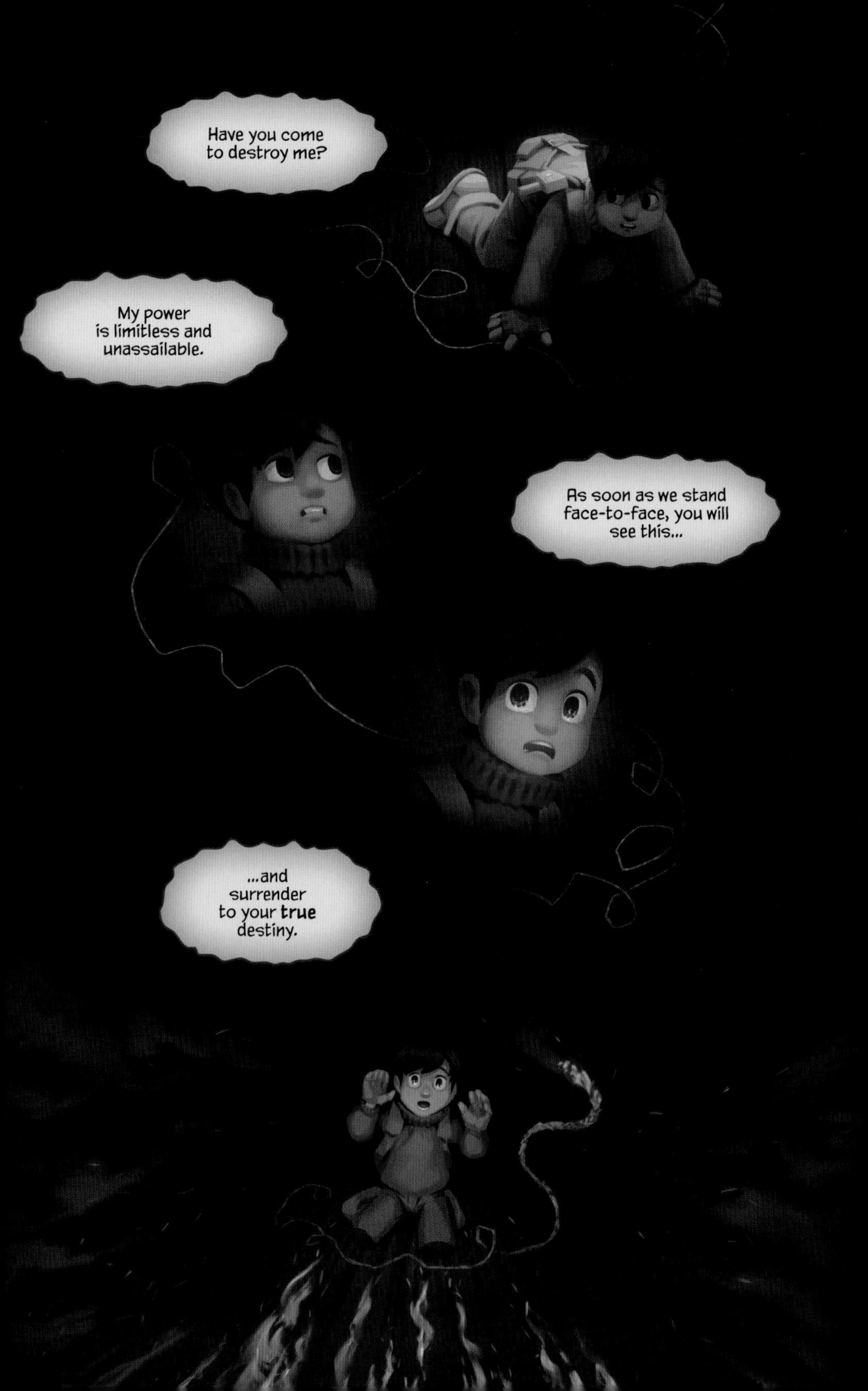

Have you come to destroy me?
My power is limitless and unassailable.
As soon as we stand face-to-face, you will see this...
...and surrender to your **true** destiny.

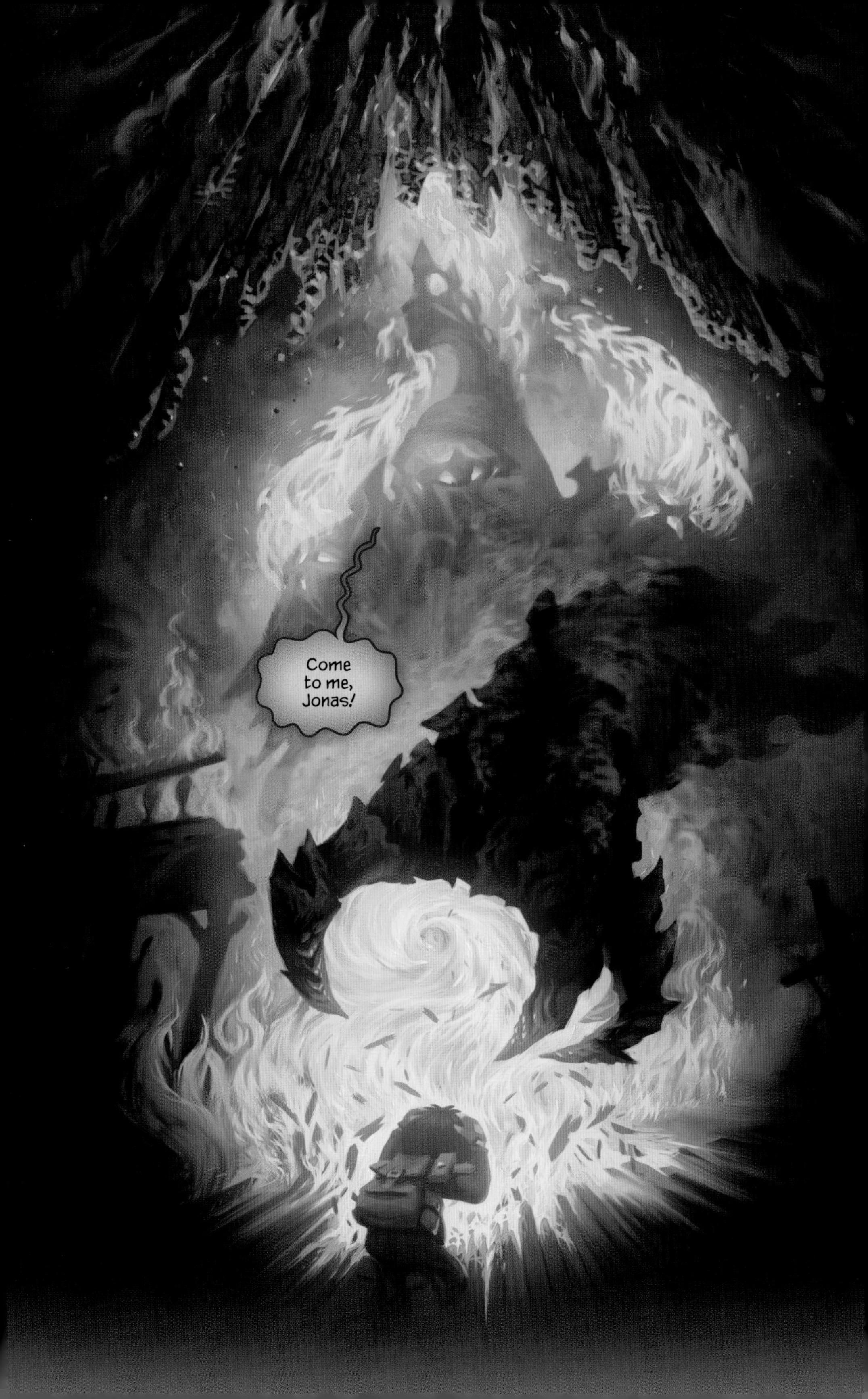
Come to me, Jonas!

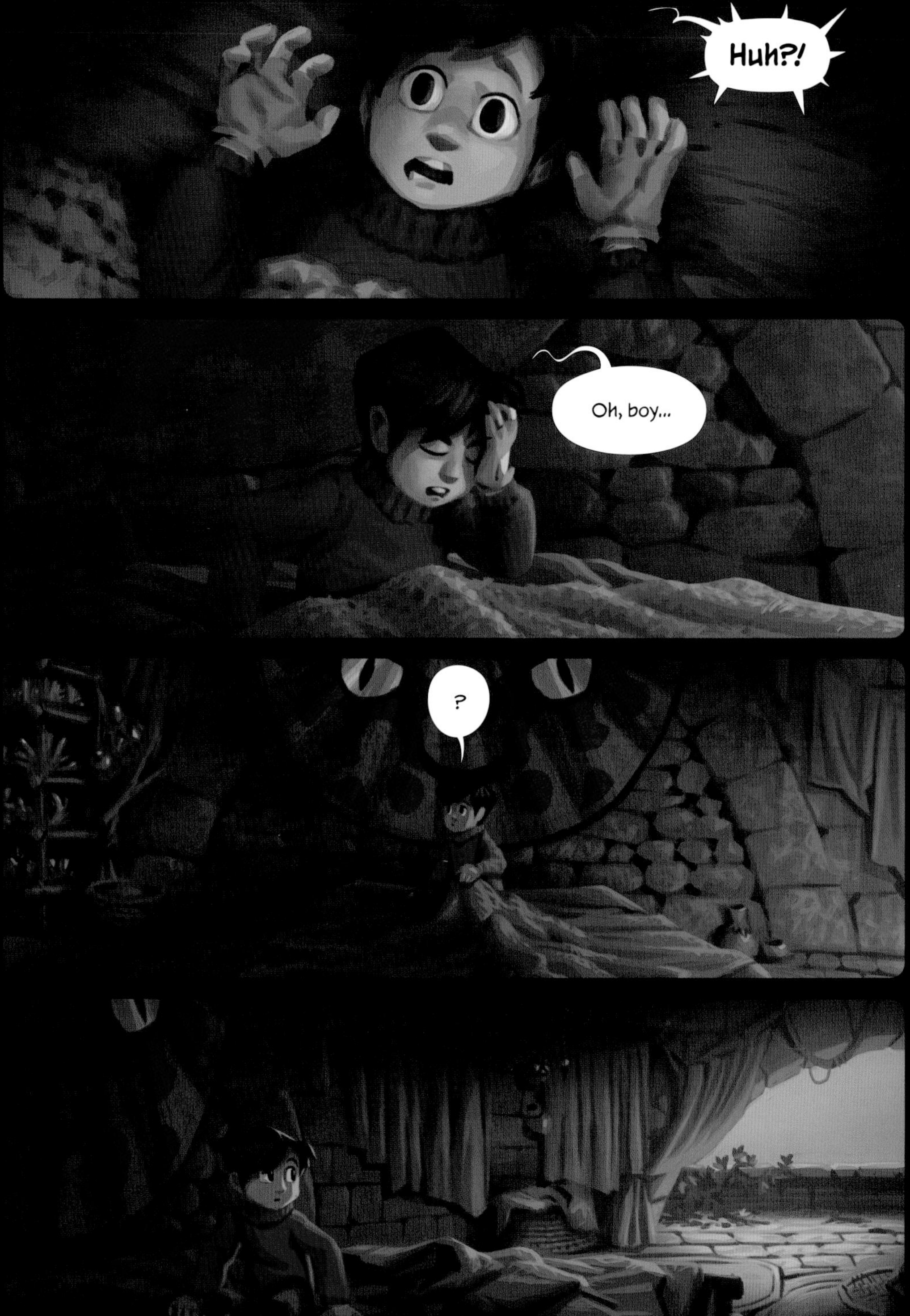
Huh?!
Oh, boy...
?

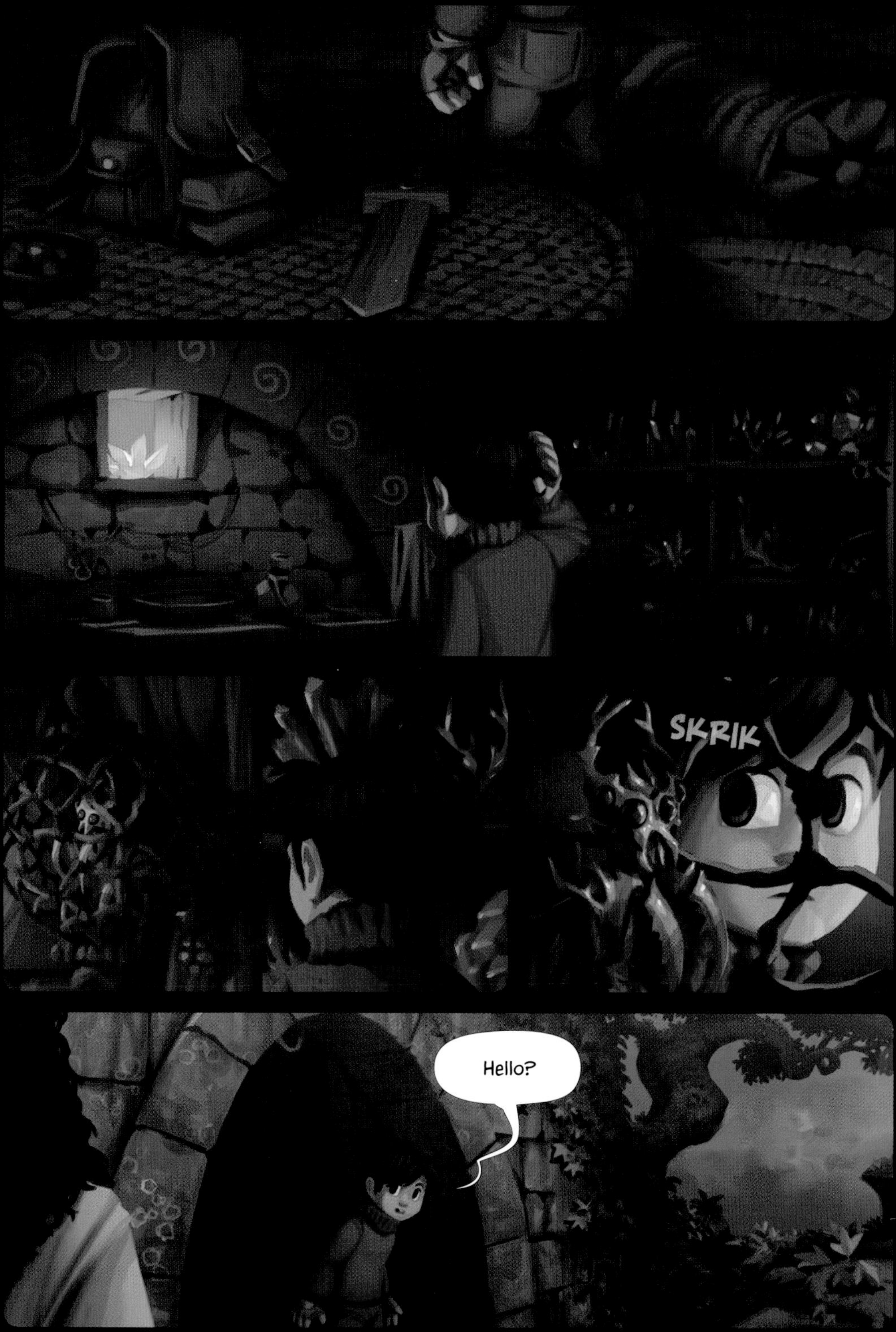
SKRIK
Hello?

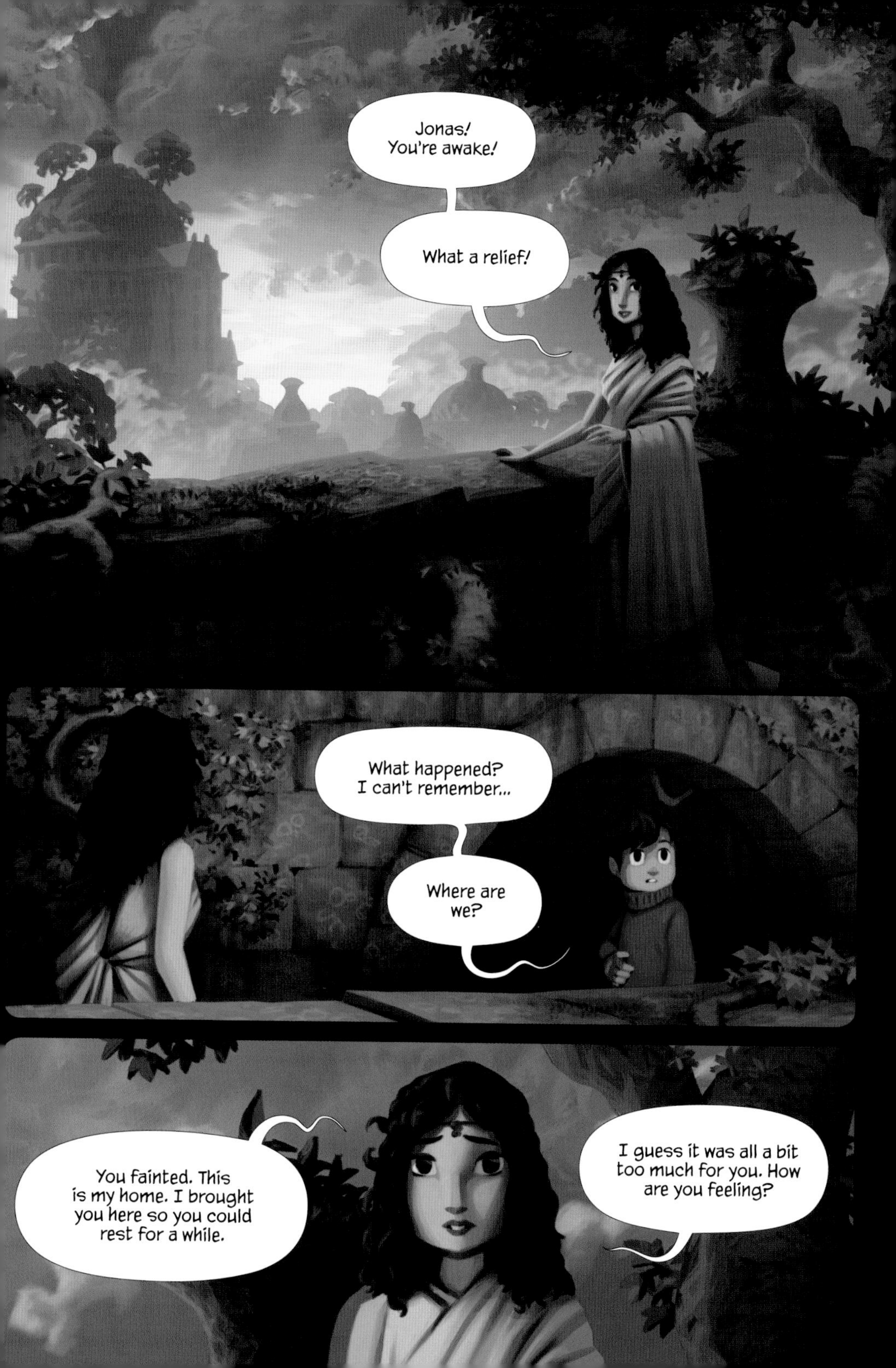
Jonas! You're awake!
What a relief!
What happened? I can't remember...
Where are we?
You fainted. This is my home. I brought you here so you could rest for a while.
I guess it was all a bit too much for you. How are you feeling?

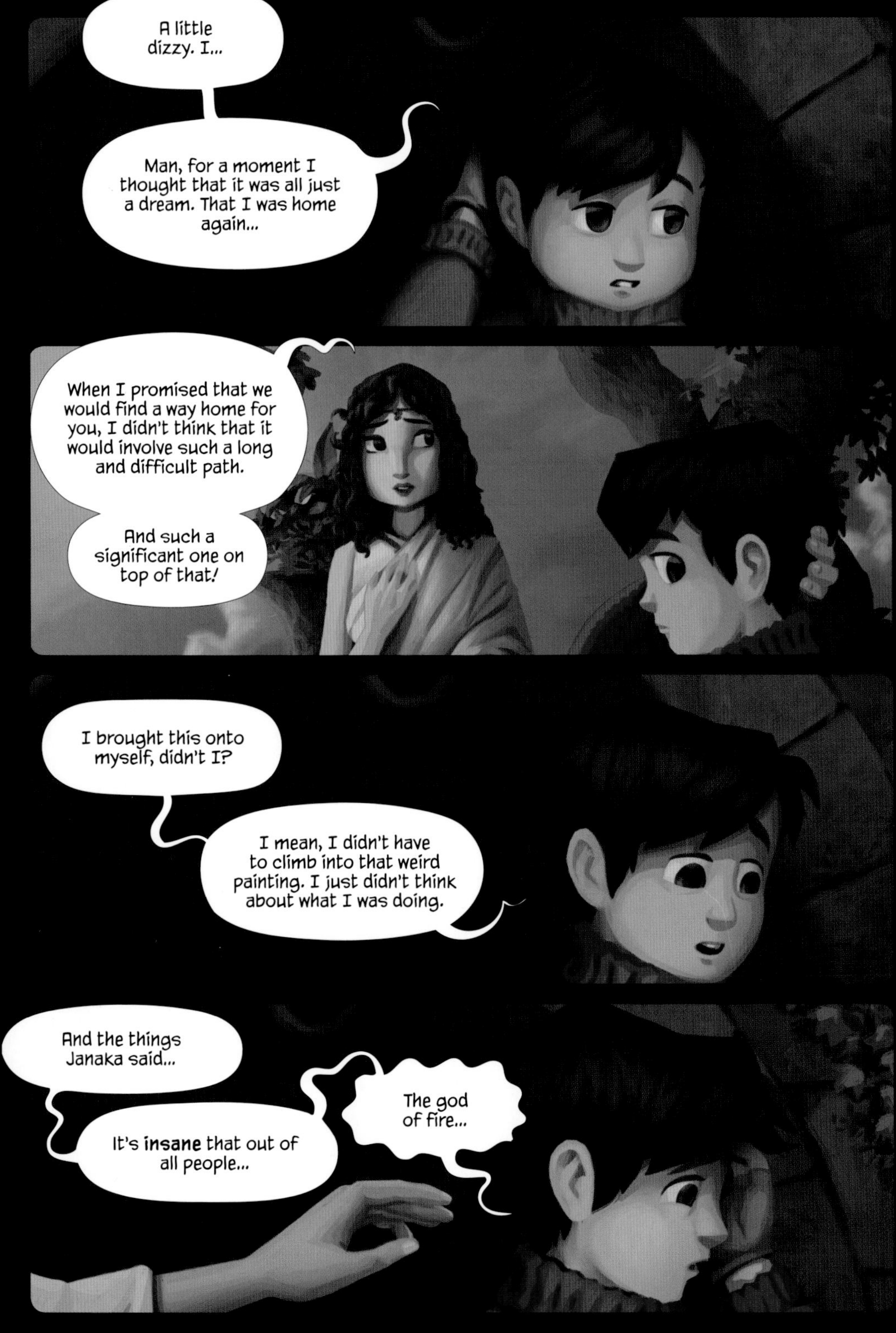
A little dizzy. I...
Man, for a moment I thought that it was all just a dream. That I was home again...
When I promised that we would find a way home for you, I didn't think that it would involve such a long and difficult path.
And such a significant one on top of that!
I brought this onto myself, didn't I?
I mean, I didn't have to climb into that weird painting. I just didn't think about what I was doing.
And the things Janaka said...
It's **insane** that out of all people...
The god of fire...

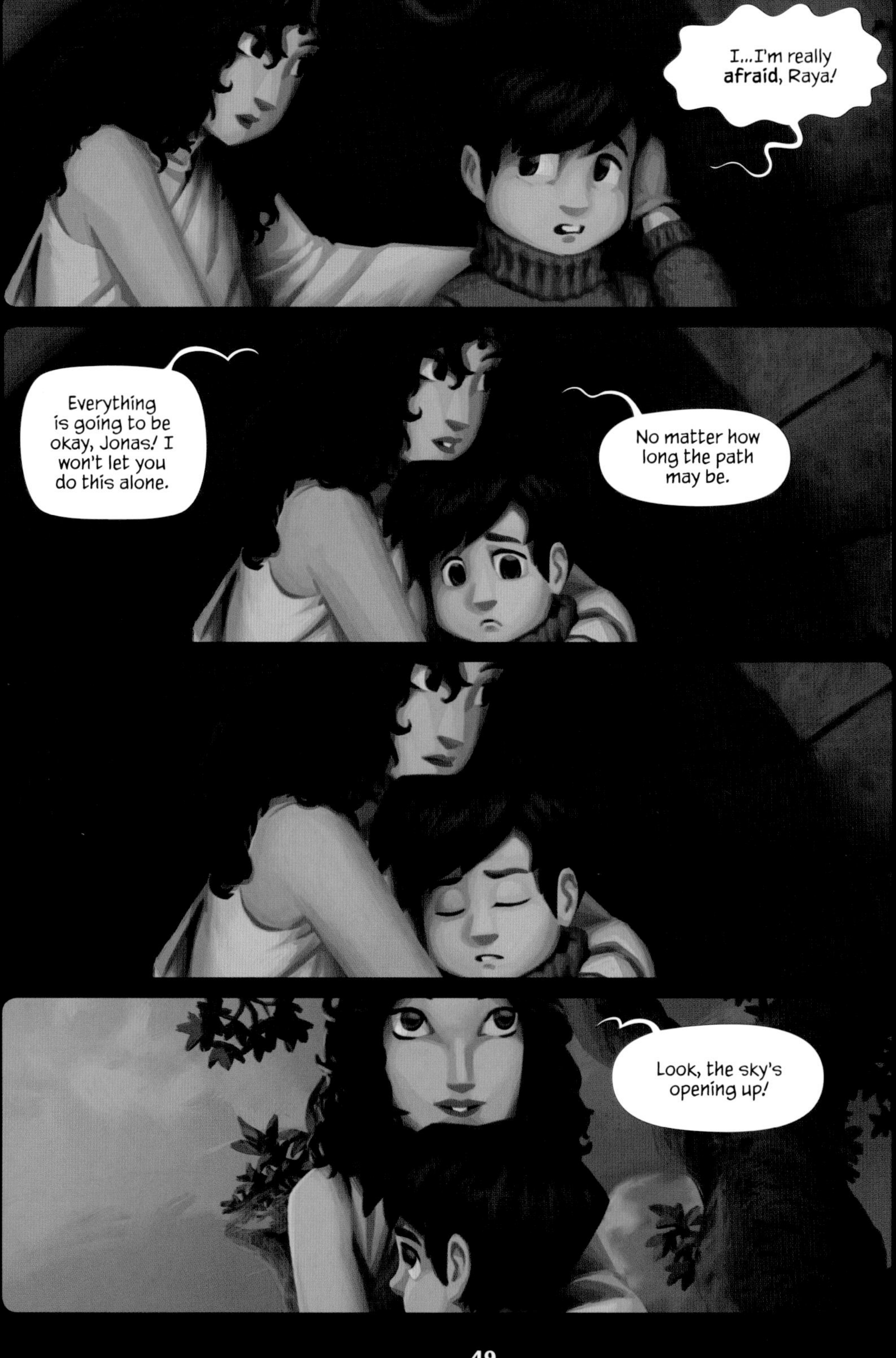
I...I'm really **afraid**, Raya!
Everything is going to be okay, Jonas! I won't let you do this alone.
No matter how long the path may be.
Look, the sky's opening up!

Oh...
From the moment that you landed at my feet, I wondered from which of these worlds you had fallen.
In...in our sky you can't see any other worlds. Not like this.
Well, maybe the moon...
Your world sounds rather remote.
I always thought that it was the only one.
Only **one** world? I'm not sure I'll ever make heads or tails out of you, Jonas!
Come, let's go! The Great Celebration has already begun!

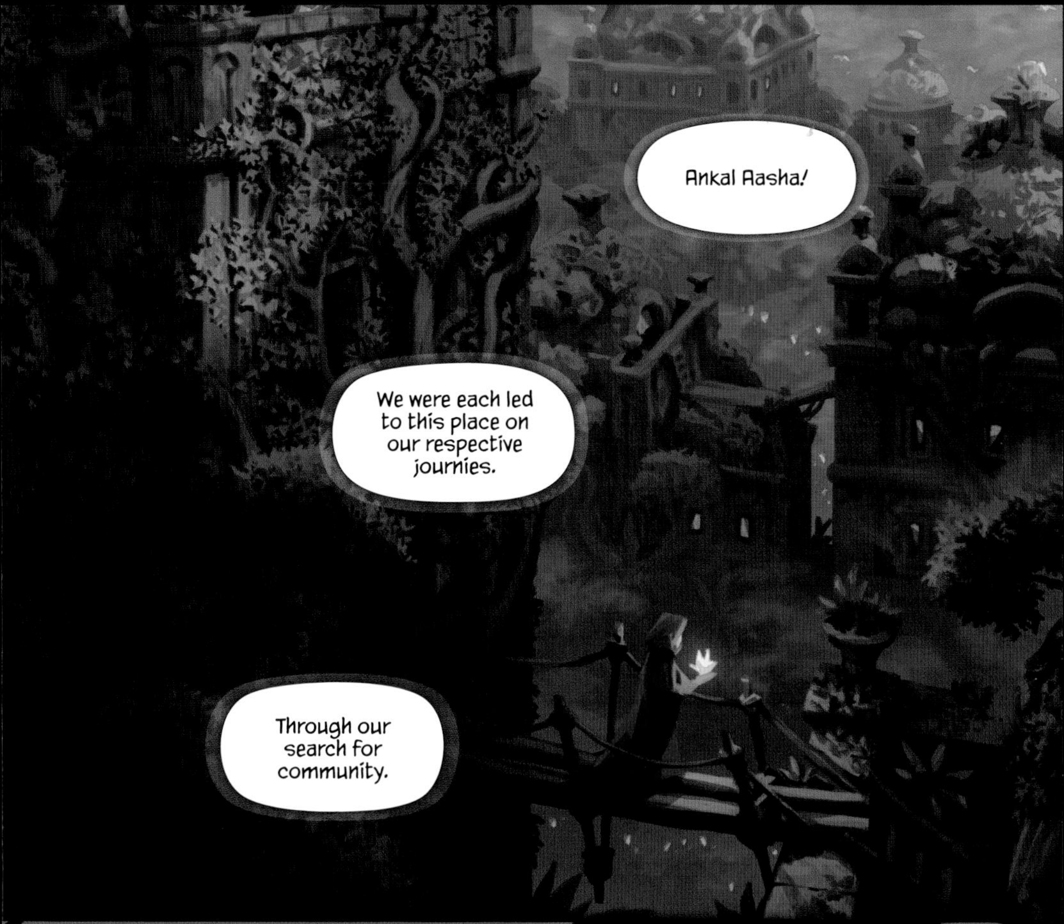
Ankal Aasha!
We were each led to this place on our respective journies.
Through our search for community.

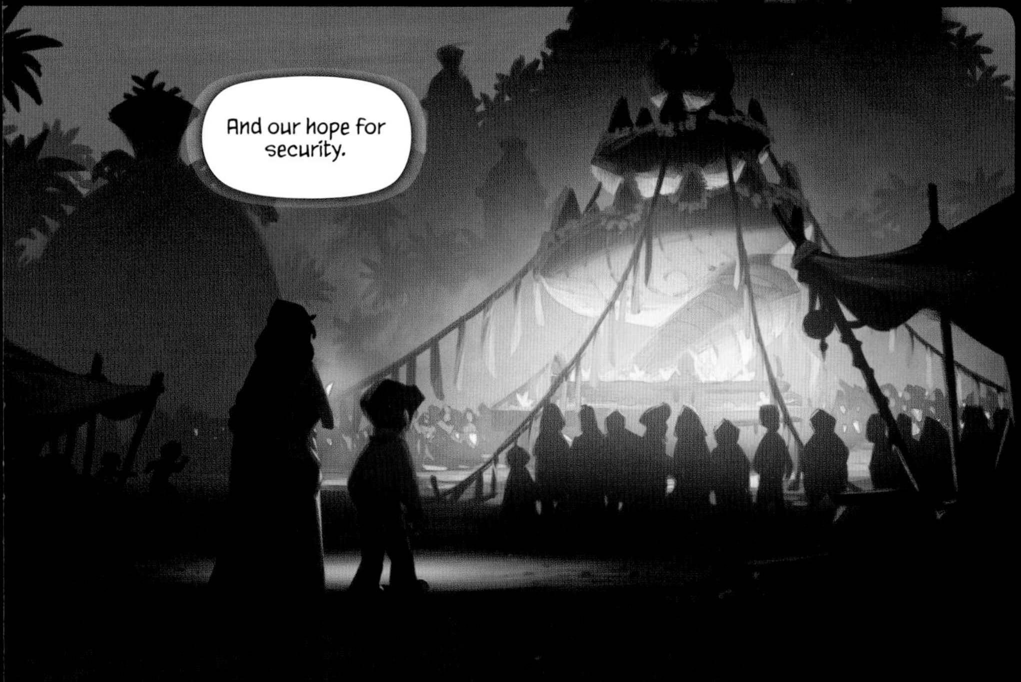
And our hope for security.

Alone, the hopes of any one of us are but a fleeting glimmer in the greater darkness that enshrouds this world.

But if we bring them together, the world will shine brightly in the brilliance of our combined hopes. The day approaches when Jiiva shall step out of this light to deliver a new dawn.

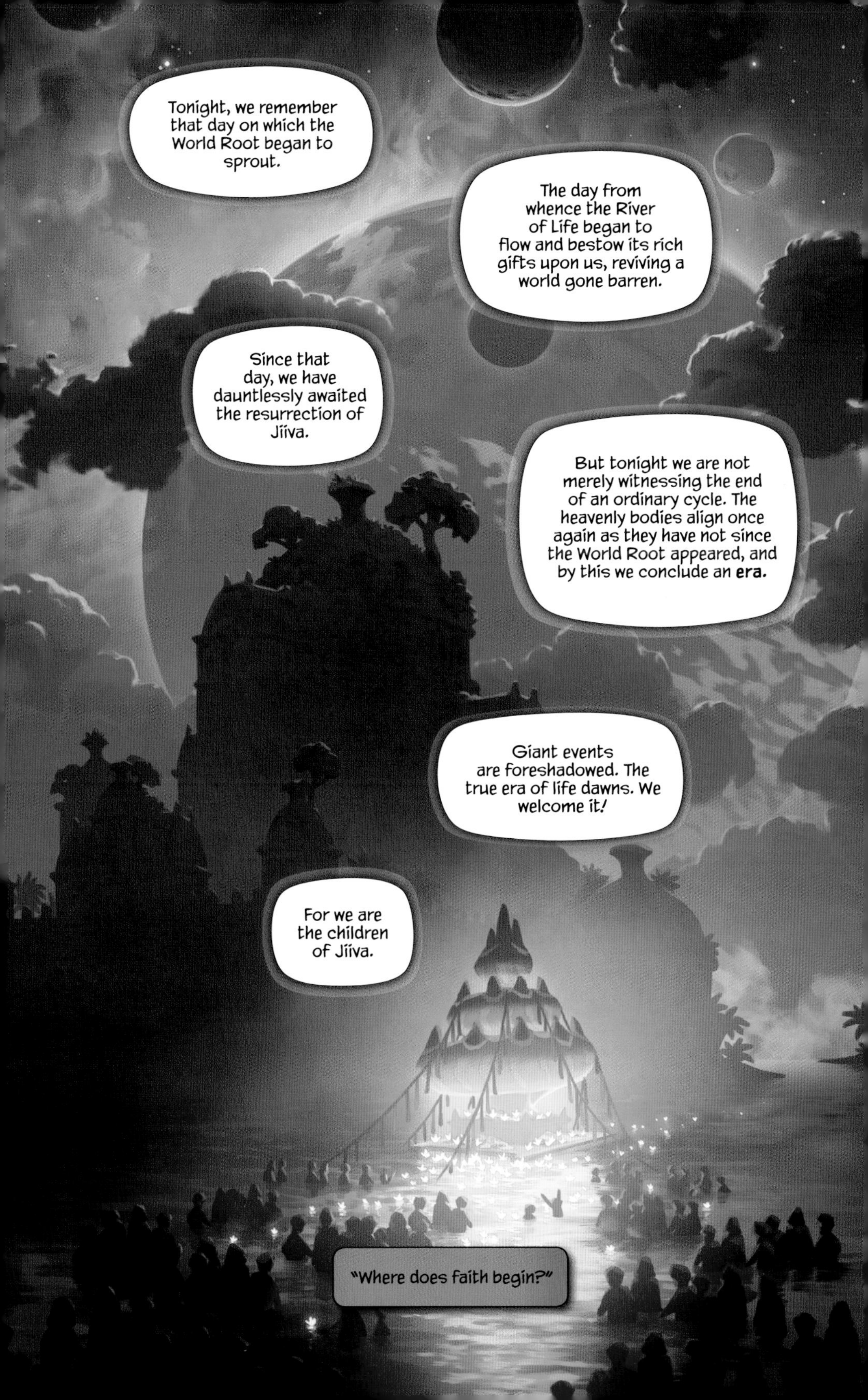
Tonight, we remember that day on which the World Root began to sprout.
The day from whence the River of Life began to flow and bestow its rich gifts upon us, reviving a world gone barren.
Since that day, we have dauntlessly awaited the resurrection of Jiíva.
But tonight we are not merely witnessing the end of an ordinary cycle. The heavenly bodies align once again as they have not since the World Root appeared, and by this we conclude an **era.**
Giant events are foreshadowed. The true era of life dawns. We welcome it!
For we are the children of Jiíva.
"Where does faith begin?"

"Don't we believe all too often in things that we merely **wish** to be true?"

"On the other hand, aren't there things that come true only **because** people believe in them so strongly?"

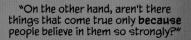

"I don't know exactly what I started to believe in that night."

"In the gods of this strange world, the prophecy Janaka and Raya constantly spoke of, or the role it held for me."

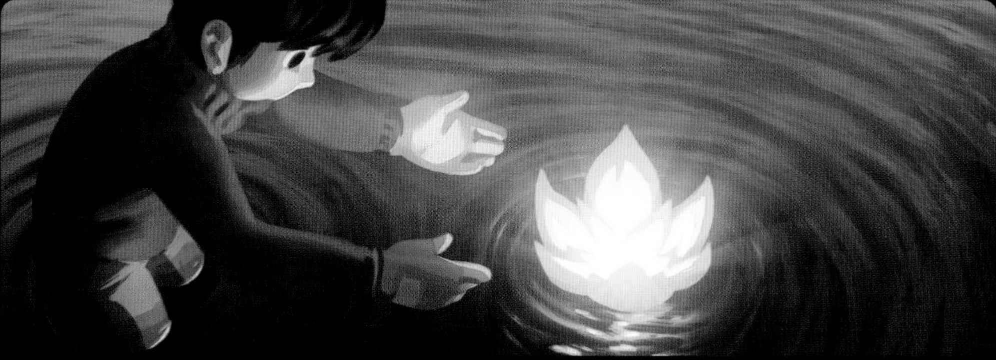

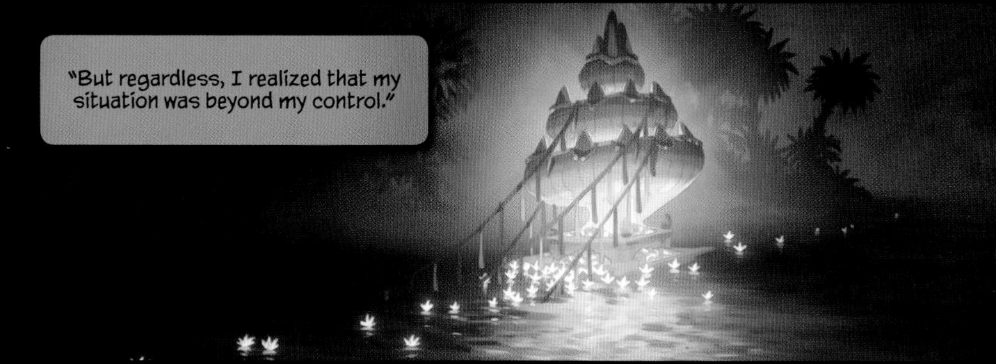
"But regardless, I realized that my situation was beyond my control."

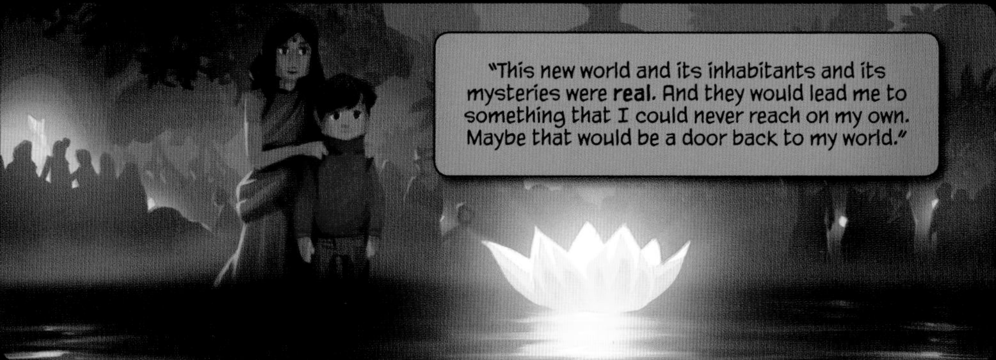
"This new world and its inhabitants and its mysteries were **real**. And they would lead me to something that I could never reach on my own. Maybe that would be a door back to my world."

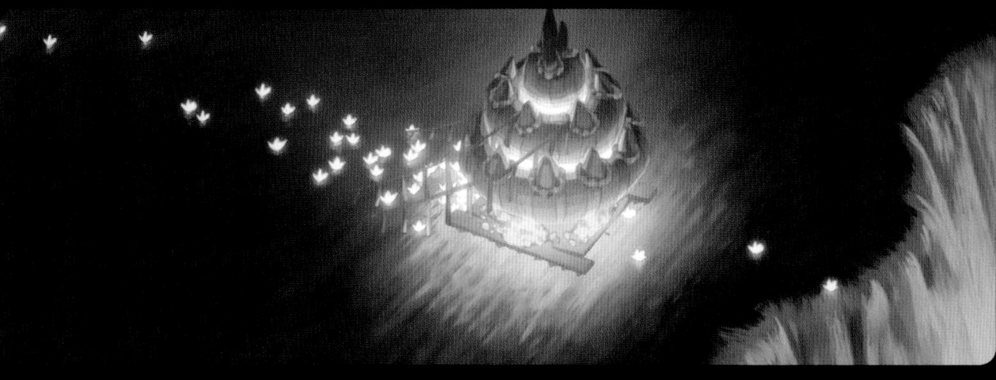

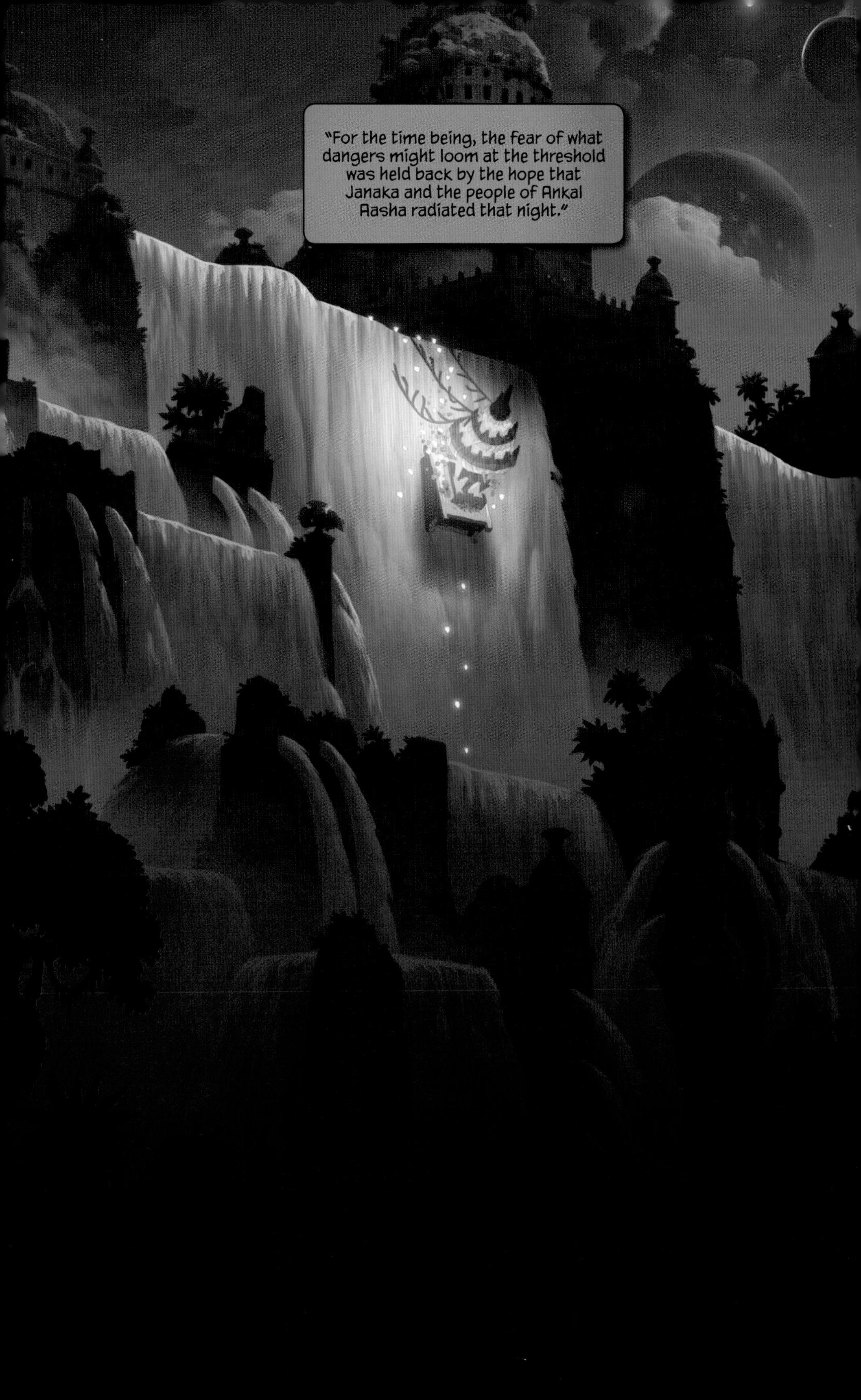
"For the time being, the fear of what dangers might loom at the threshold was held back by the hope that Janaka and the people of Ankal Aasha radiated that night."

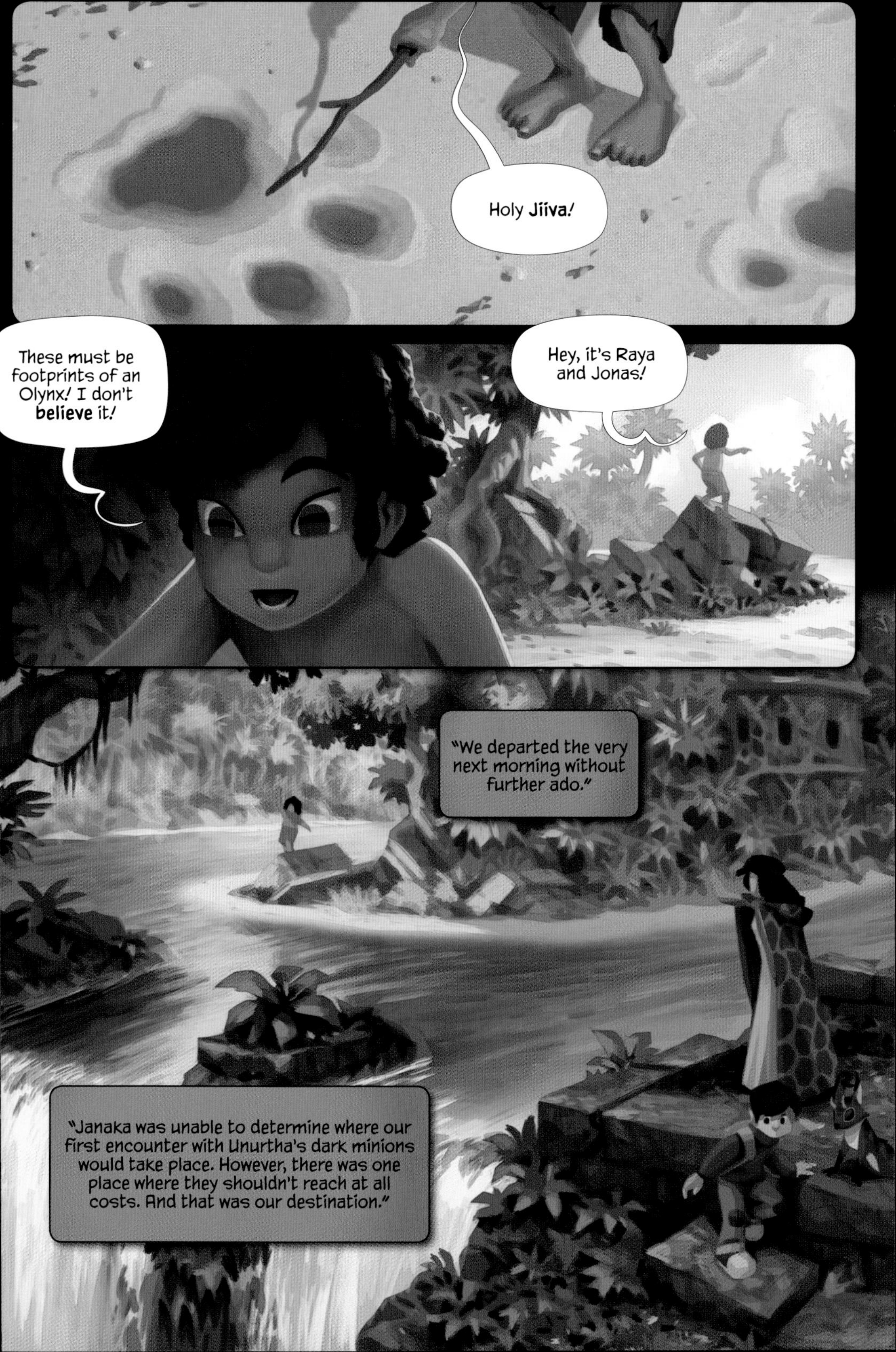
Holy **Jiiva!**
These must be footprints of an Olynx! I don't **believe** it!
Hey, it's Raya and Jonas!
"We departed the very next morning without further ado."
"Janaka was unable to determine where our first encounter with Unurtha's dark minions would take place. However, there was one place where they shouldn't reach at all costs. And that was our destination."

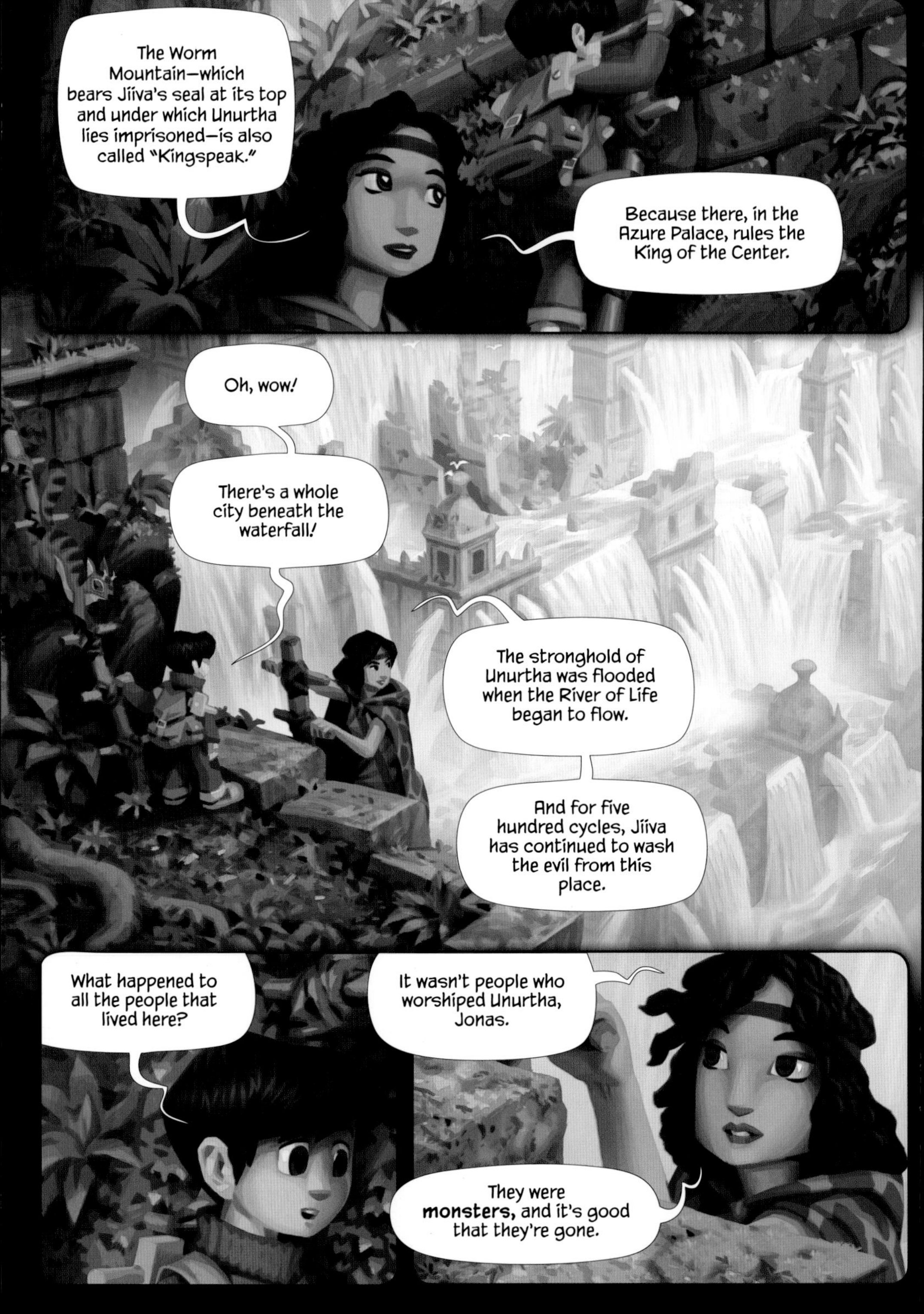
The Worm Mountain—which bears Jiiva's seal at its top and under which Unurtha lies imprisoned—is also called "Kingspeak."
Because there, in the Azure Palace, rules the King of the Center.
Oh, wow!
There's a whole city beneath the waterfall!
The stronghold of Unurtha was flooded when the River of Life began to flow.
And for five hundred cycles, Jiiva has continued to wash the evil from this place.
What happened to all the people that lived here?
It wasn't people who worshiped Unurtha, Jonas.
They were **monsters,** and it's good that they're gone.

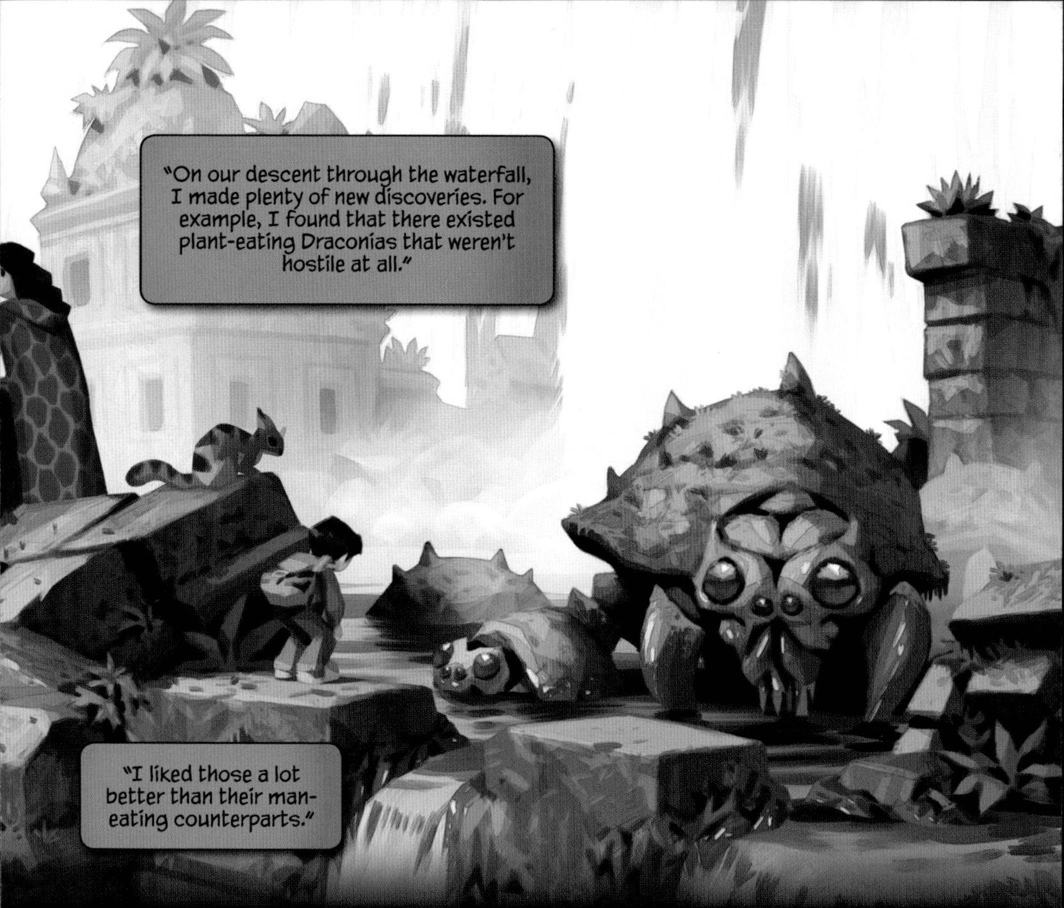
"On our descent through the waterfall, I made plenty of new discoveries. For example, I found that there existed plant-eating Draconias that weren't hostile at all."
"I liked those a lot better than their man-eating counterparts."

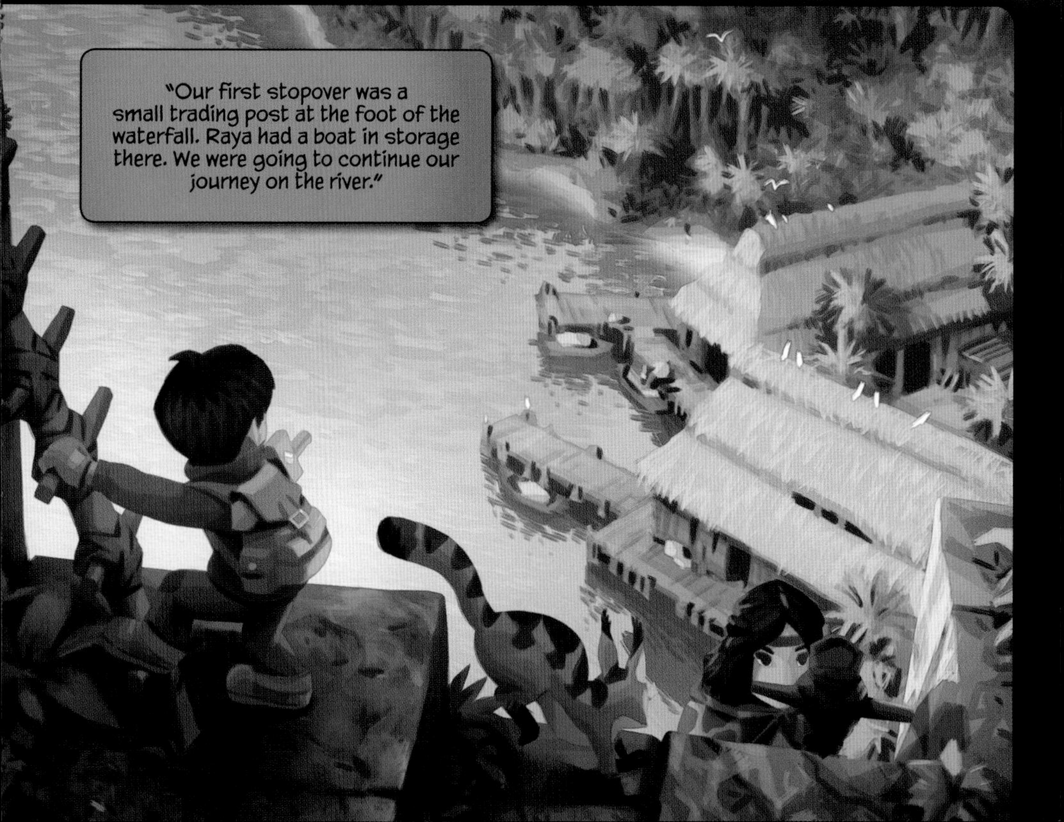
"Our first stopover was a small trading post at the foot of the waterfall. Raya had a boat in storage there. We were going to continue our journey on the river."

A strange fellow you're traveling with, Raya! Looks like a runaway to me.
What are you looking for in the north? Are you heading for Kingspeak? You mustn't have been there for **ages**, surely!
Nosy as usual, Shandar! Our destination is none of your business!
Thanks for maintaining my boat, and for the supplies. I think we've got everything. We'll cut loose immediately.
Oh, no thanks needed, Raya! Just take care if you are traveling to Kingspeak.
The merchants bring strange tales...it's not like it used to be!
We'll take care! Goodbye, Shandar!
Farewell! And may the Wanderer keep an eye on you both!

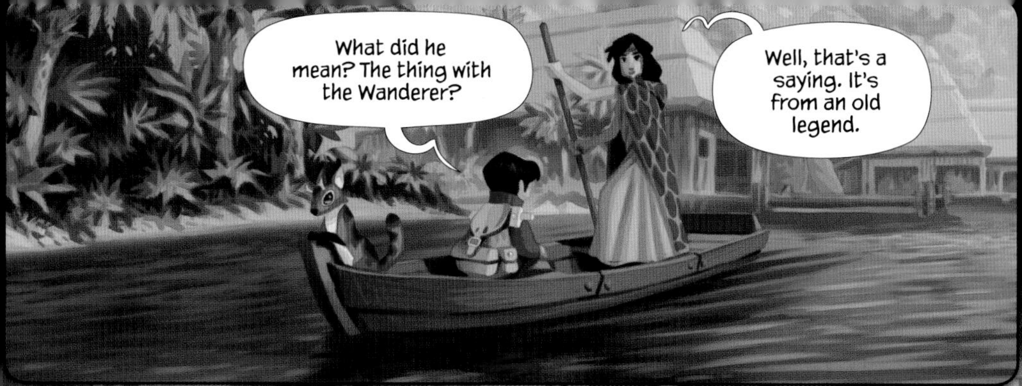
What did he mean? The thing with the Wanderer?
Well, that's a saying. It's from an old legend.
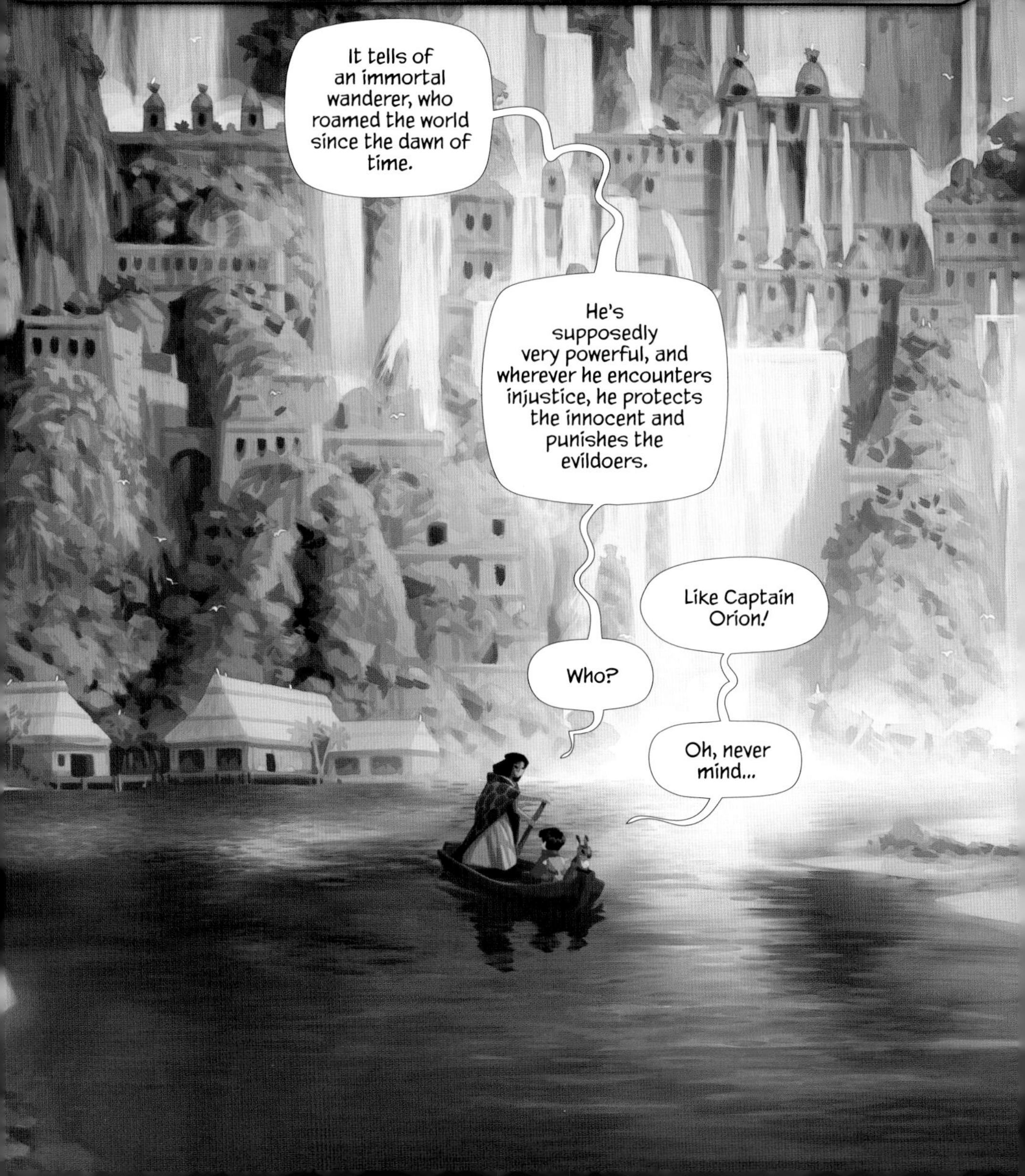
It tells of an immortal wanderer, who roamed the world since the dawn of time.
He's supposedly very powerful, and wherever he encounters injustice, he protects the innocent and punishes the evildoers.
Like Captain Orion!
Who?
Oh, never mind...

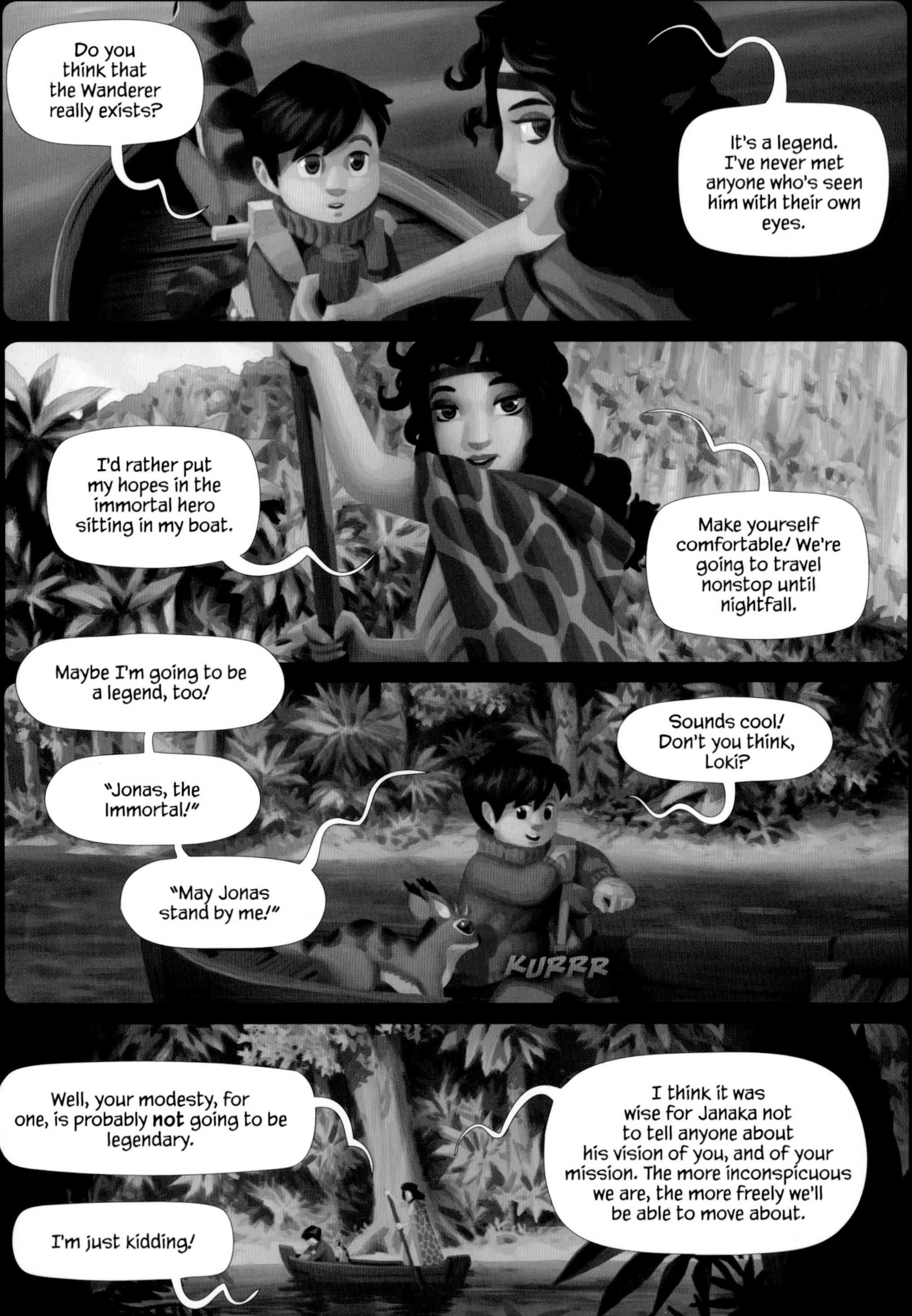
Do you think that the Wanderer really exists?
It's a legend. I've never met anyone who's seen him with their own eyes.
I'd rather put my hopes in the immortal hero sitting in my boat.
Make yourself comfortable! We're going to travel nonstop until nightfall.
Maybe I'm going to be a legend, too!
"Jonas, the Immortal!"
"May Jonas stand by me!"
Sounds cool! Don't you think, Loki?
KURRR
Well, your modesty, for one, is probably **not** going to be legendary.
I'm just kidding!
I think it was wise for Janaka not to tell anyone about his vision of you, and of your mission. The more inconspicuous we are, the more freely we'll be able to move about.

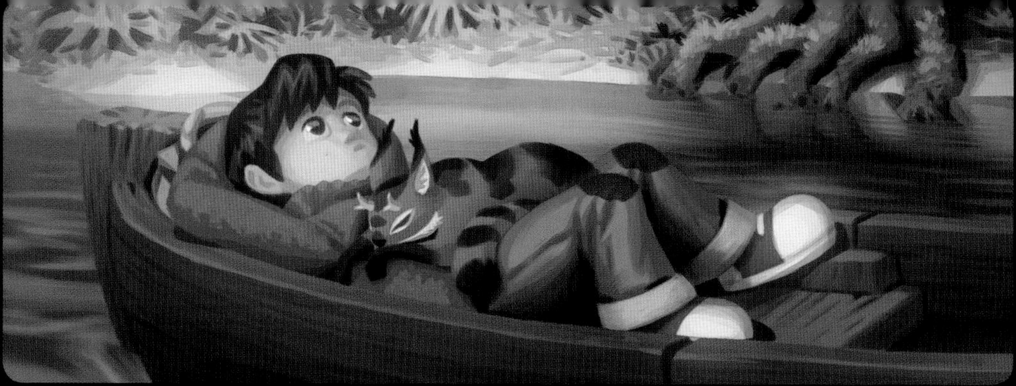

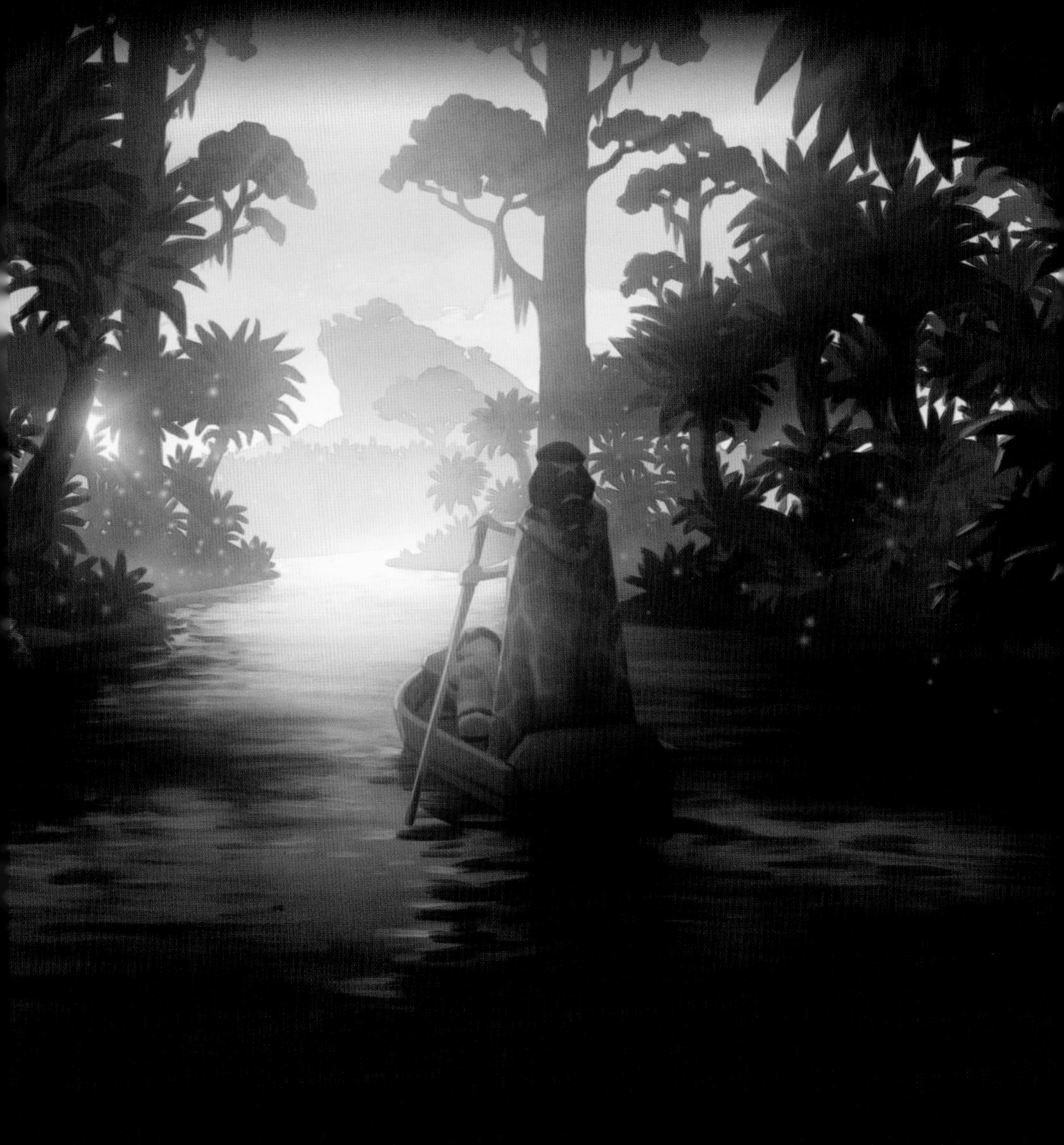

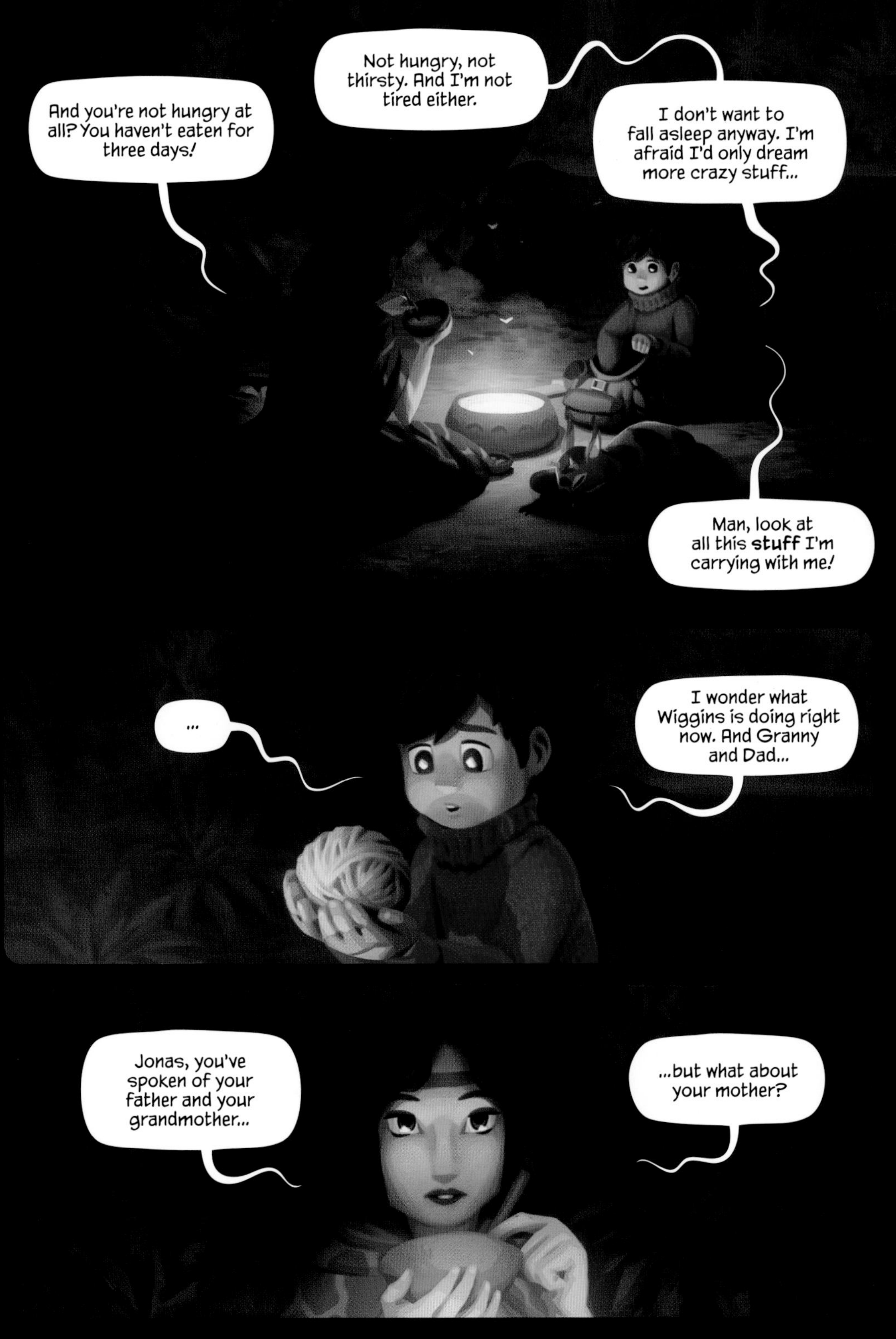
And you're not hungry at all? You haven't eaten for three days!
Not hungry, not thirsty. And I'm not tired either.
I don't want to fall asleep anyway. I'm afraid I'd only dream more crazy stuff...
Man, look at all this **stuff** I'm carrying with me!
...
I wonder what Wiggins is doing right now. And Granny and Dad...
Jonas, you've spoken of your father and your grandmother...
...but what about your mother?

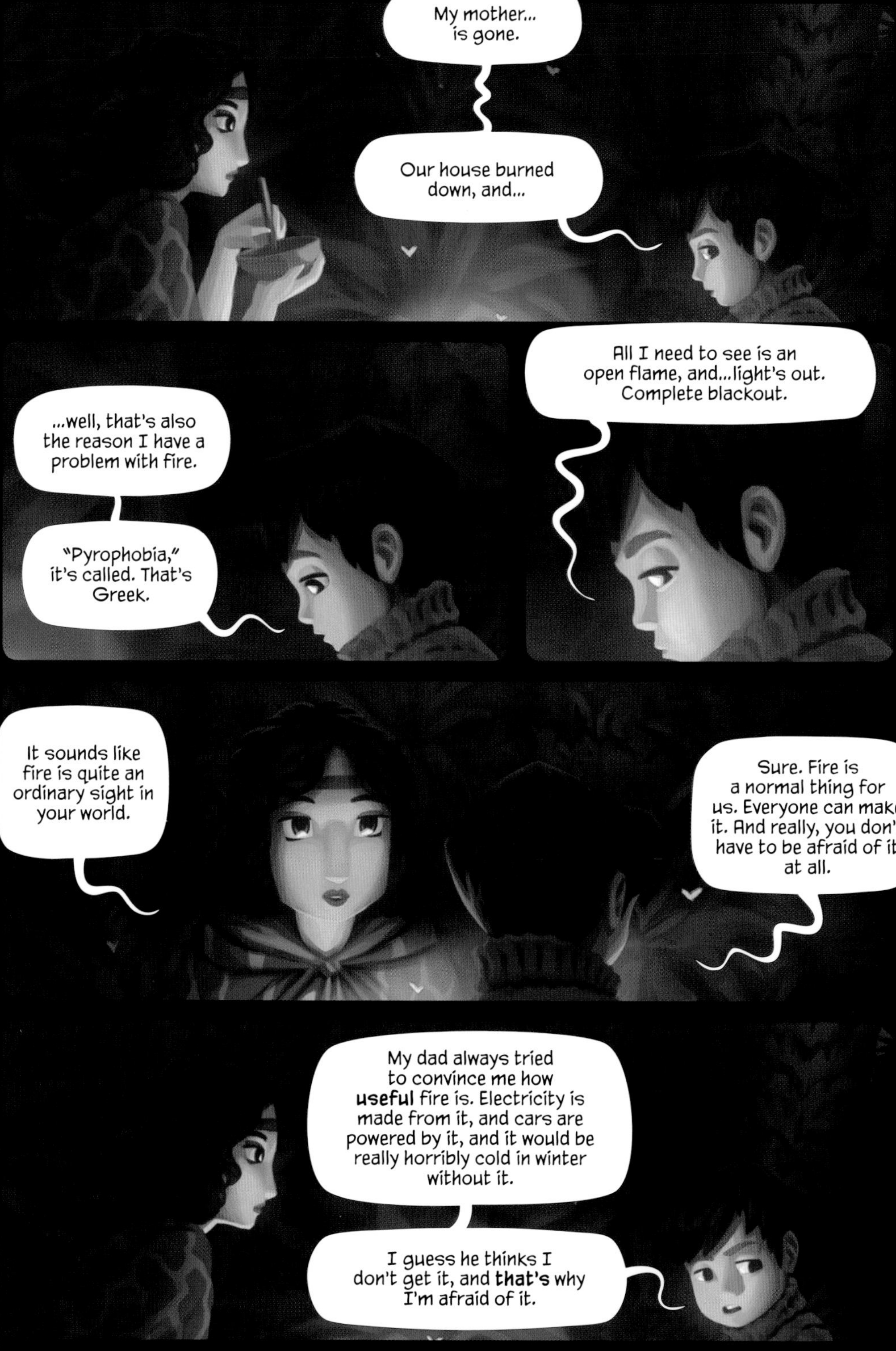
My mother... is gone.
Our house burned down, and...
...well, that's also the reason I have a problem with fire.
"Pyrophobia," it's called. That's Greek.
All I need to see is an open flame, and...light's out. Complete blackout.
It sounds like fire is quite an ordinary sight in your world.
Sure. Fire is a normal thing for us. Everyone can make it. And really, you don't have to be afraid of it at all.
My dad always tried to convince me how **useful** fire is. Electricity is made from it, and cars are powered by it, and it would be really horribly cold in winter without it.
I guess he thinks I don't get it, and **that's** why I'm afraid of it.

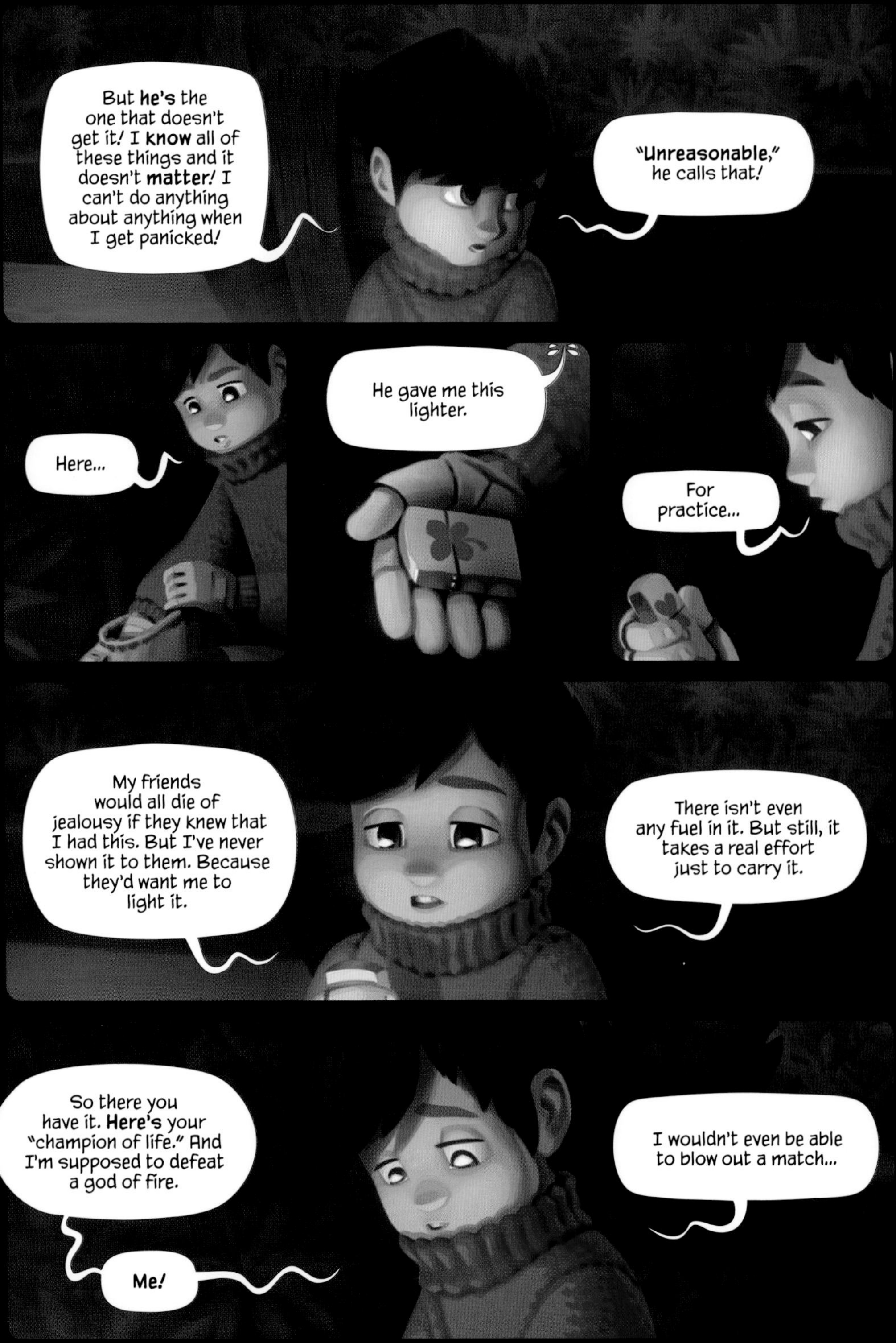

But **he's** the one that doesn't get it! I **know** all of these things and it doesn't **matter**! I can't do anything about anything when I get panicked!
"**Unreasonable,**" he calls that!
Here...
He gave me this lighter.
For practice...
My friends would all die of jealousy if they knew that I had this. But I've never shown it to them. Because they'd want me to light it.
There isn't even any fuel in it. But still, it takes a real effort just to carry it.
So there you have it. **Here's** your "champion of life." And I'm supposed to defeat a god of fire.
Me!
I wouldn't even be able to blow out a match...

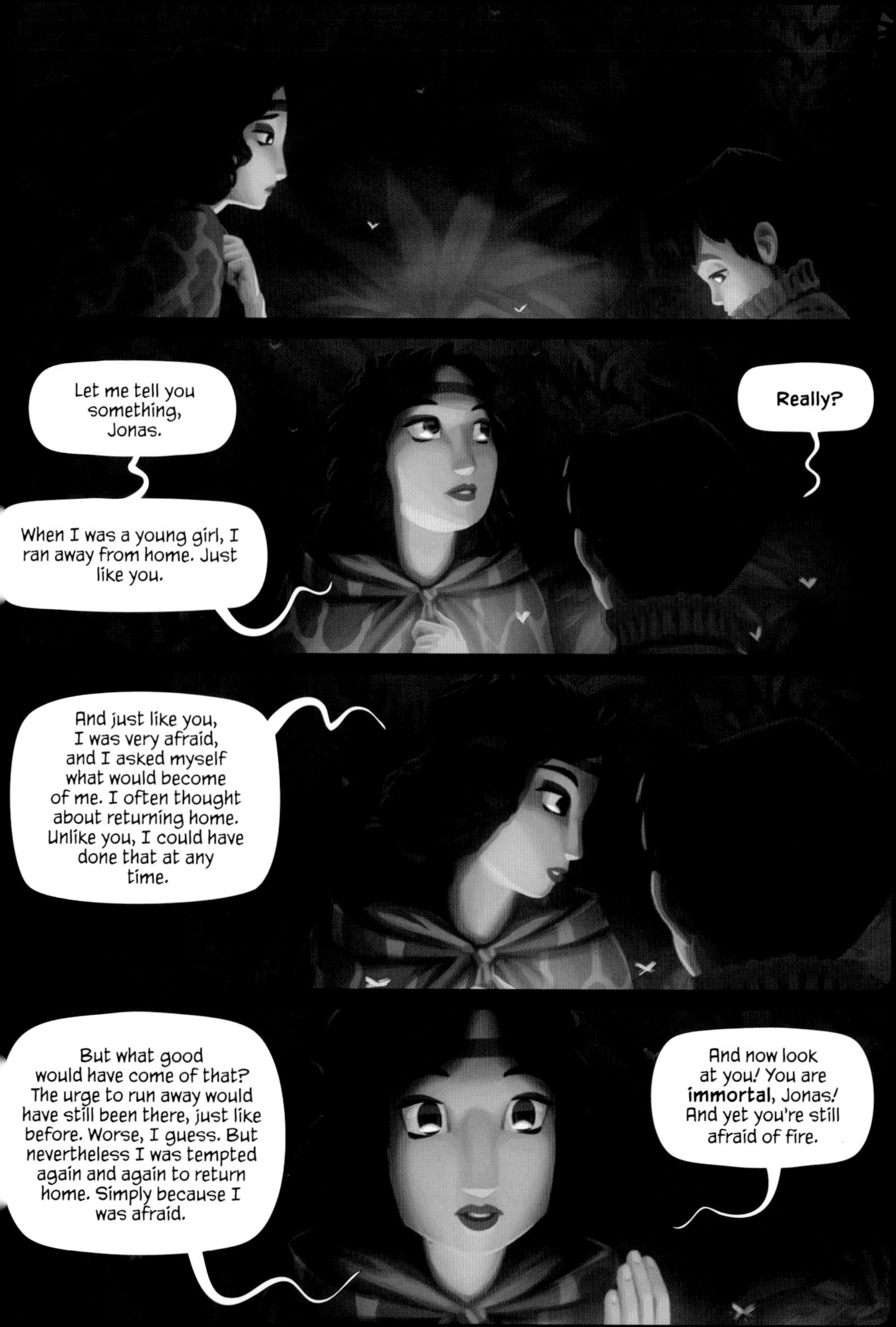
Let me tell you something, Jonas.
Really?
When I was a young girl, I ran away from home. Just like you.
And just like you, I was very afraid, and I asked myself what would become of me. I often thought about returning home. Unlike you, I could have done that at any time.
But what good would have come of that? The urge to run away would have still been there, just like before. Worse, I guess. But nevertheless I was tempted again and again to return home. Simply because I was afraid.
And now look at you! You are **immortal**, Jonas! And yet you're still afraid of fire.

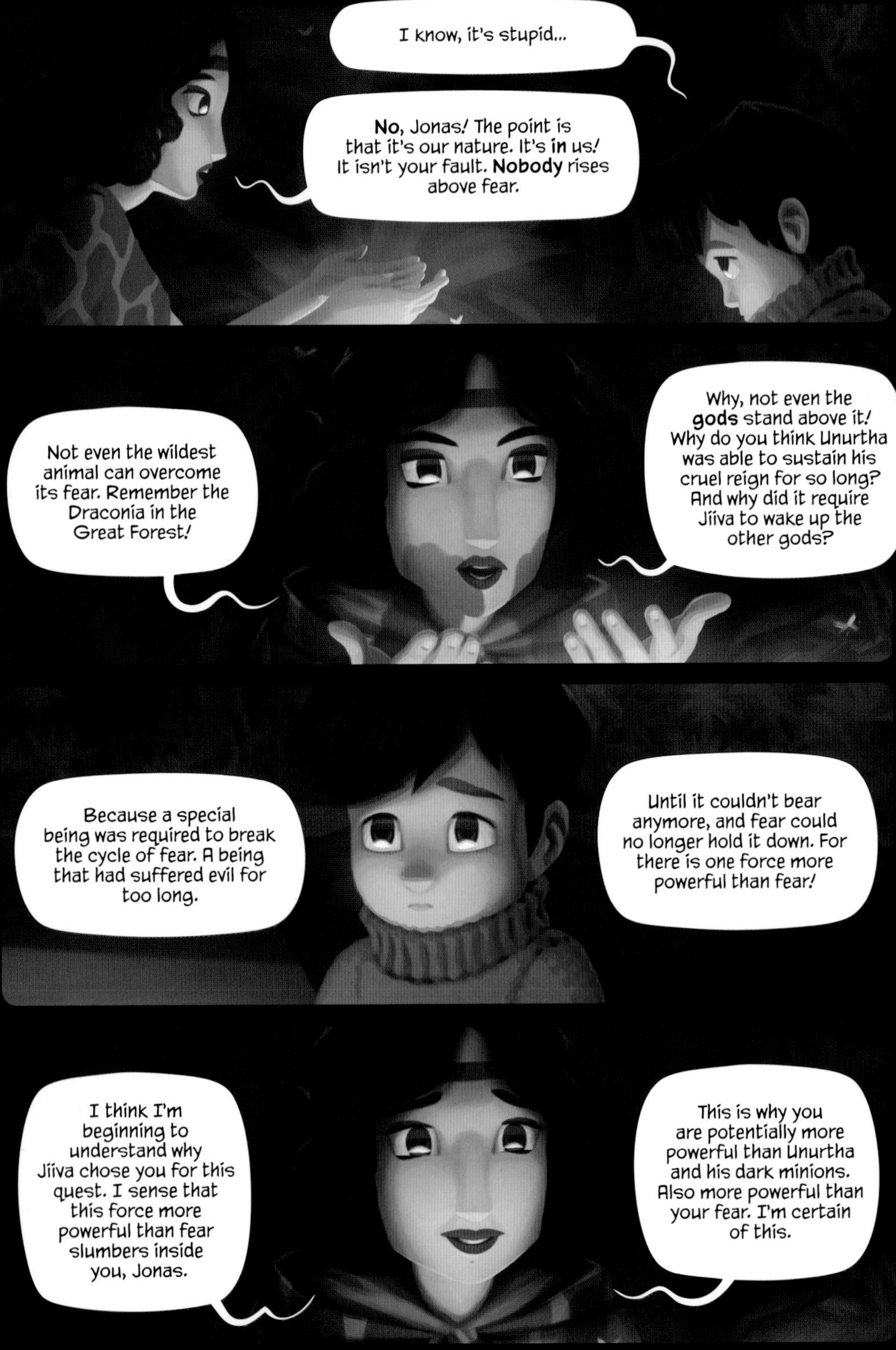

I know, it's stupid...
No, Jonas! The point is that it's our nature. It's **in** us! It isn't your fault. **Nobody** rises above fear.
Not even the wildest animal can overcome its fear. Remember the Draconia in the Great Forest!
Why, not even the **gods** stand above it! Why do you think Unurtha was able to sustain his cruel reign for so long? And why did it require Jiiva to wake up the other gods?
Because a special being was required to break the cycle of fear. A being that had suffered evil for too long.
Until it couldn't bear anymore, and fear could no longer hold it down. For there is one force more powerful than fear!
I think I'm beginning to understand why Jiiva chose you for this quest. I sense that this force more powerful than fear slumbers inside you, Jonas.
This is why you are potentially more powerful than Unurtha and his dark minions. Also more powerful than your fear. I'm certain of this.

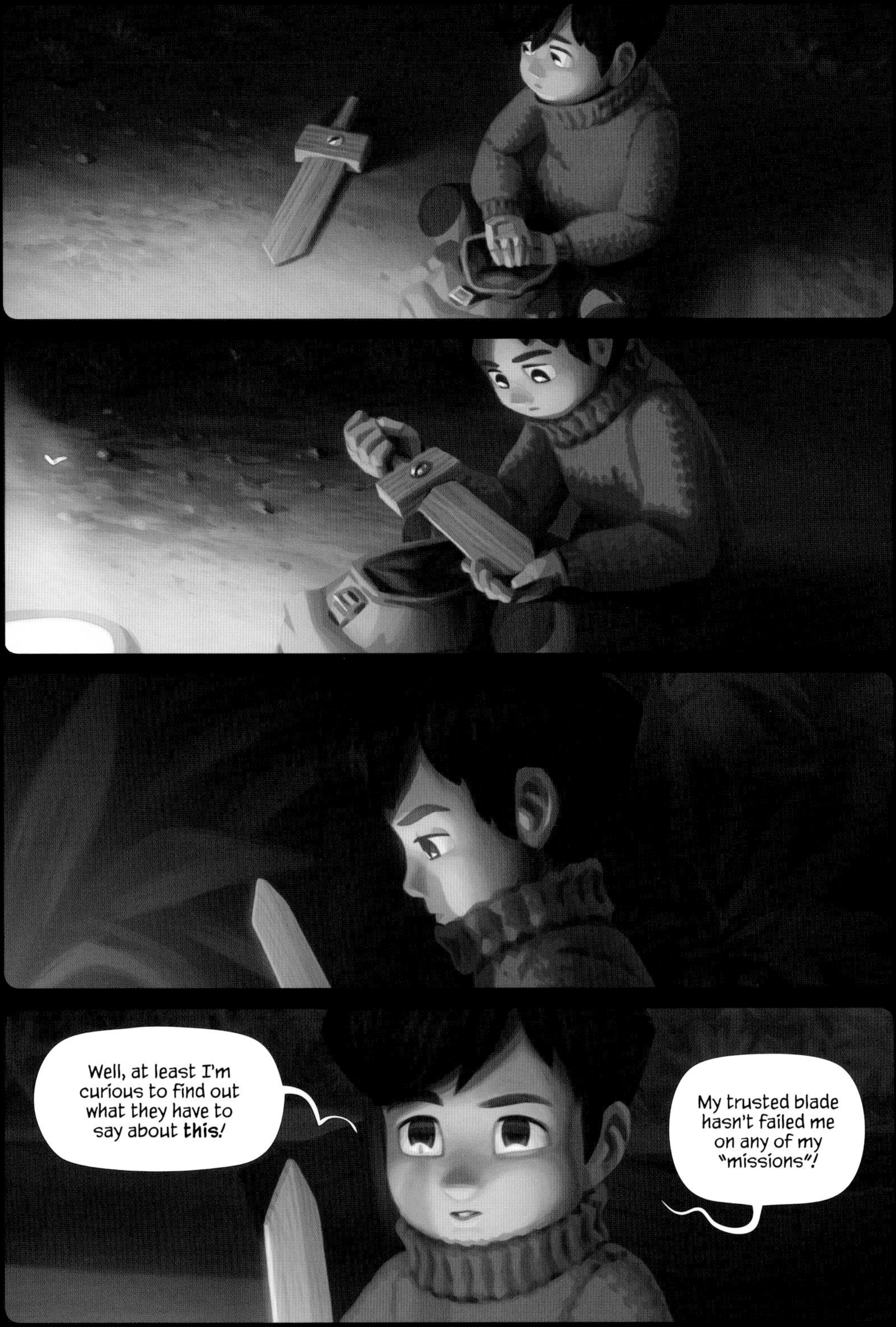
Well, at least I'm curious to find out what they have to say about **this**!
My trusted blade hasn't failed me on any of my "missions"!

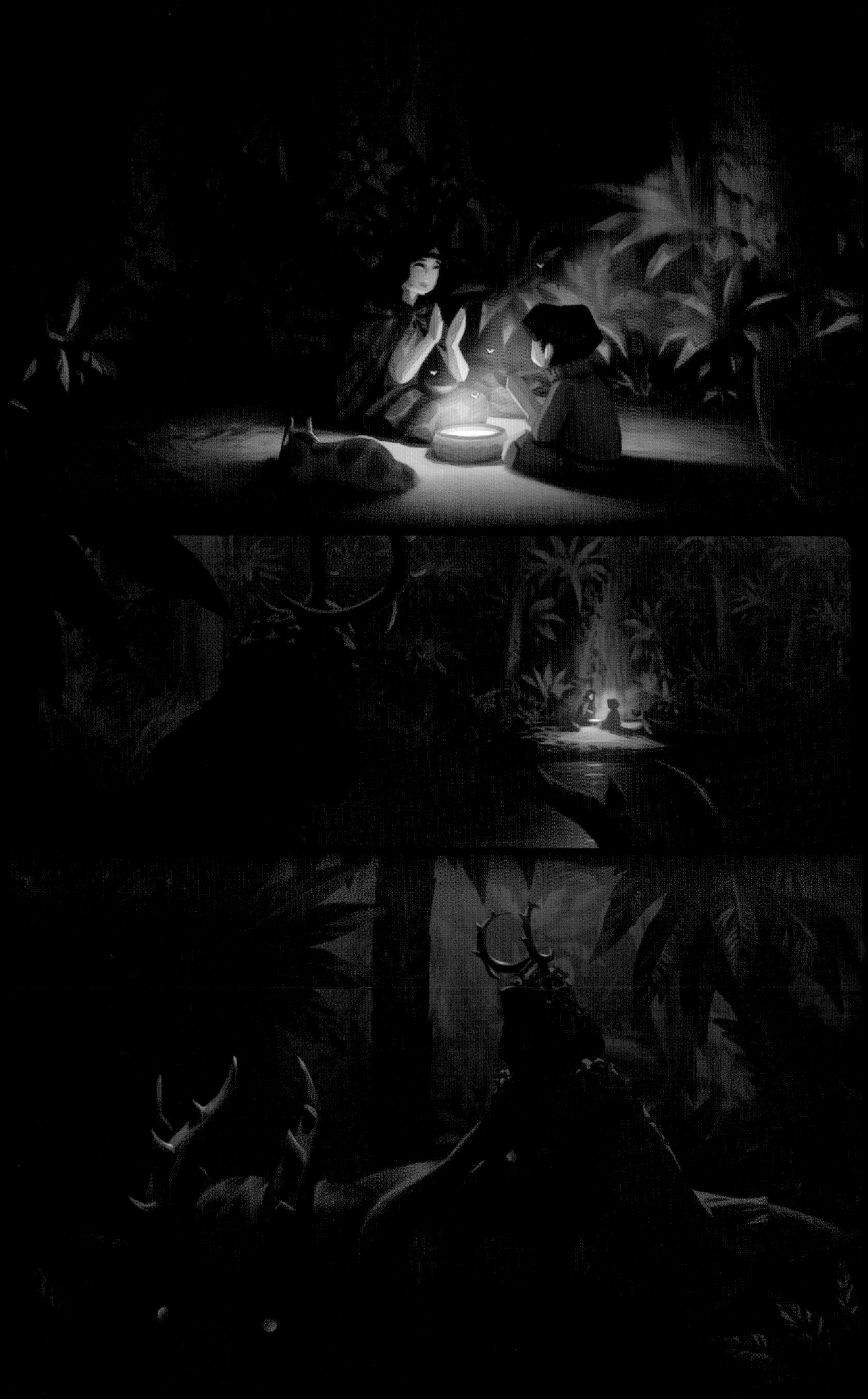

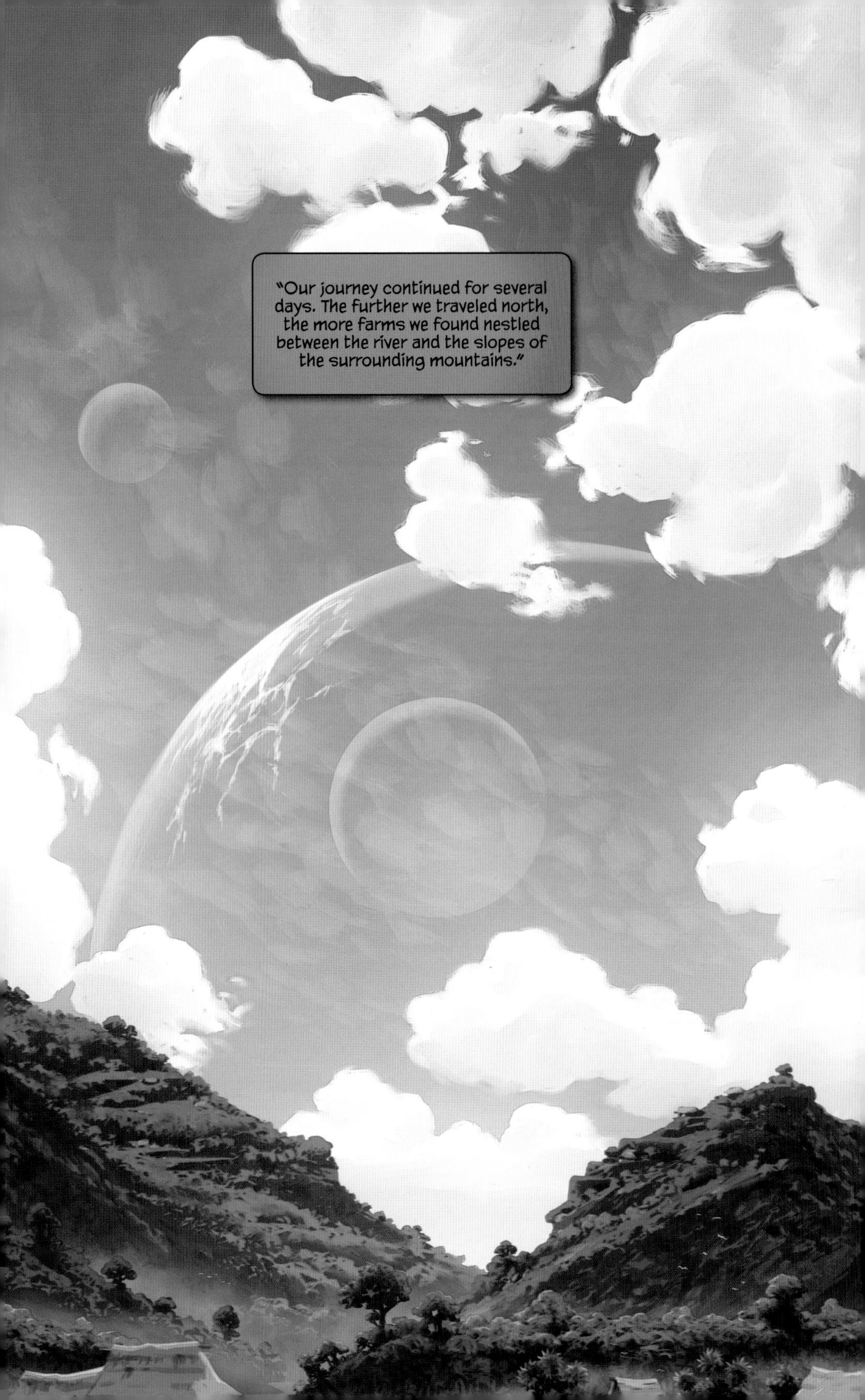
"Our journey continued for several days. The further we traveled north, the more farms we found nestled between the river and the slopes of the surrounding mountains."

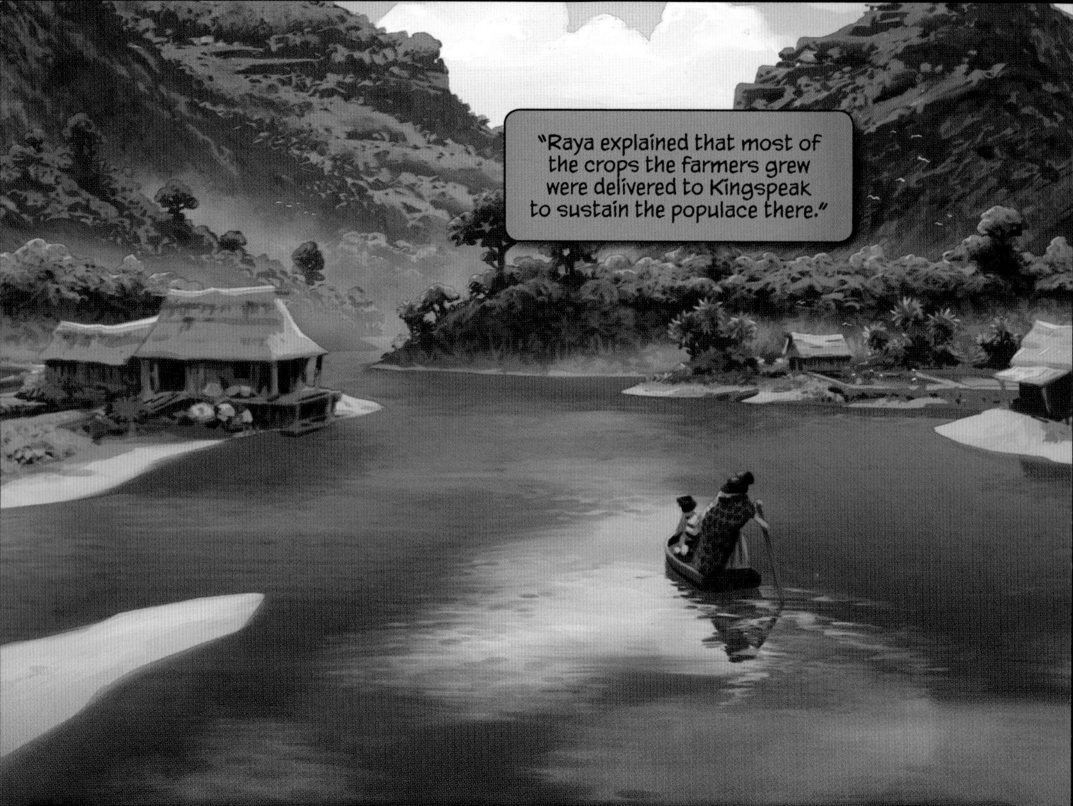
"Raya explained that most of the crops the farmers grew were delivered to Kingspeak to sustain the populace there."
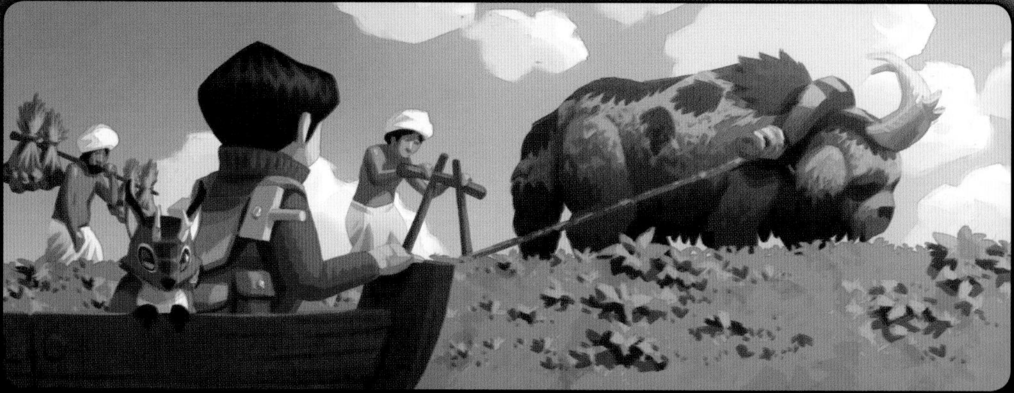
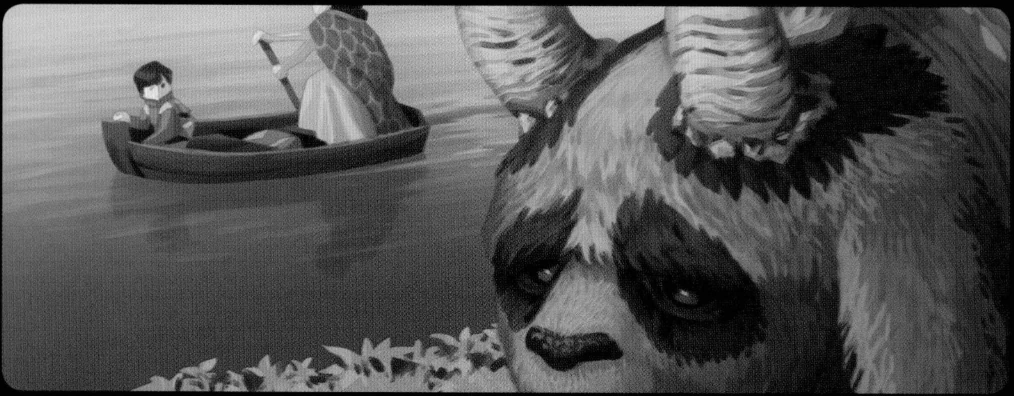

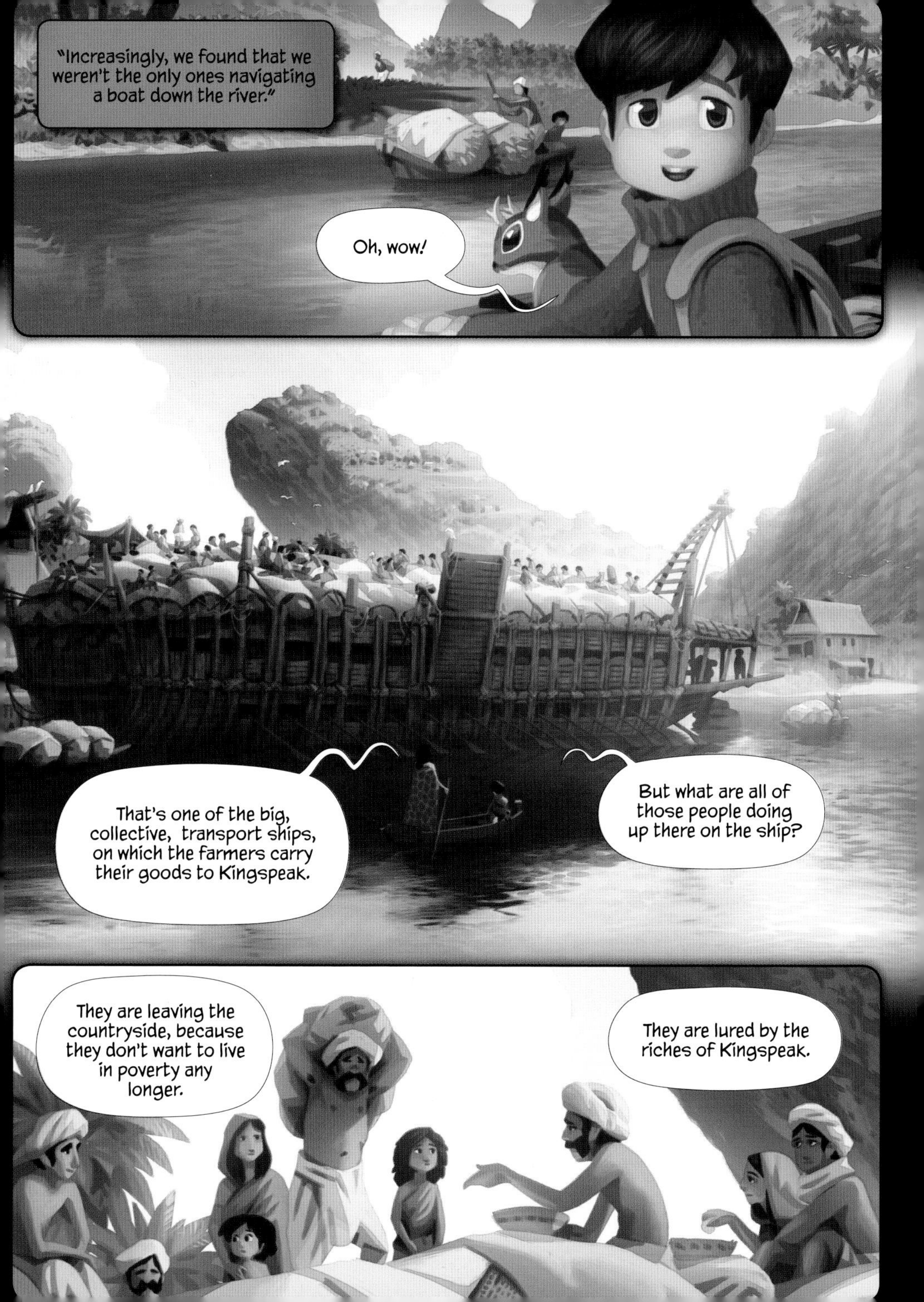
"Increasingly, we found that we weren't the only ones navigating a boat down the river."
Oh, wow!
That's one of the big, collective, transport ships, on which the farmers carry their goods to Kingspeak.
But what are all of those people doing up there on the ship?
They are leaving the countryside, because they don't want to live in poverty any longer.
They are lured by the riches of Kingspeak.

We will join them, Jonas. The water's getting too deep for me here, anyway, and that ship travels directly to Kingspeak.
What, us board that ship? **Awesome!!!**
Thank you! Your boat is in good hands!
Passengers have to travel on the roof. The stairway's over there.

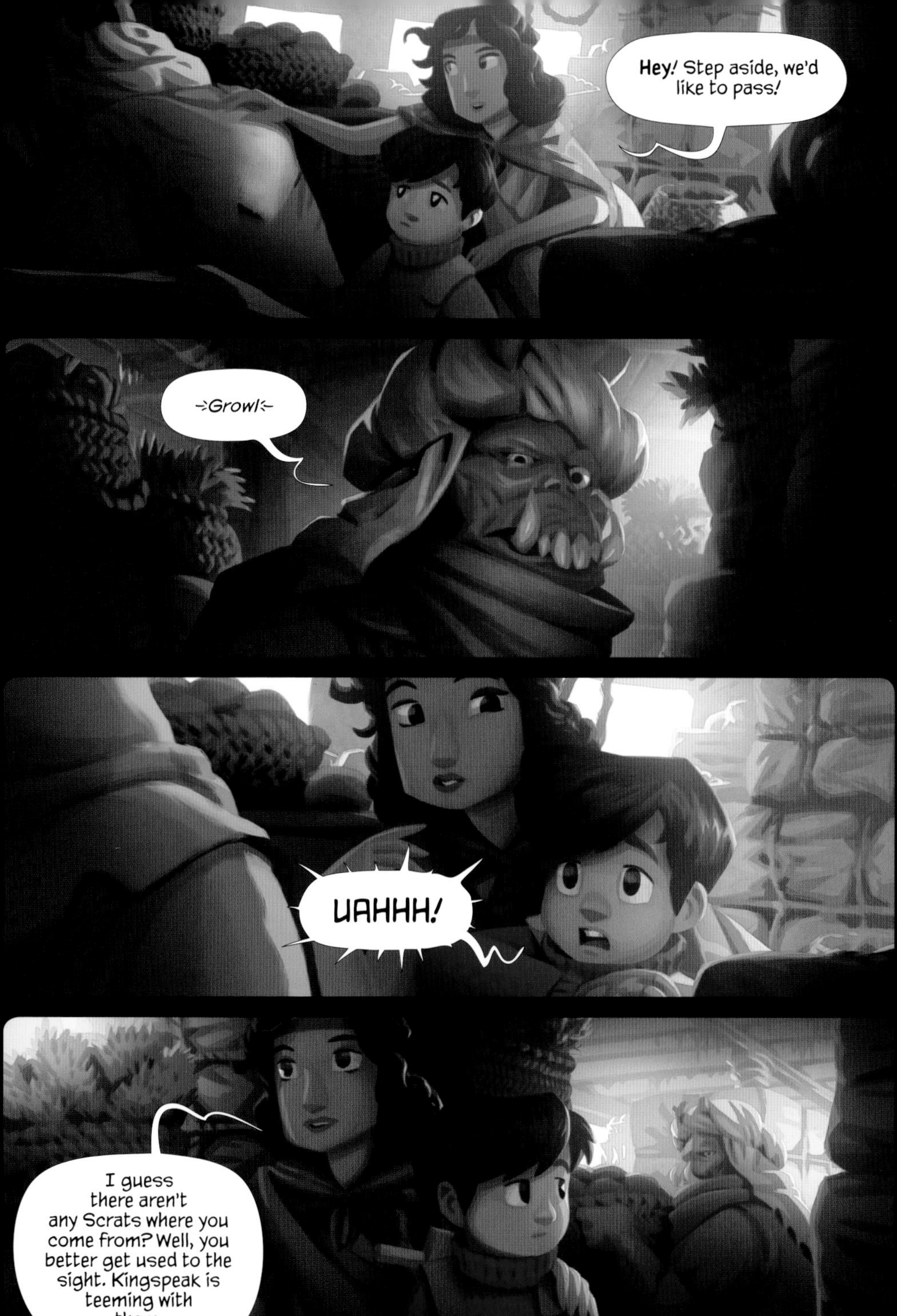
Hey! Step aside, we'd like to pass!
-Growl-
UAHHH!
I guess there aren't any Scrats where you come from? Well, you better get used to the sight. Kingspeak is teeming with them.

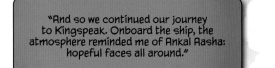

"And so we continued our journey to Kingspeak. Onboard the ship, the atmosphere reminded me of Ankal Aasha: hopeful faces all around."

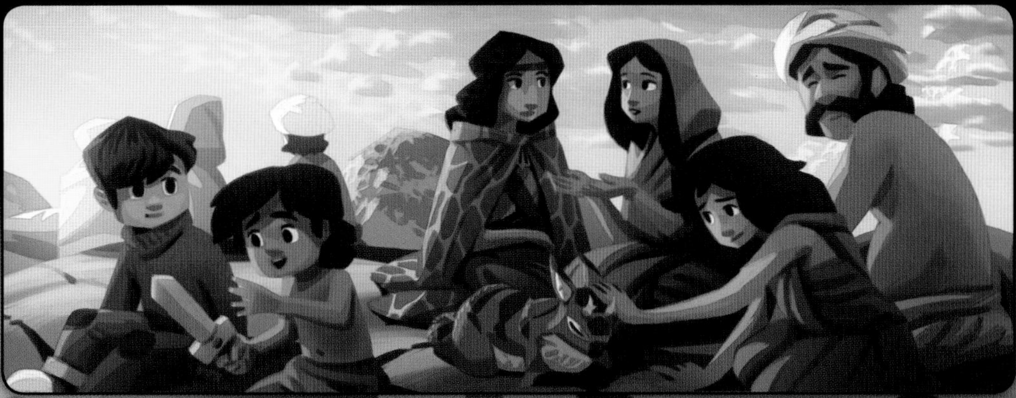

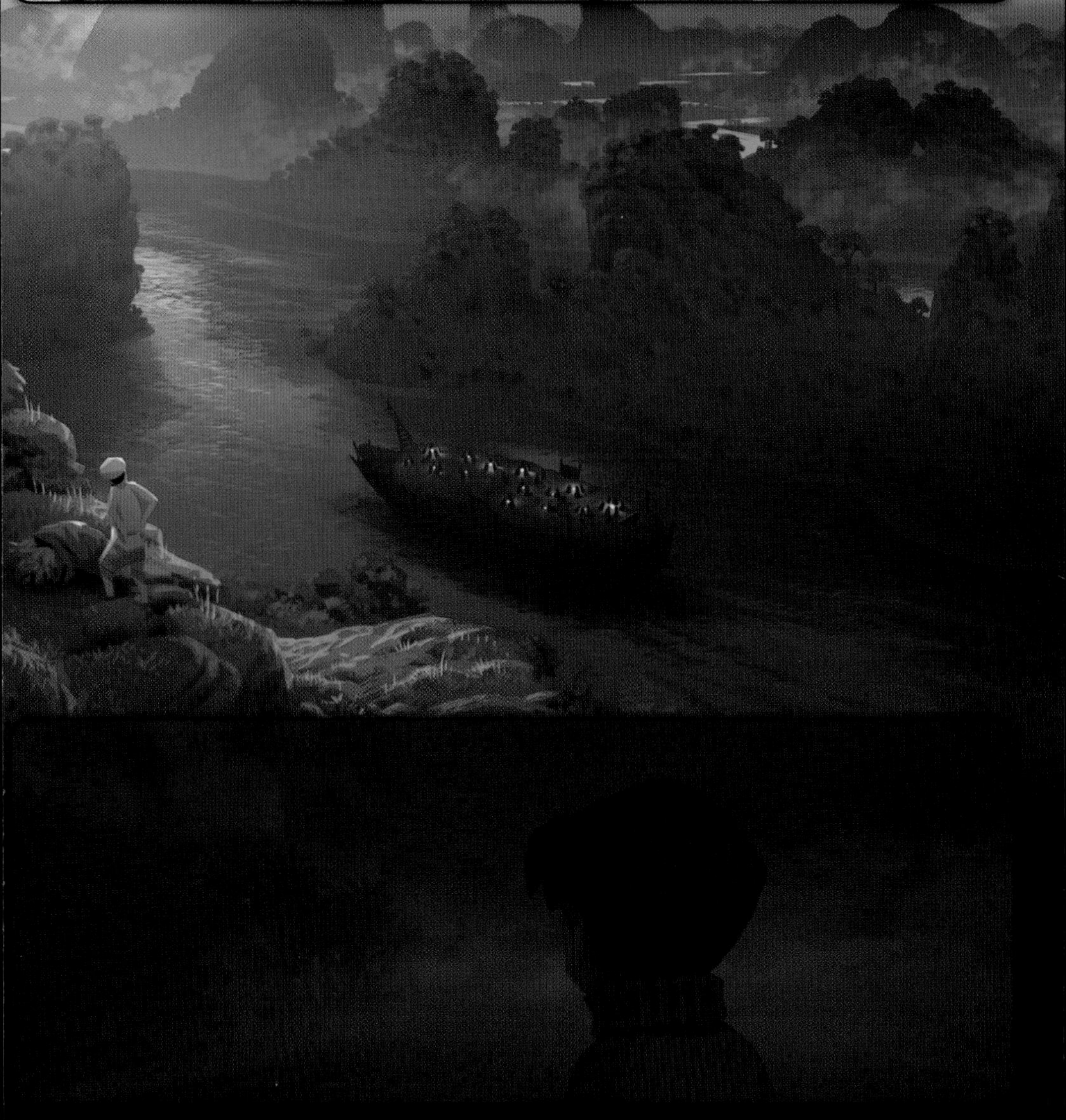

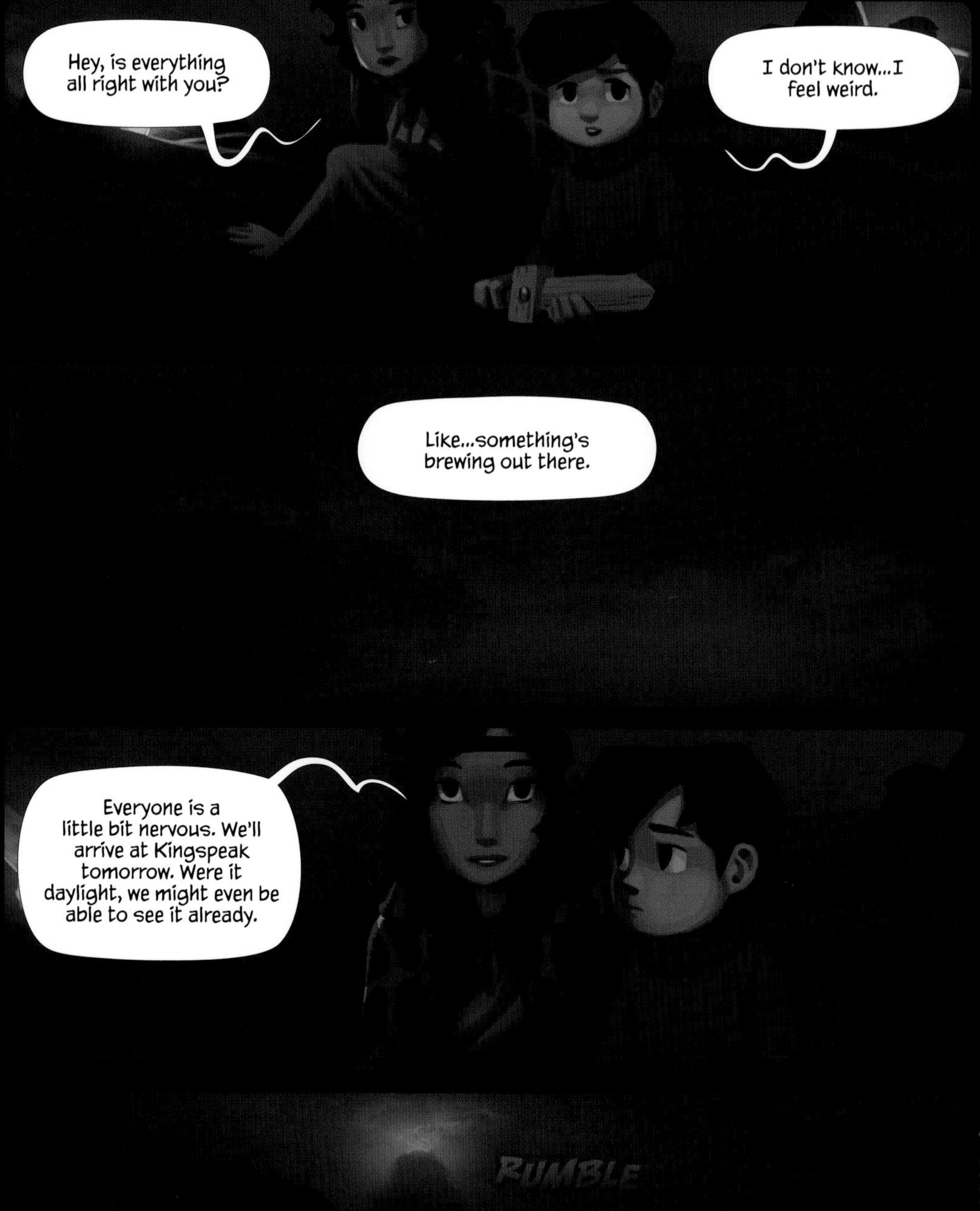
Hey, is everything all right with you?
I don't know...I feel weird.
Like...something's brewing out there.
Everyone is a little bit nervous. We'll arrive at Kingspeak tomorrow. Were it daylight, we might even be able to see it already.
RUMBLE

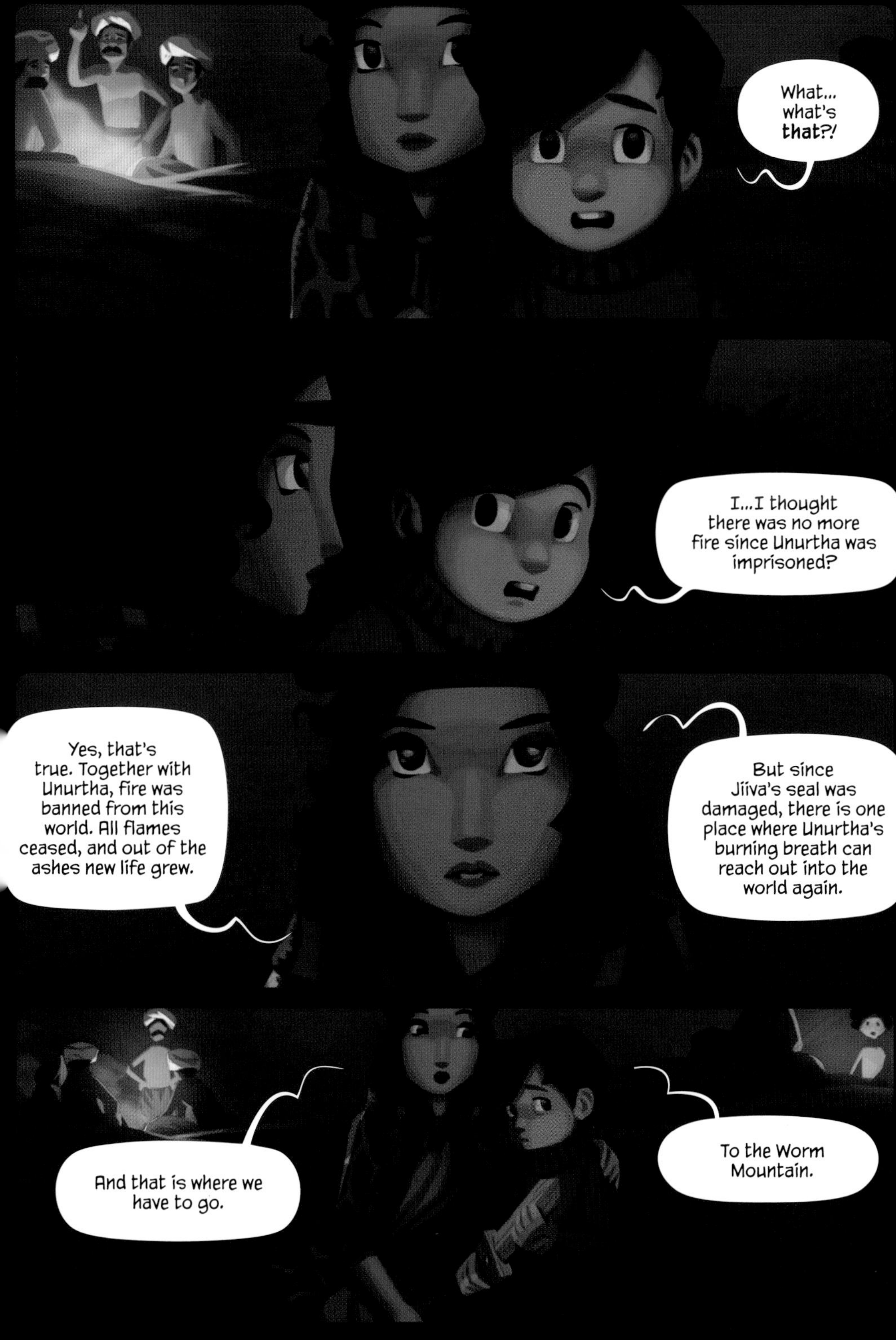
What... what's **that?!**
I...I thought there was no more fire since Unurtha was imprisoned?
Yes, that's true. Together with Unurtha, fire was banned from this world. All flames ceased, and out of the ashes new life grew.
But since Jiiva's seal was damaged, there is one place where Unurtha's burning breath can reach out into the world again.
And that is where we have to go.
To the Worm Mountain.

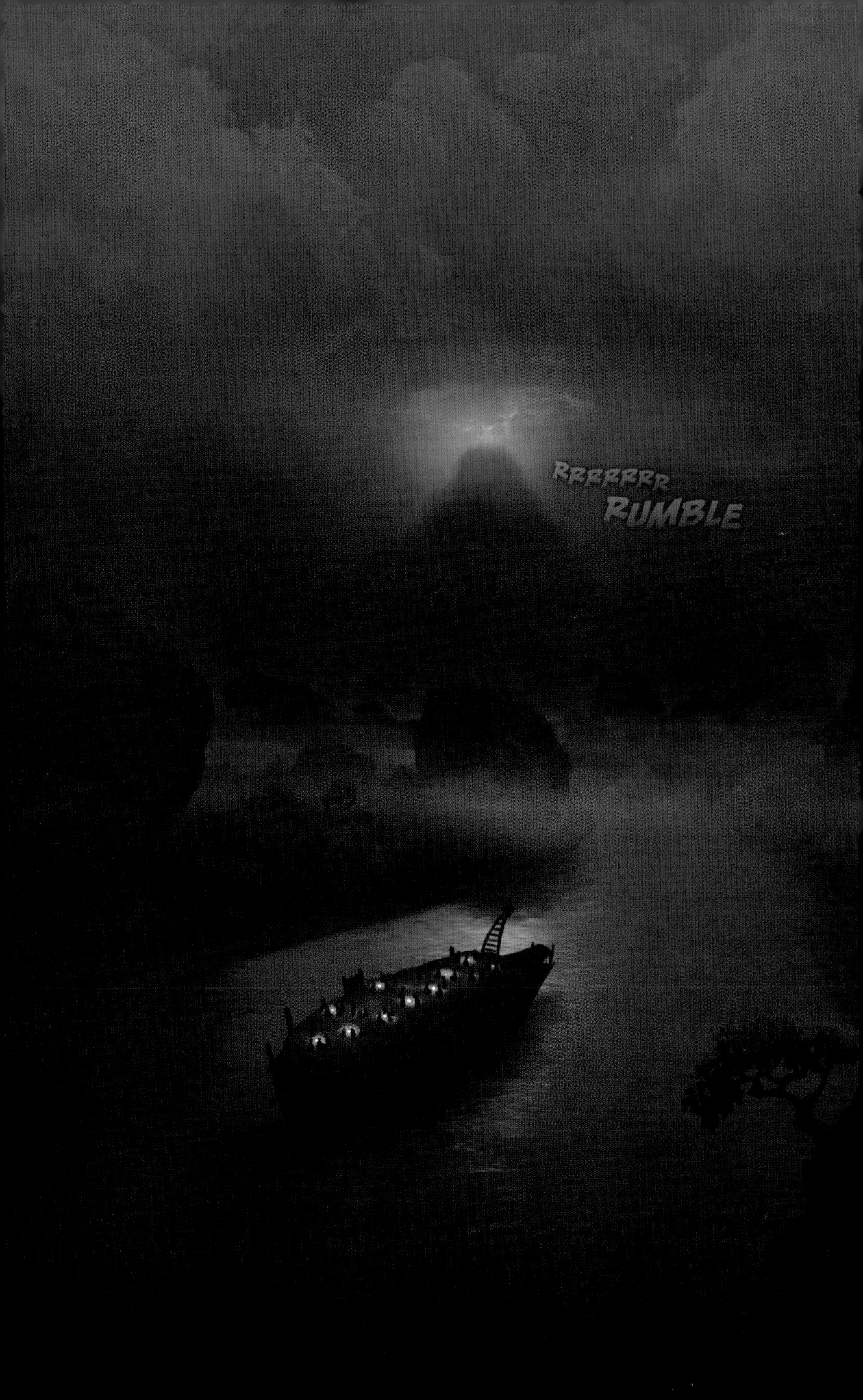
RRRRRRR
RUMBLE

A Look at the
Very Beginning of
The Wormworld Saga

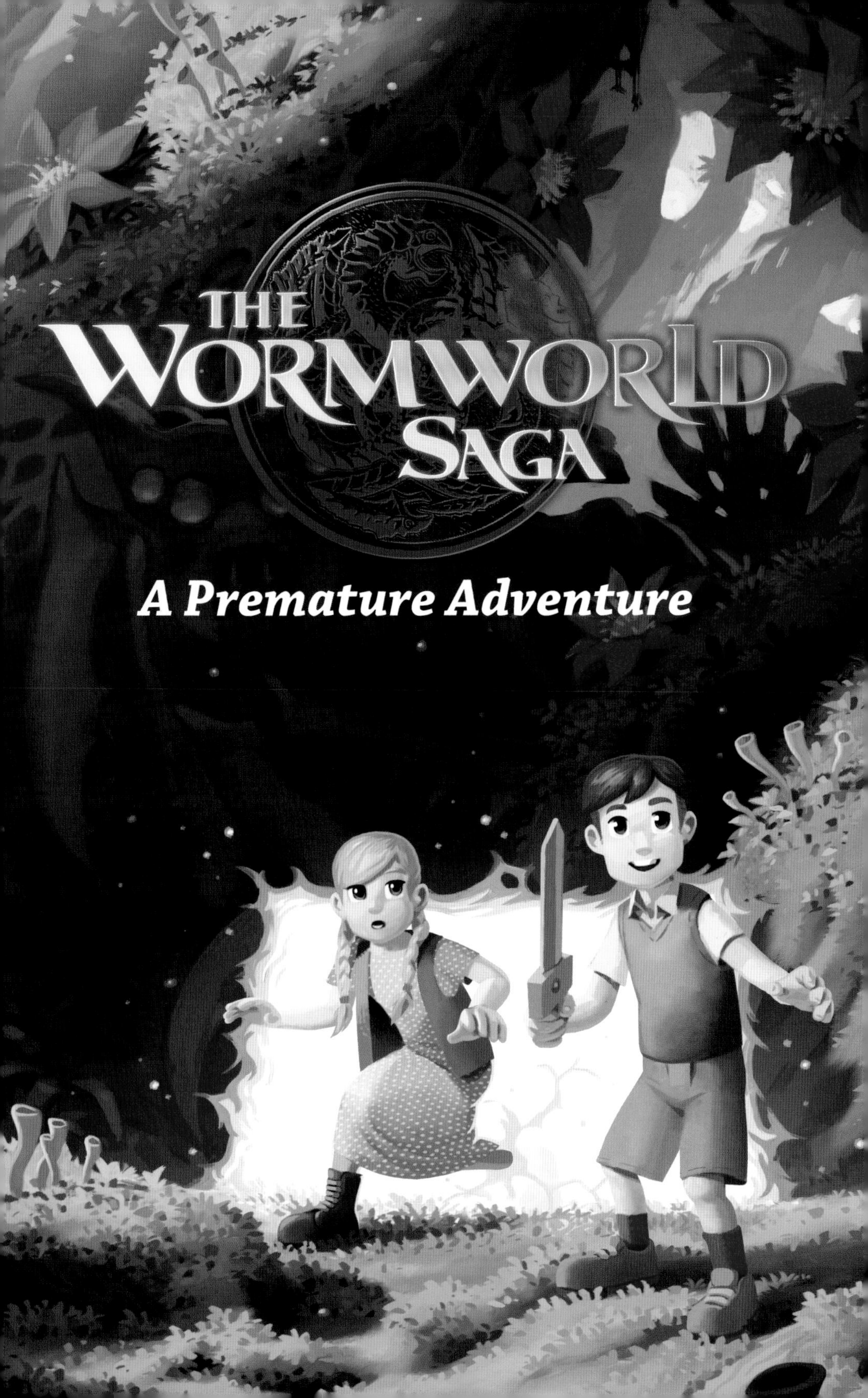
THE WORMWORLD SAGA
A Premature Adventure

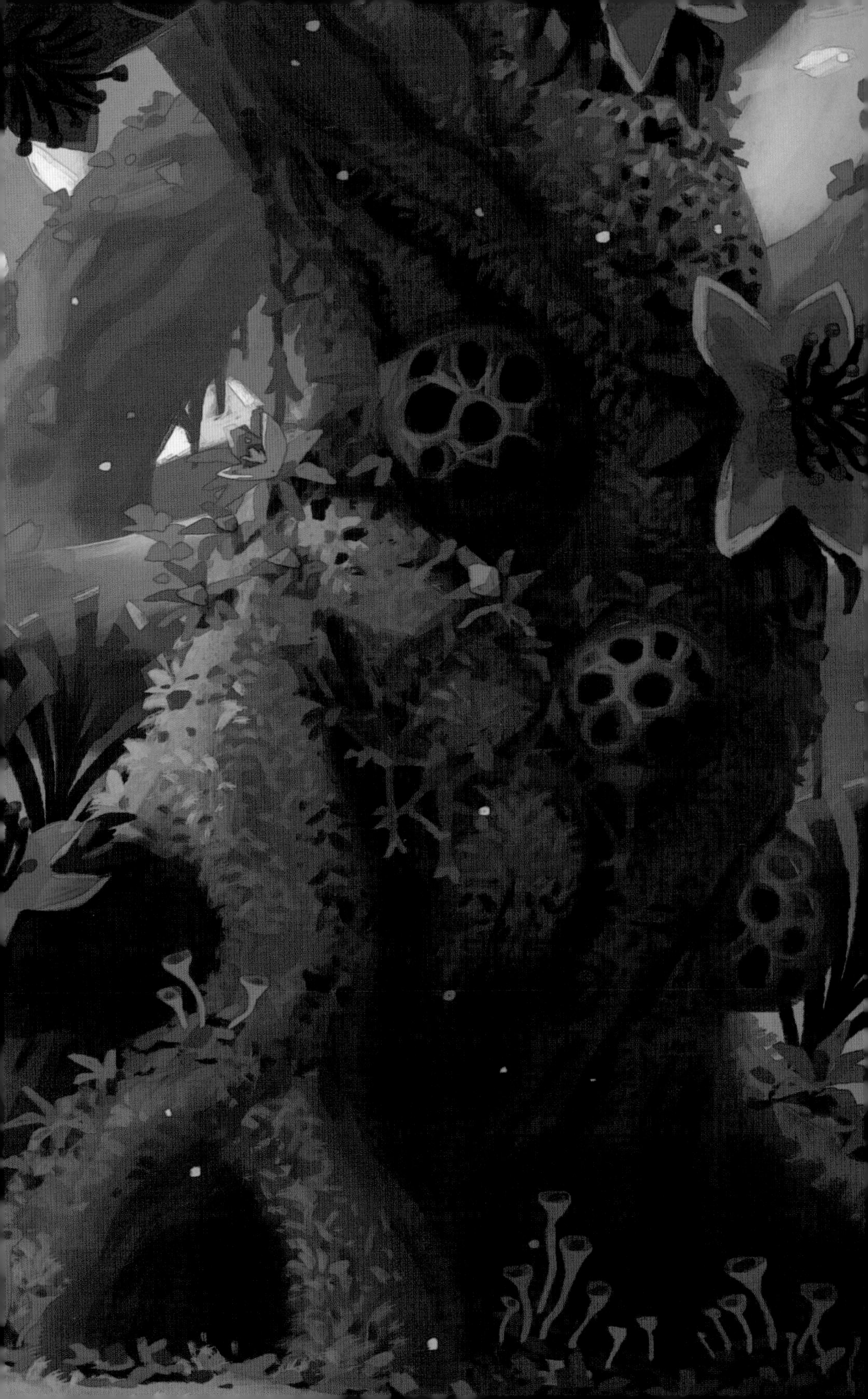

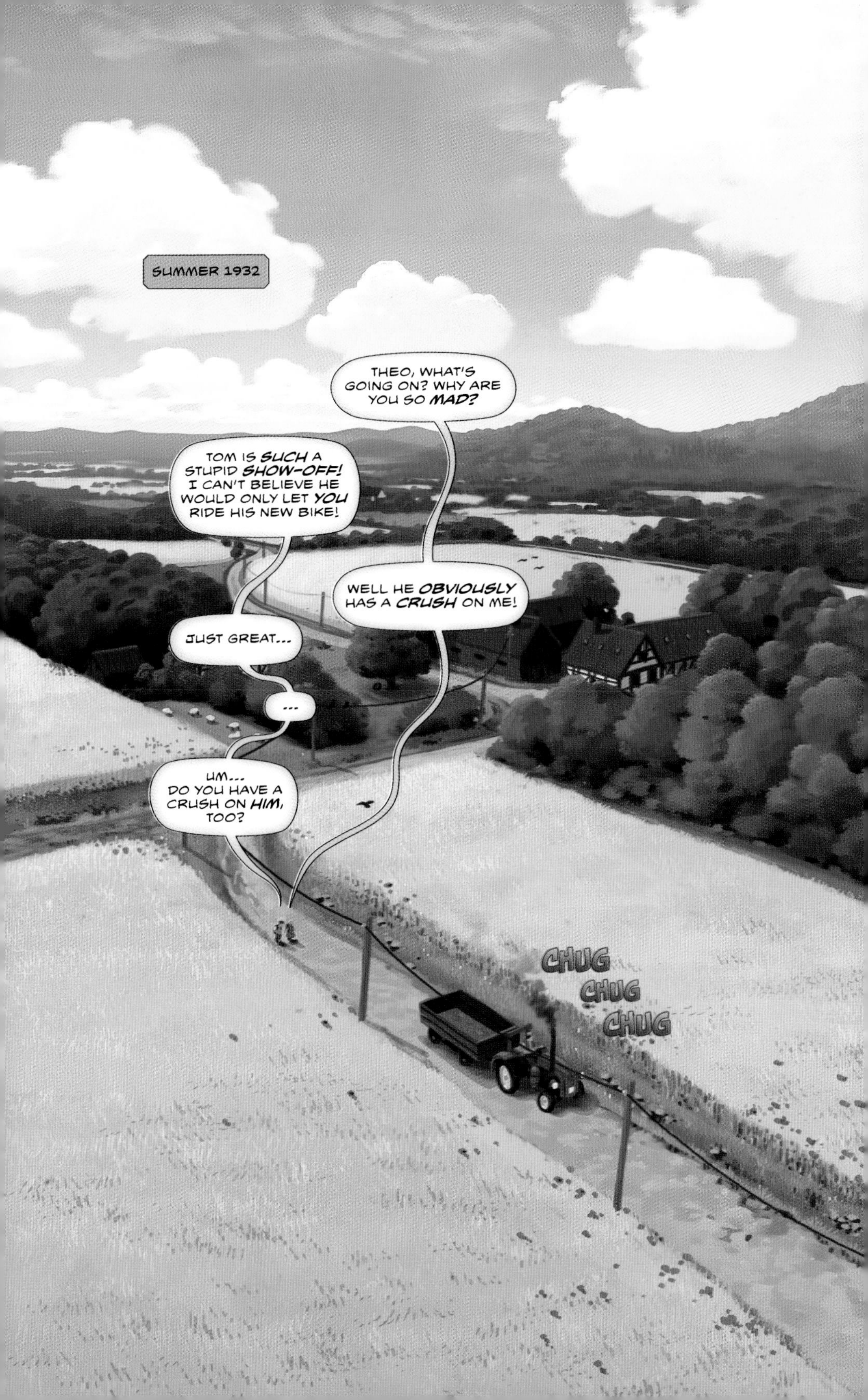
SUMMER 1932
THEO, WHAT'S GOING ON? WHY ARE YOU SO MAD?
TOM IS SUCH A STUPID SHOW-OFF! I CAN'T BELIEVE HE WOULD ONLY LET YOU RIDE HIS NEW BIKE!
WELL HE OBVIOUSLY HAS A CRUSH ON ME!
JUST GREAT...
...
UM... DO YOU HAVE A CRUSH ON HIM, TOO?
CHUG
CHUG
CHUG

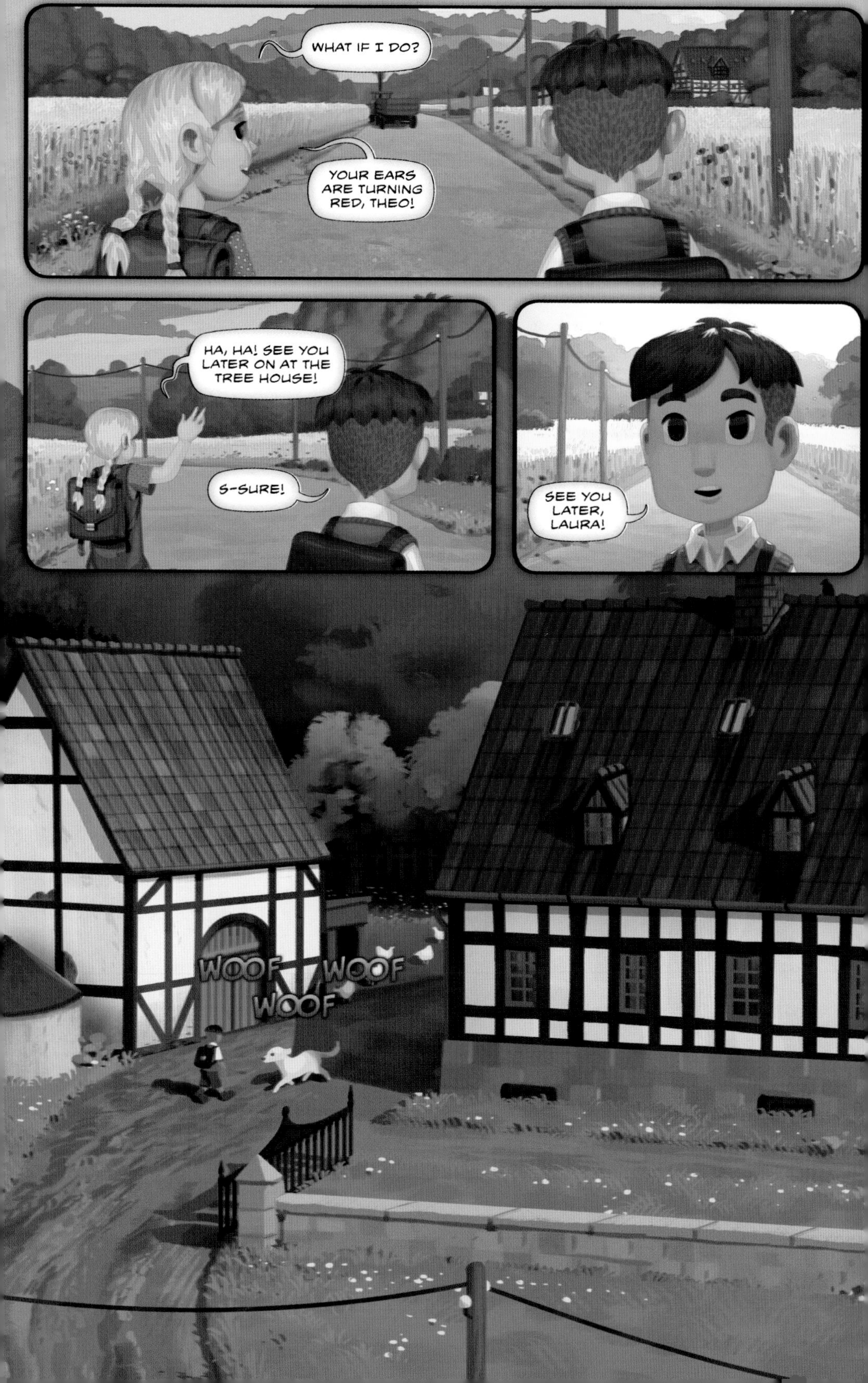
WHAT IF I DO?
YOUR EARS ARE TURNING RED, THEO!
HA, HA! SEE YOU LATER ON AT THE TREE HOUSE!
S-SURE!
SEE YOU LATER, LAURA!
WOOF WOOF WOOF

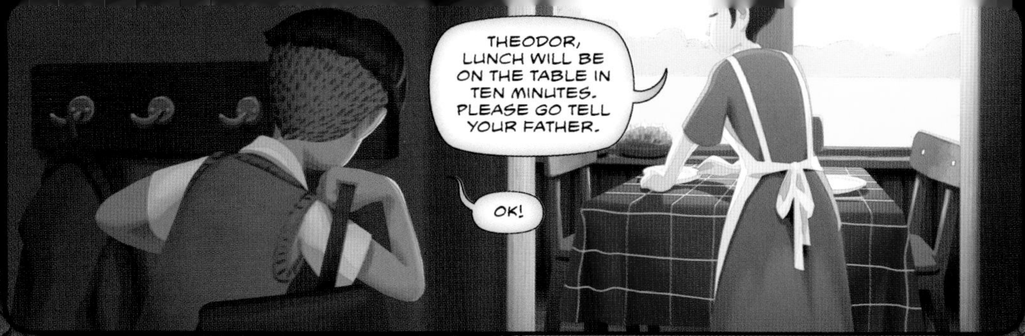
THEODOR, LUNCH WILL BE ON THE TABLE IN TEN MINUTES. PLEASE GO TELL YOUR FATHER.
OK!

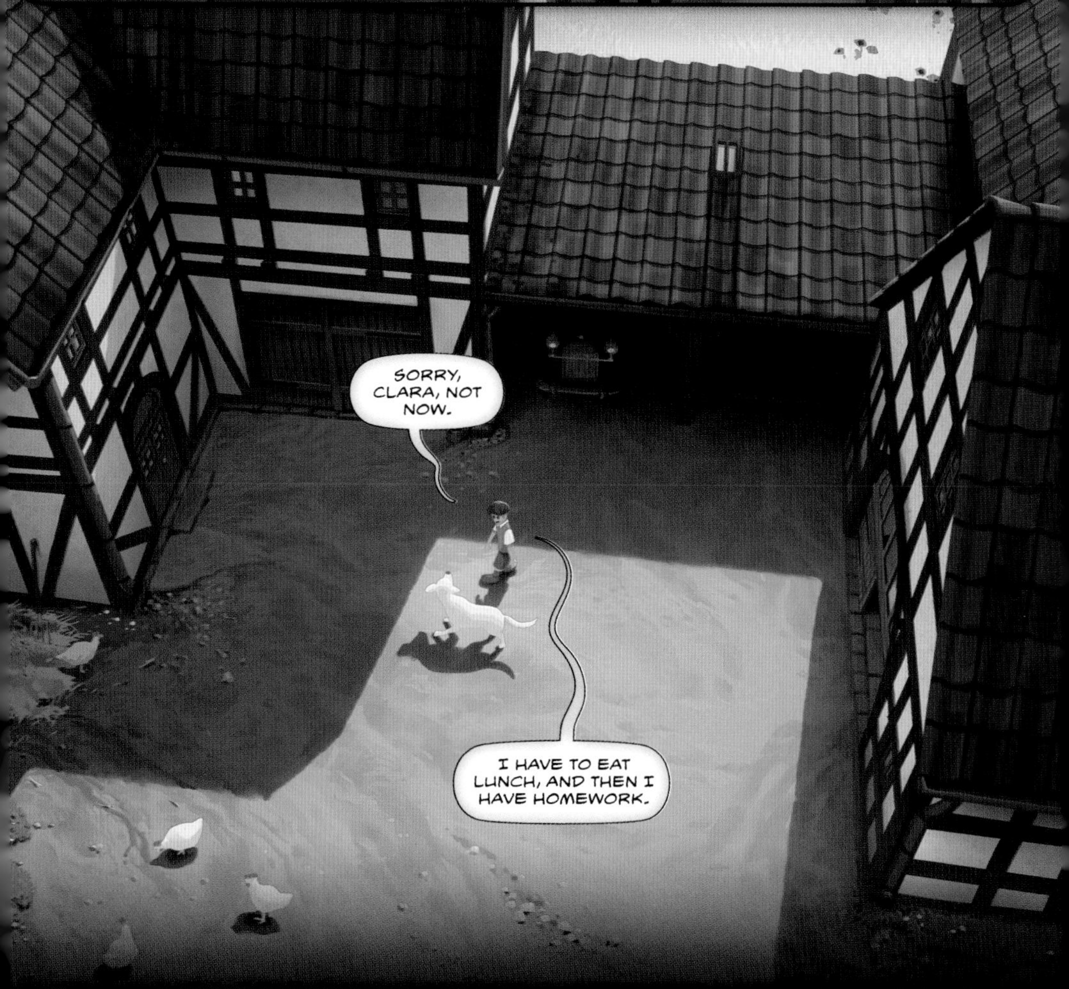
SORRY, CLARA, NOT NOW.
I HAVE TO EAT LUNCH, AND THEN I HAVE HOMEWORK.

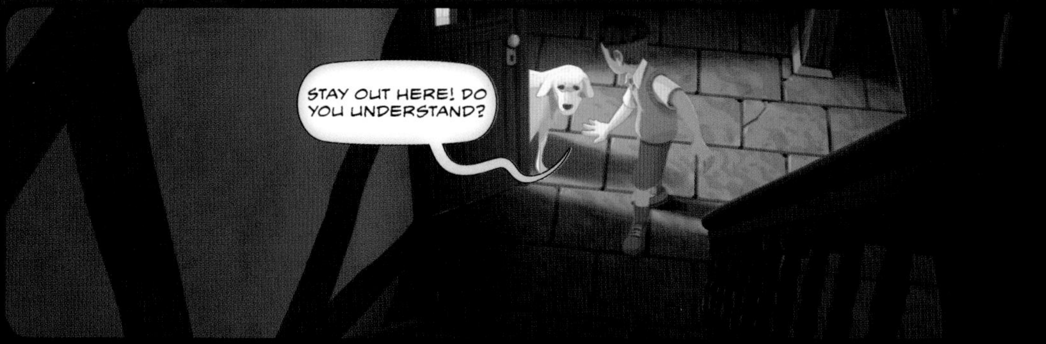
STAY OUT HERE! DO YOU UNDERSTAND?

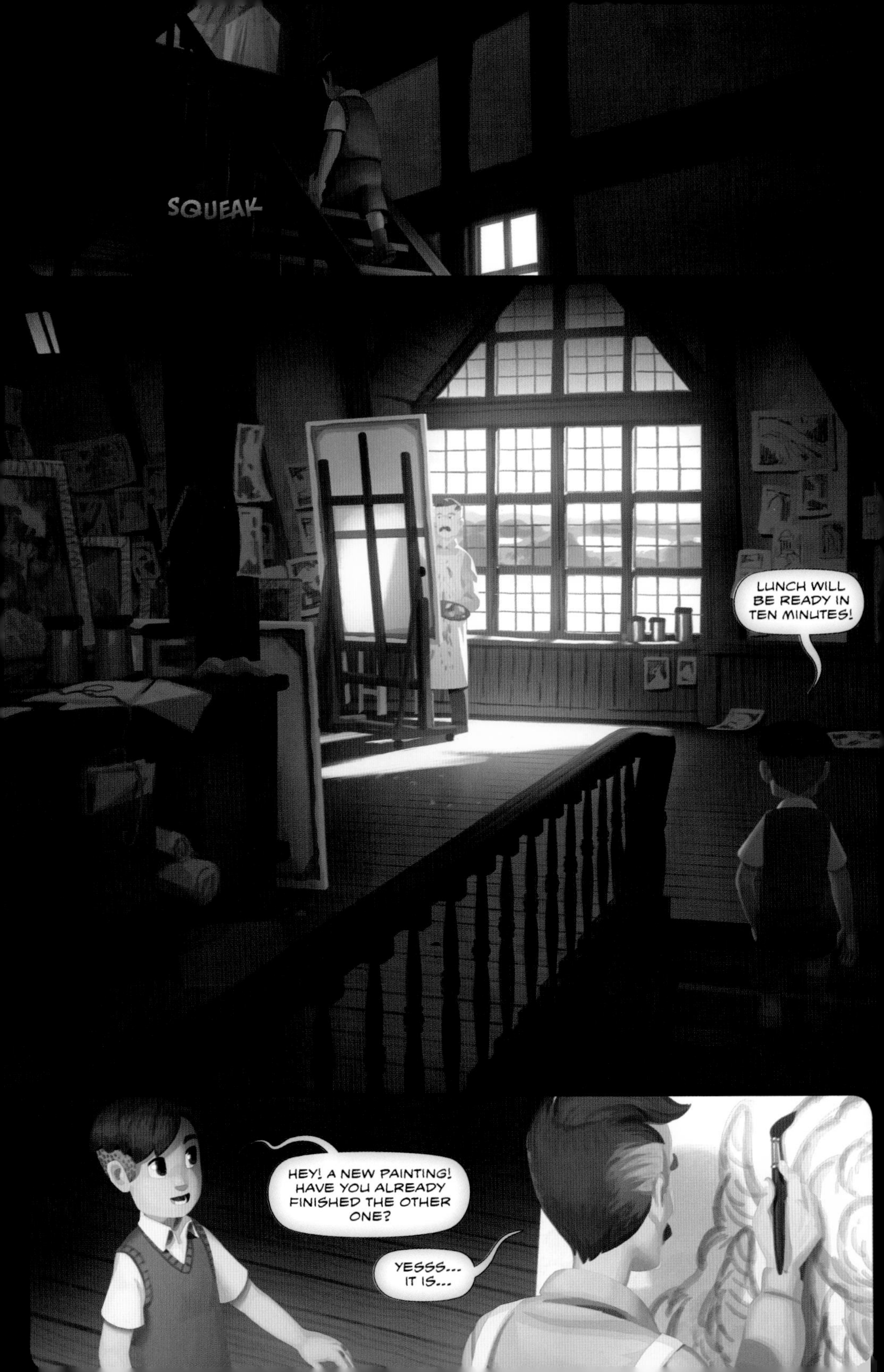
SQUEAK
LUNCH WILL BE READY IN TEN MINUTES!
HEY! A NEW PAINTING! HAVE YOU ALREADY FINISHED THE OTHER ONE?
YESSS... IT IS...

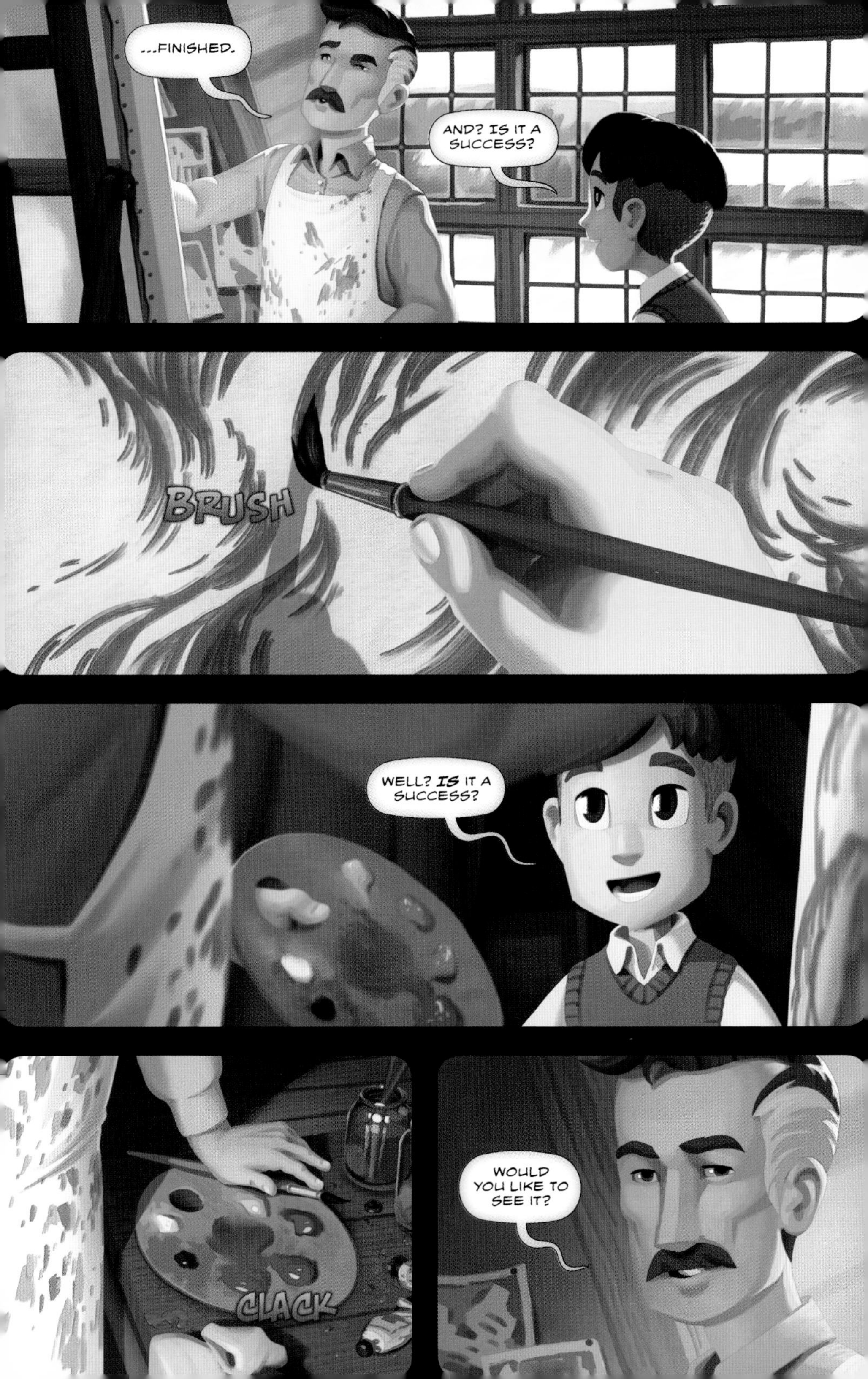
...FINISHED.
AND? IS IT A SUCCESS?
BRUSH
WELL? *IS* IT A SUCCESS?
CLACK
WOULD YOU LIKE TO SEE IT?

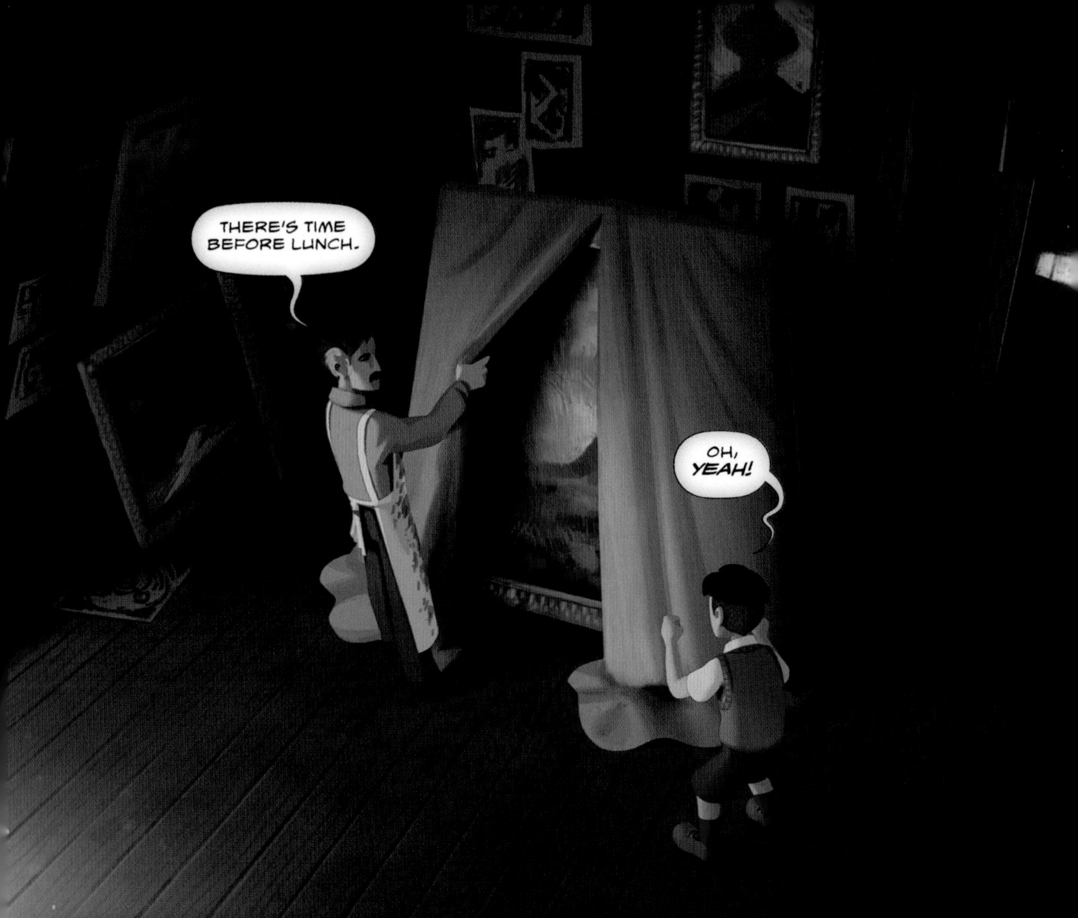
THERE'S TIME BEFORE LUNCH.
OH, YEAH!

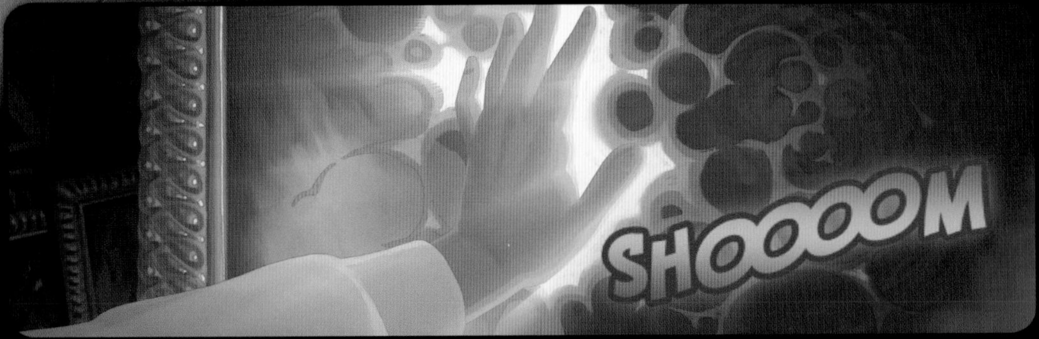
SHOOOOM

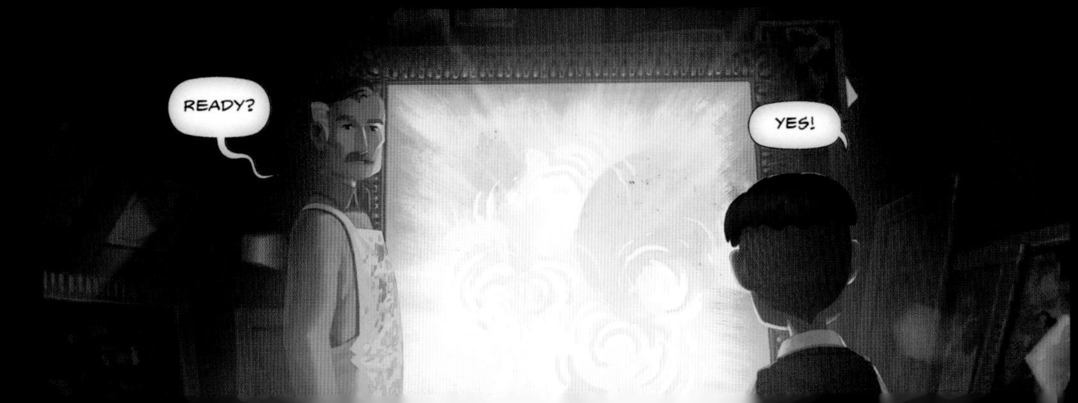
READY?
YES!

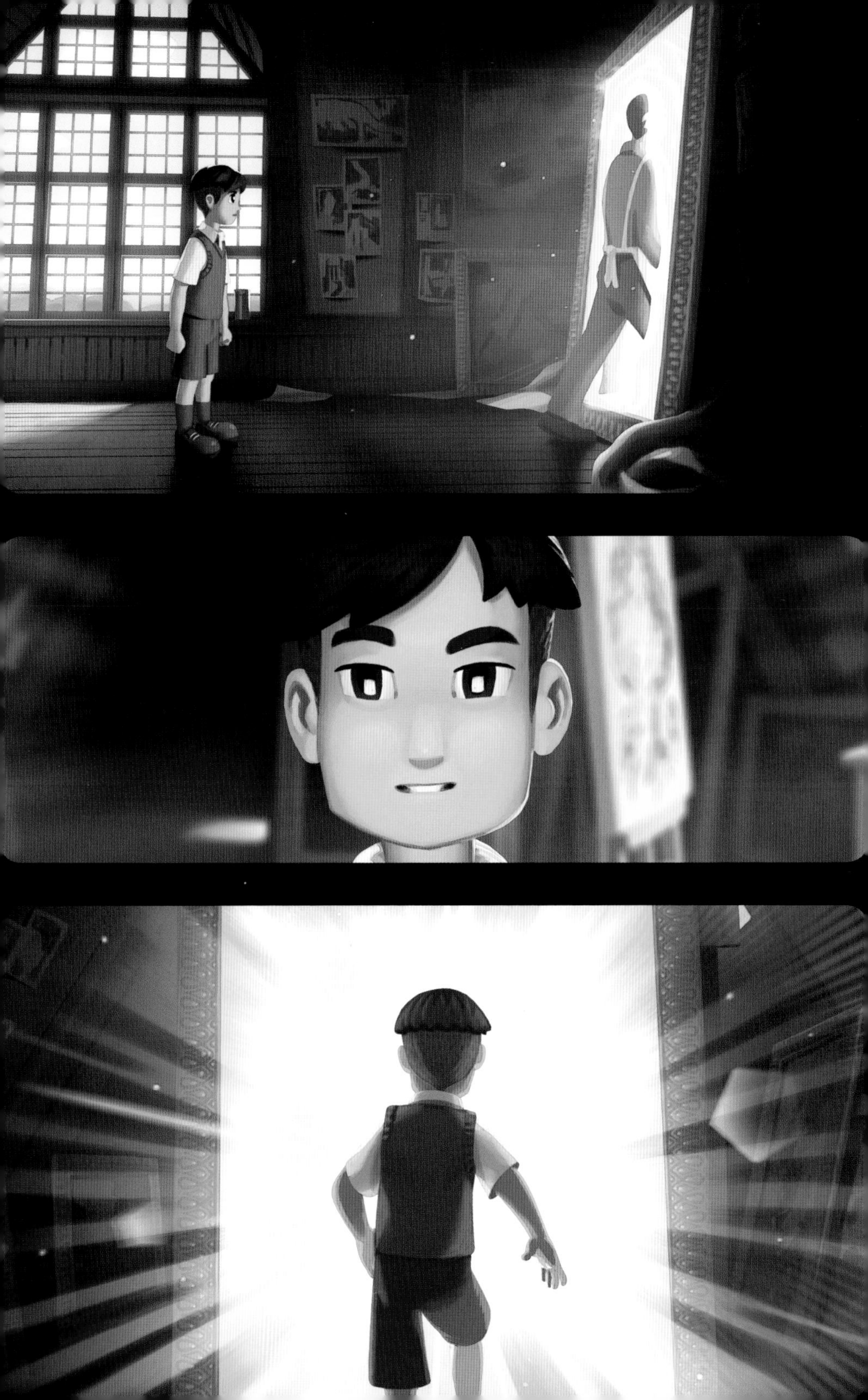

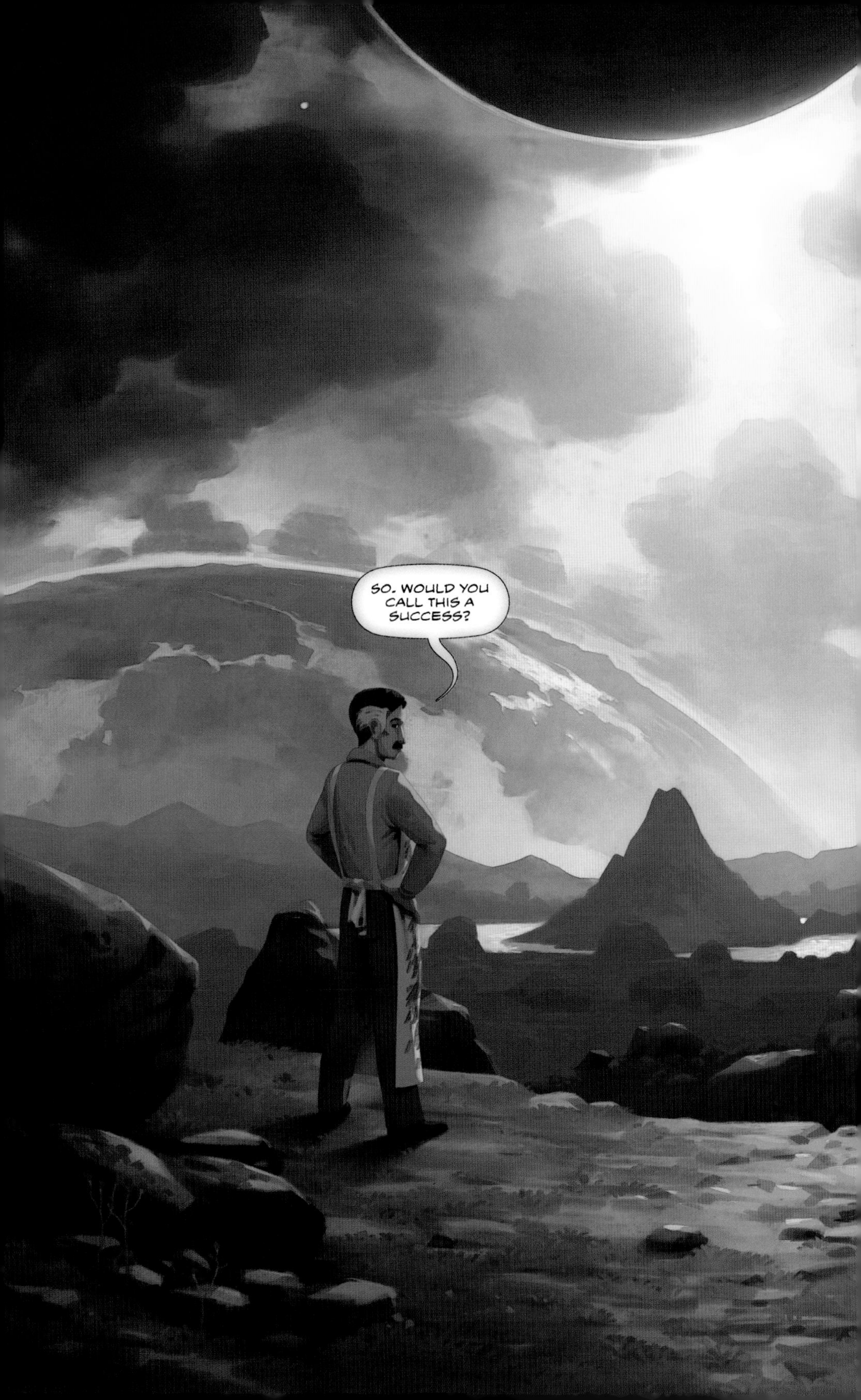
SO. WOULD YOU CALL THIS A SUCCESS?

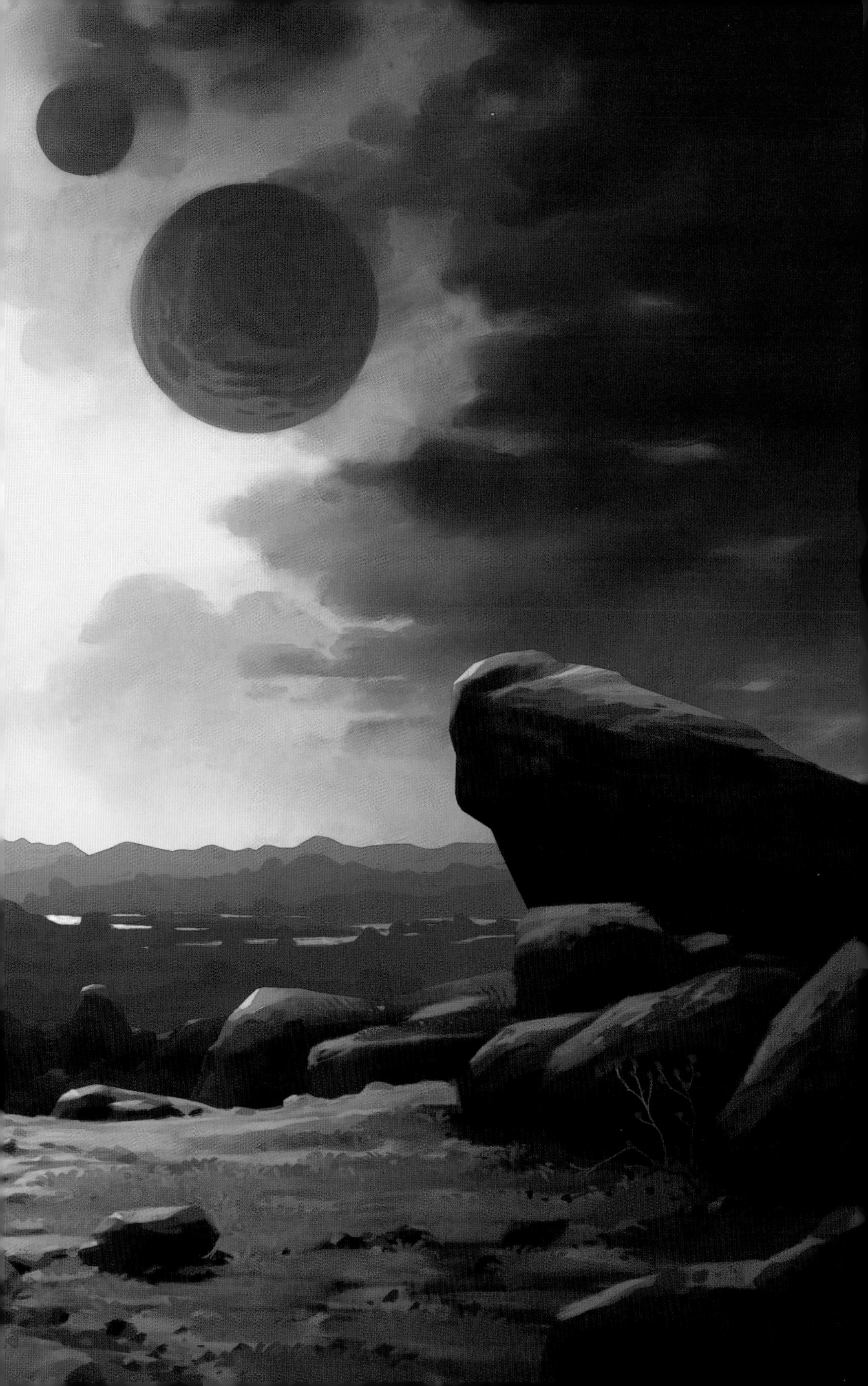

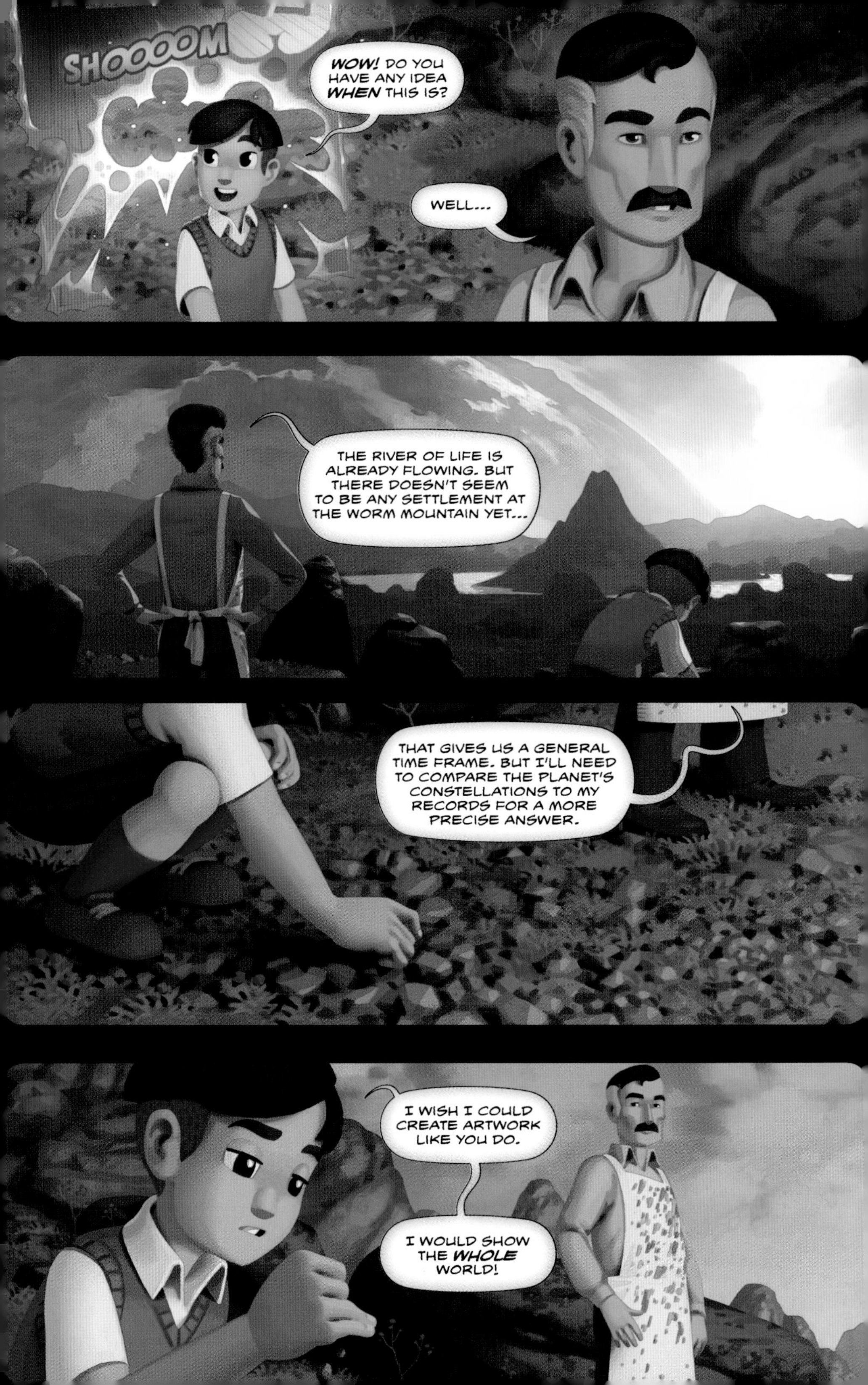
SHOOOOM
WOW! DO YOU HAVE ANY IDEA WHEN THIS IS?
WELL...
THE RIVER OF LIFE IS ALREADY FLOWING. BUT THERE DOESN'T SEEM TO BE ANY SETTLEMENT AT THE WORM MOUNTAIN YET...
THAT GIVES US A GENERAL TIME FRAME. BUT I'LL NEED TO COMPARE THE PLANET'S CONSTELLATIONS TO MY RECORDS FOR A MORE PRECISE ANSWER.
I WISH I COULD CREATE ARTWORK LIKE YOU DO.
I WOULD SHOW THE WHOLE WORLD!

THEODOR! AS I'VE TOLD YOU COUNTLESS TIMES, ***NOBODY*** BUT US CAN EVER KNOW ABOUT THIS WORLD.
THE CONSEQUENCES WOULD BE FAR TOO GREAT.
SHOOOOM
NOW COME!
IT'S TIME FOR LUNCH!

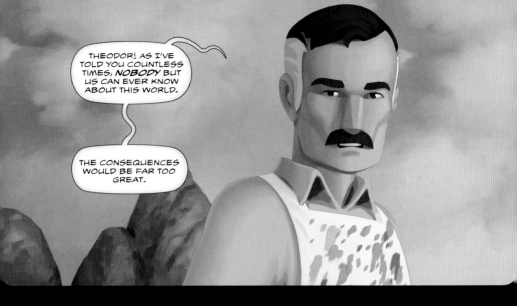

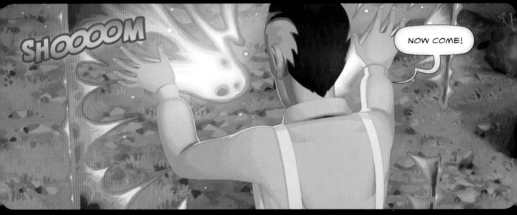

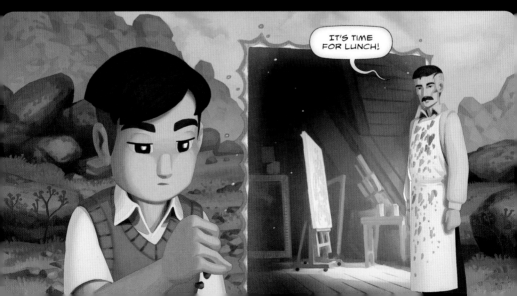

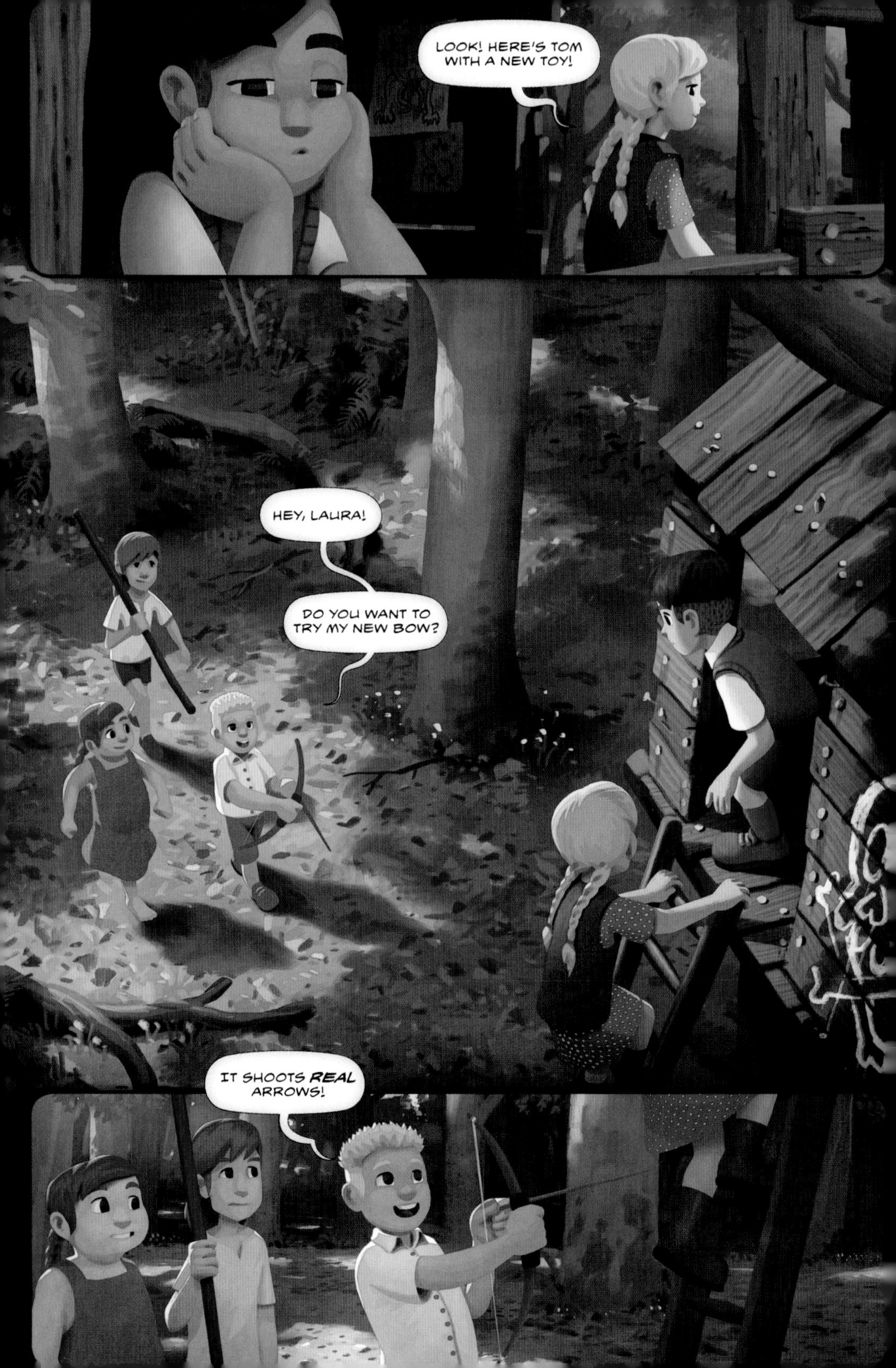
LOOK! HERE'S TOM WITH A NEW TOY!
HEY, LAURA!
DO YOU WANT TO TRY MY NEW BOW?
IT SHOOTS *REAL* ARROWS!

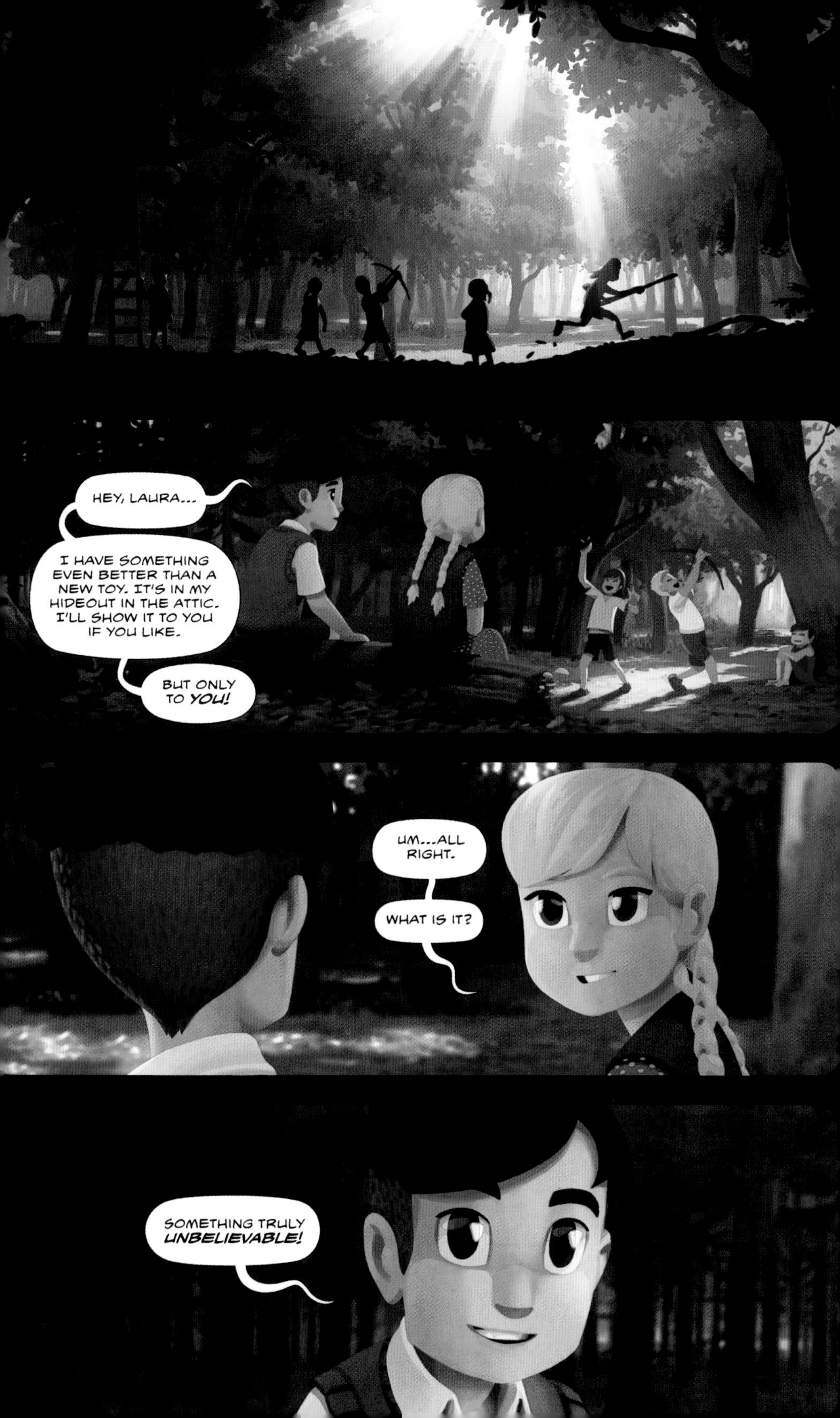
HEY, LAURA...
I HAVE SOMETHING EVEN BETTER THAN A NEW TOY. IT'S IN MY HIDEOUT IN THE ATTIC. I'LL SHOW IT TO YOU IF YOU LIKE.
BUT ONLY TO ***YOU!***
UM...ALL RIGHT.
WHAT IS IT?
SOMETHING TRULY ***UNBELIEVABLE!***

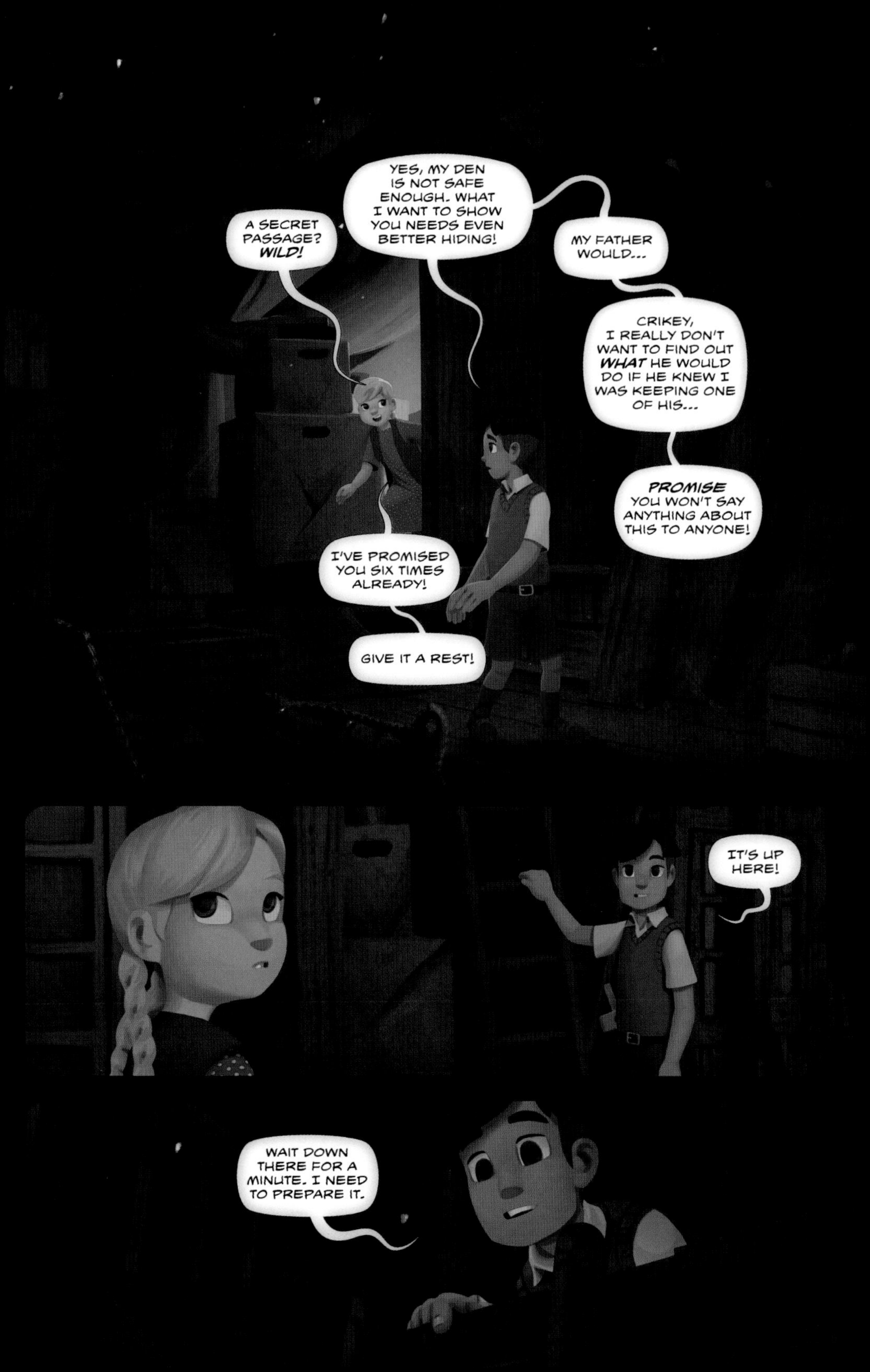
A SECRET PASSAGE? ***WILD!***
YES, MY DEN IS NOT SAFE ENOUGH. WHAT I WANT TO SHOW YOU NEEDS EVEN BETTER HIDING!
MY FATHER WOULD...
CRIKEY, I REALLY DON'T WANT TO FIND OUT ***WHAT*** HE WOULD DO IF HE KNEW I WAS KEEPING ONE OF HIS...
PROMISE YOU WON'T SAY ANYTHING ABOUT THIS TO ANYONE!
I'VE PROMISED YOU SIX TIMES ALREADY!
GIVE IT A REST!
IT'S UP HERE!
WAIT DOWN THERE FOR A MINUTE. I NEED TO PREPARE IT.

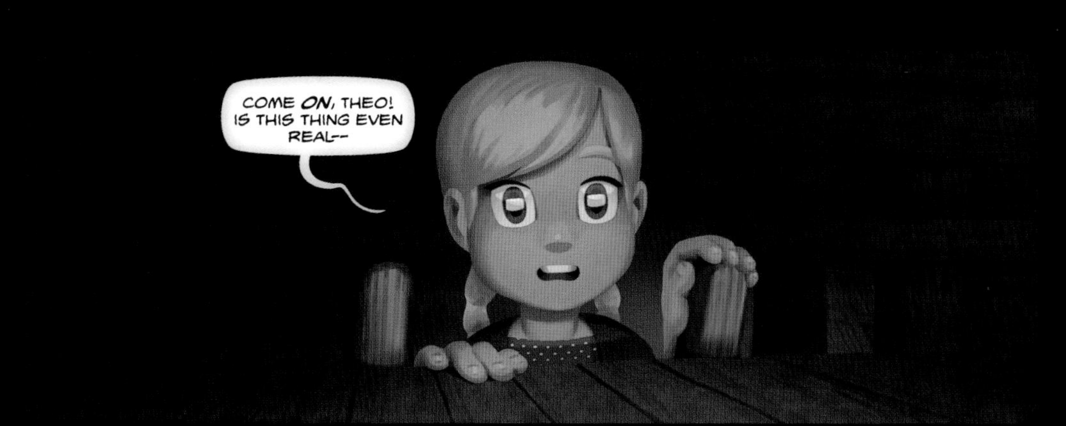
COME ON, THEO! IS THIS THING EVEN REAL--

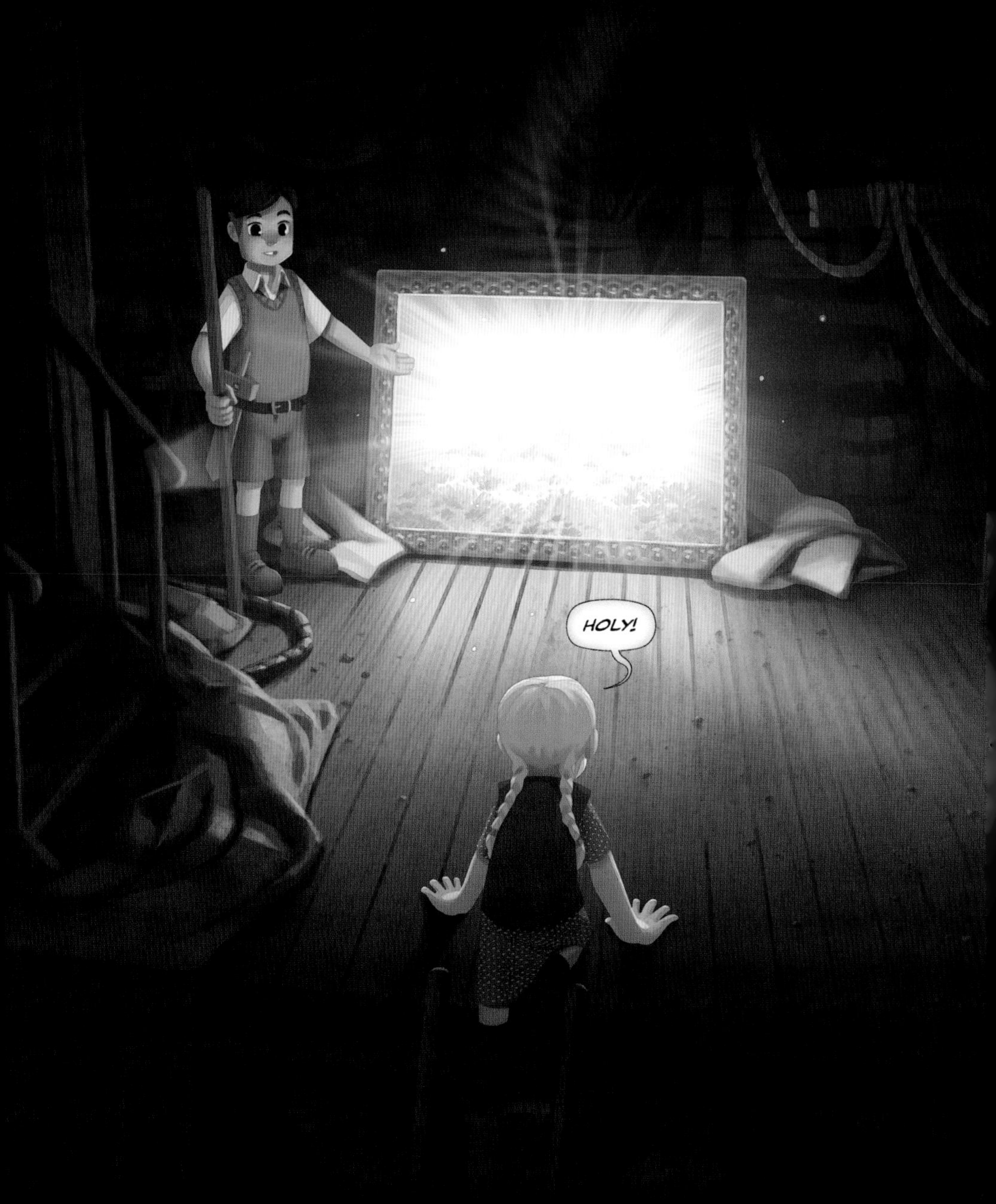
HOLY!

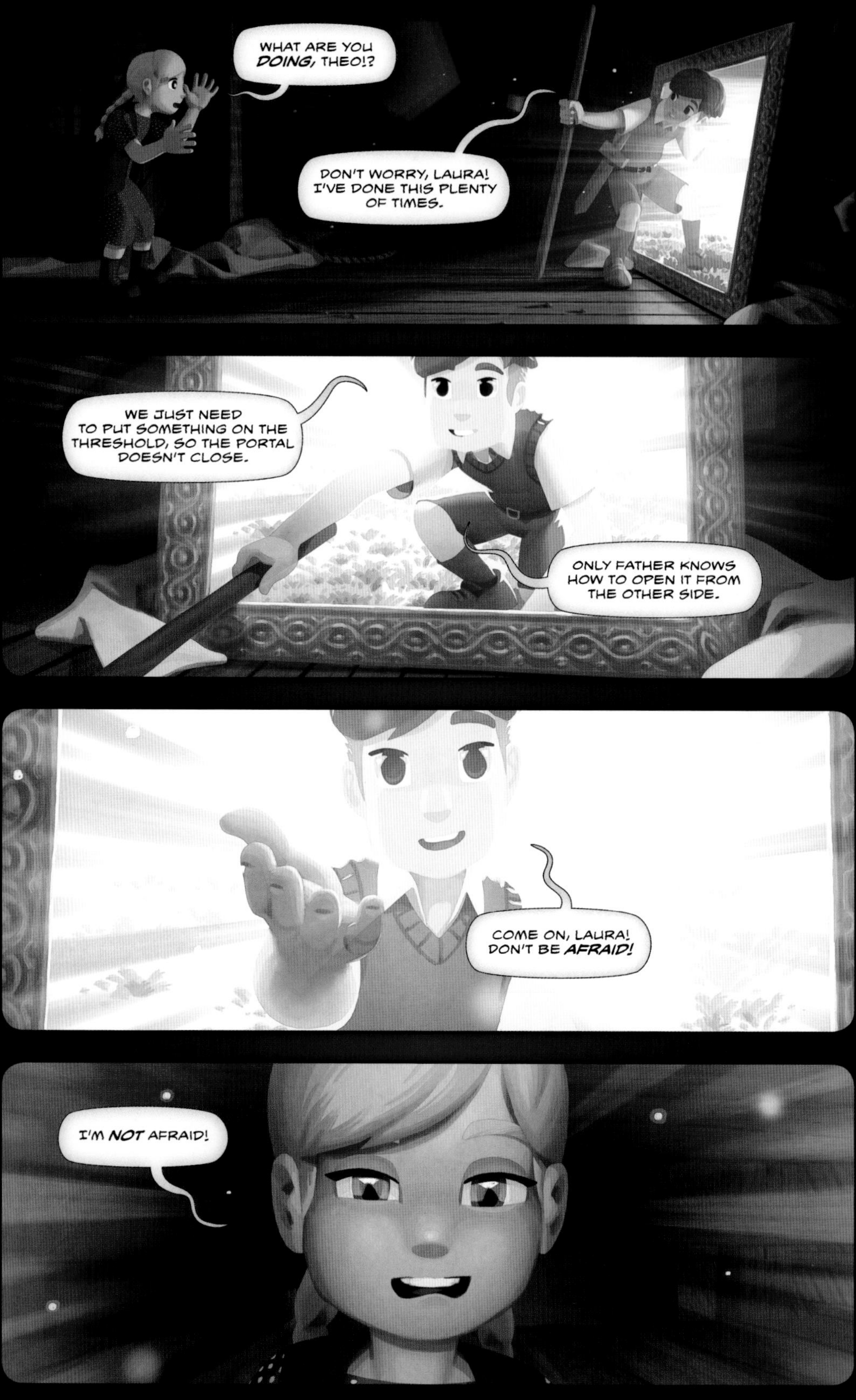
WHAT ARE YOU *DOING*, THEO!?
DON'T WORRY, LAURA! I'VE DONE THIS PLENTY OF TIMES.
WE JUST NEED TO PUT SOMETHING ON THE THRESHOLD, SO THE PORTAL DOESN'T CLOSE.
ONLY FATHER KNOWS HOW TO OPEN IT FROM THE OTHER SIDE.
COME ON, LAURA! DON'T BE *AFRAID!*
I'M *NOT* AFRAID!

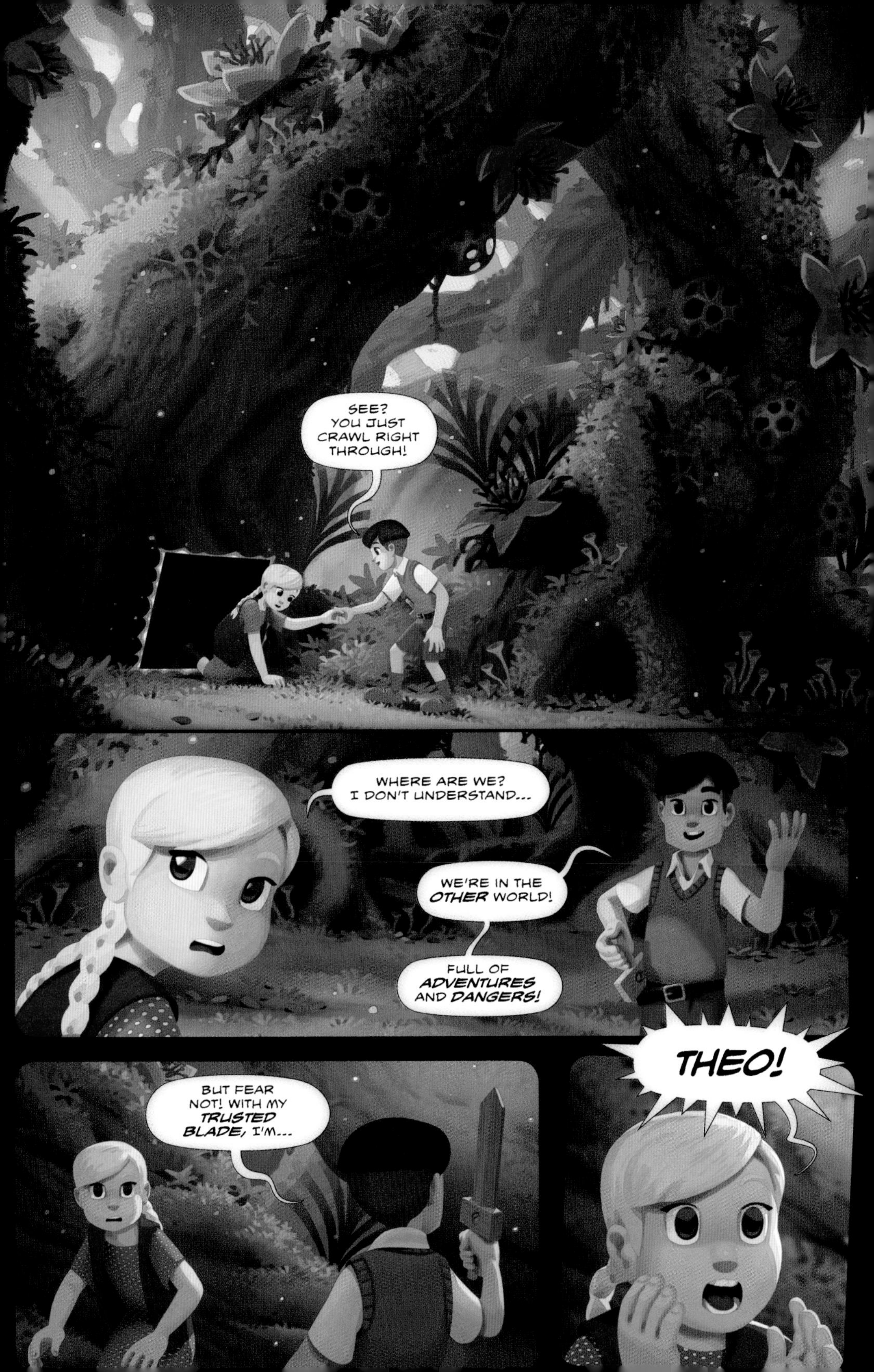
SEE? YOU JUST CRAWL RIGHT THROUGH!
WHERE ARE WE? I DON'T UNDERSTAND...
WE'RE IN THE *OTHER* WORLD!
FULL OF *ADVENTURES* AND *DANGERS!*
BUT FEAR NOT! WITH MY *TRUSTED BLADE,* I'M...
THEO!

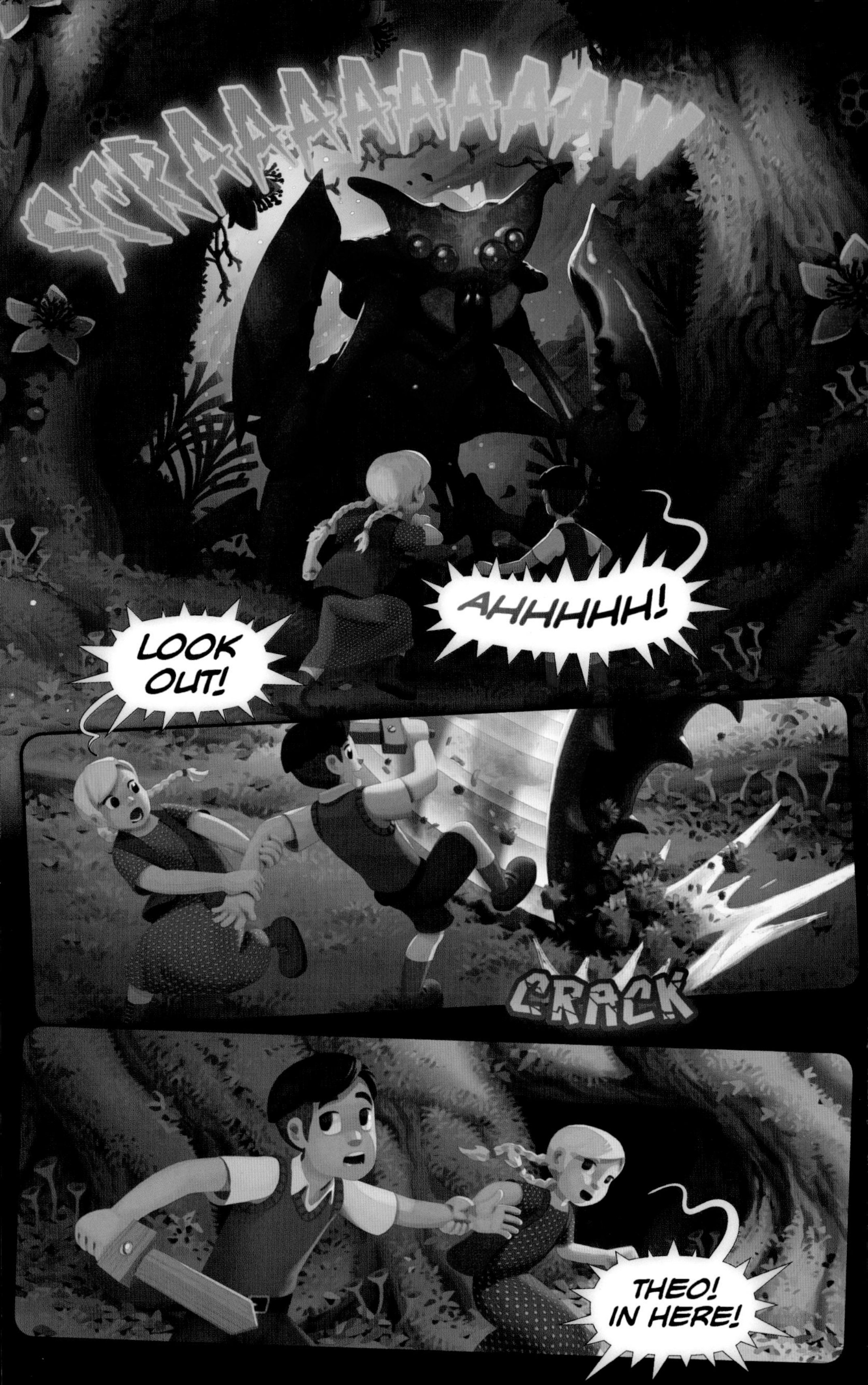
SCRAAAAAAAAAAW
AHHHHH!
LOOK OUT!
CRACK
THEO! IN HERE!

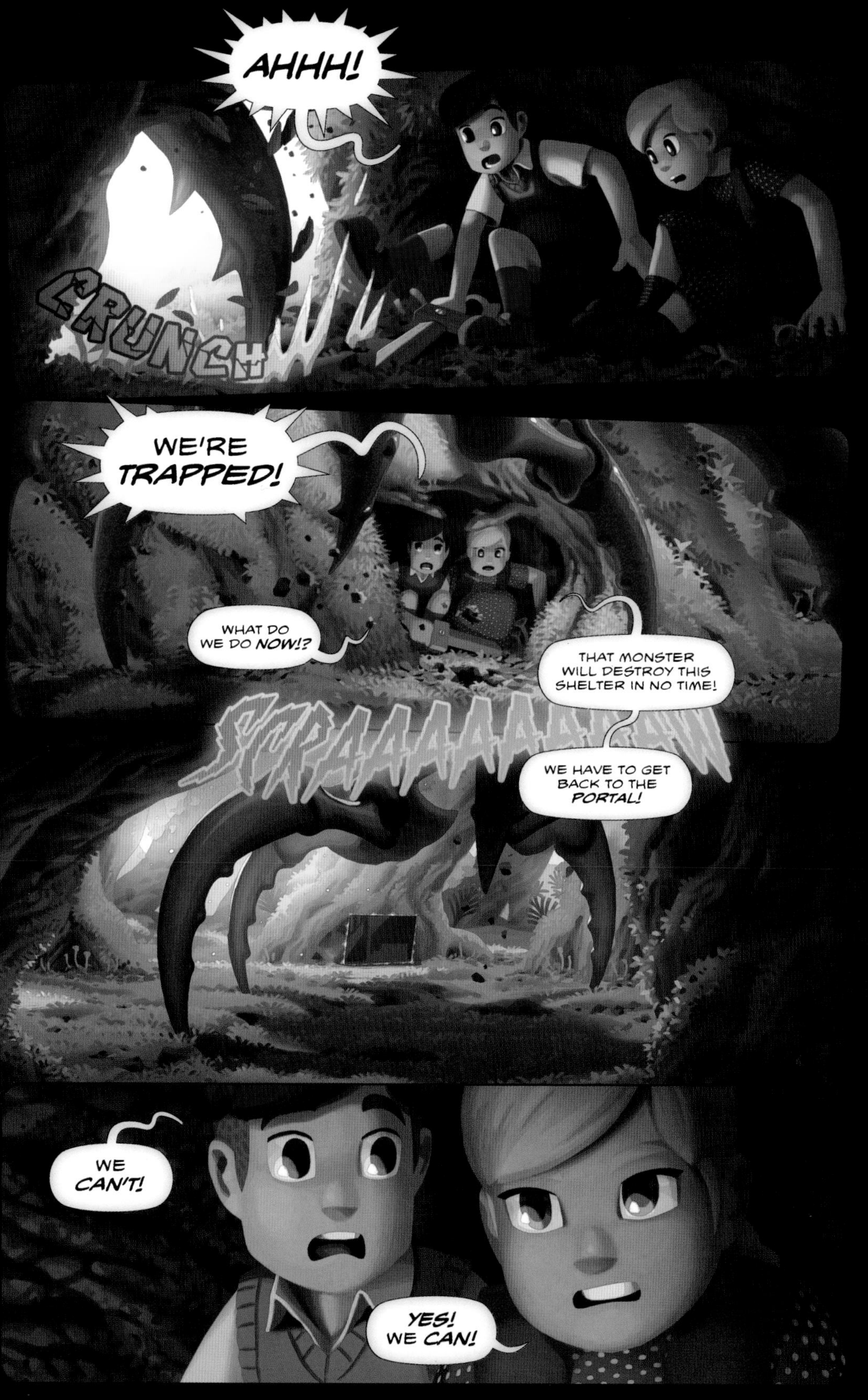
AHHH!
CRUNCH
WE'RE TRAPPED!
WHAT DO WE DO NOW!?
THAT MONSTER WILL DESTROY THIS SHELTER IN NO TIME!
WE HAVE TO GET BACK TO THE PORTAL!
WE CAN'T!
YES! WE CAN!

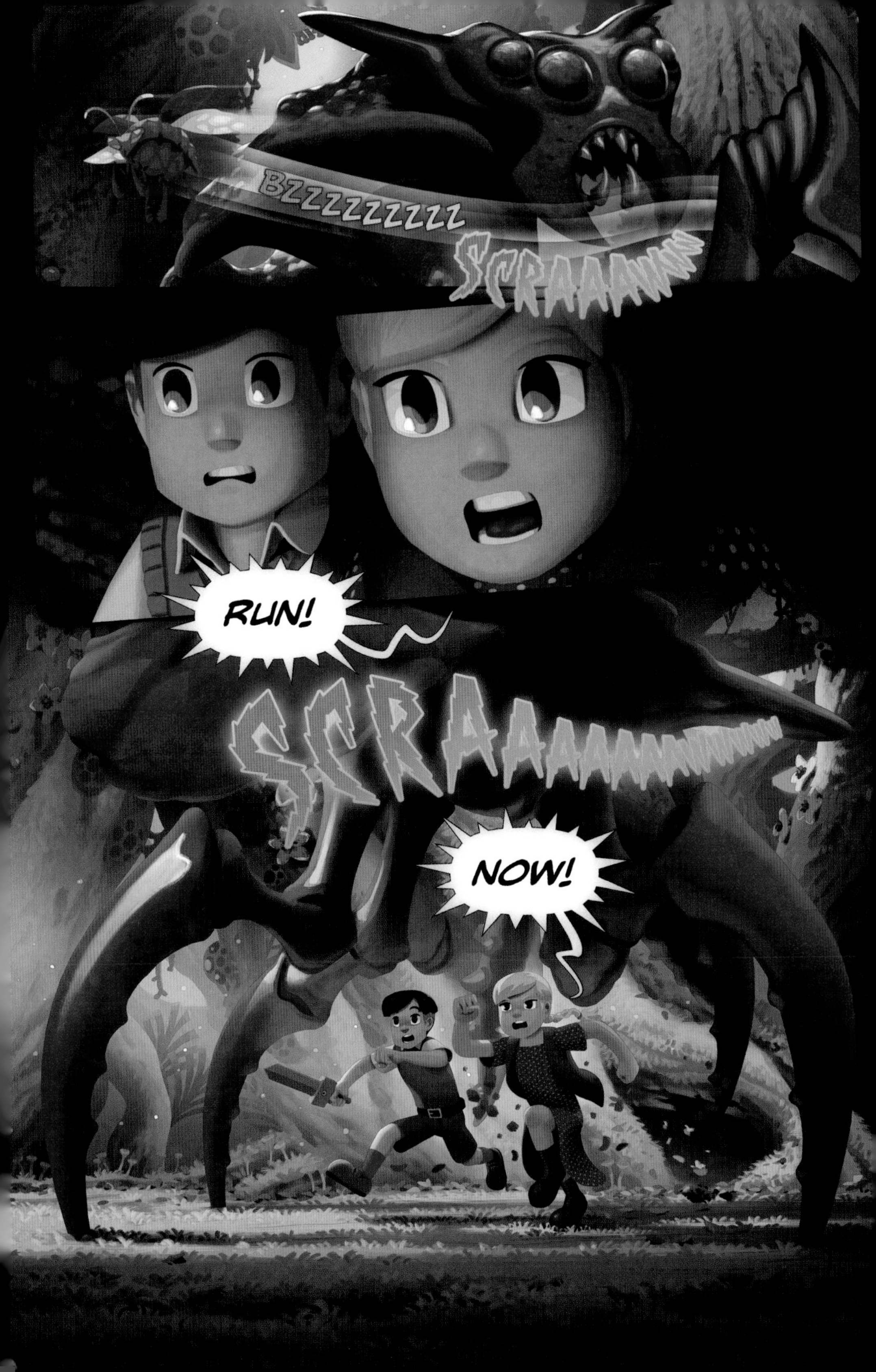
BZZZZZZZZZ
SCRAAAW
RUN!
SCRAAAAAW
NOW!

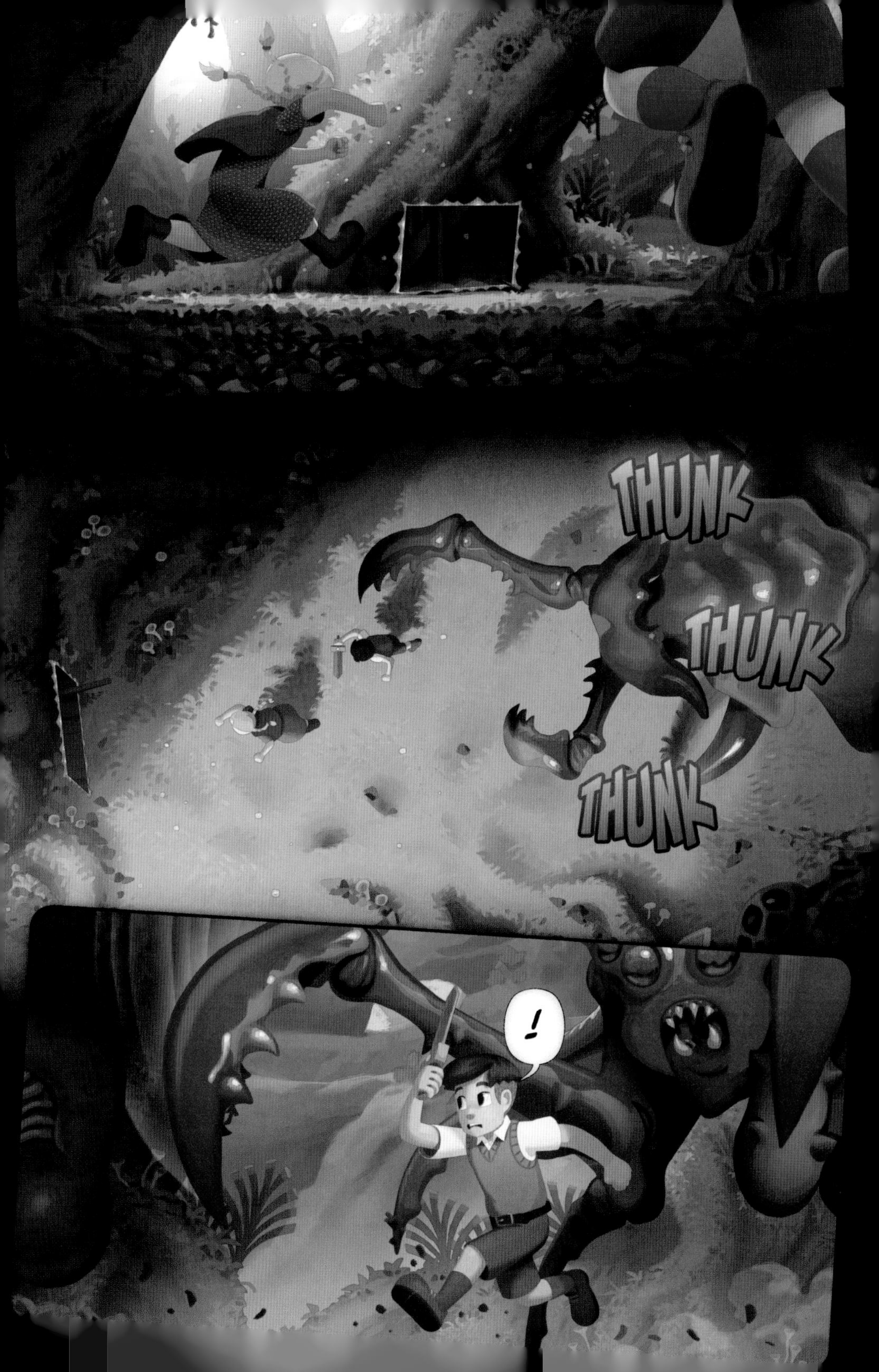
THUNK
THUNK
THUNK
!

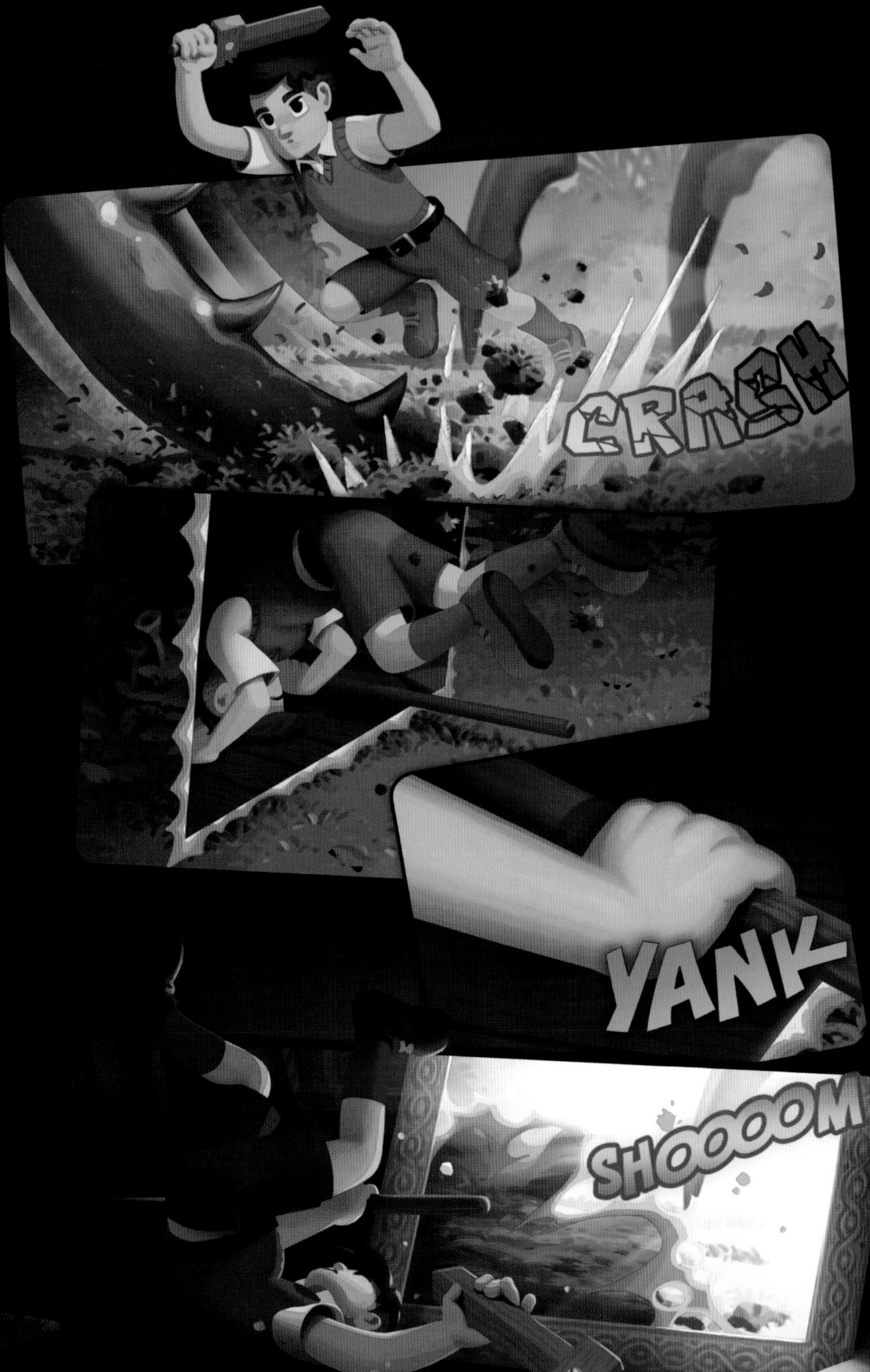
CRRRSH
YANK
SHOOOOM

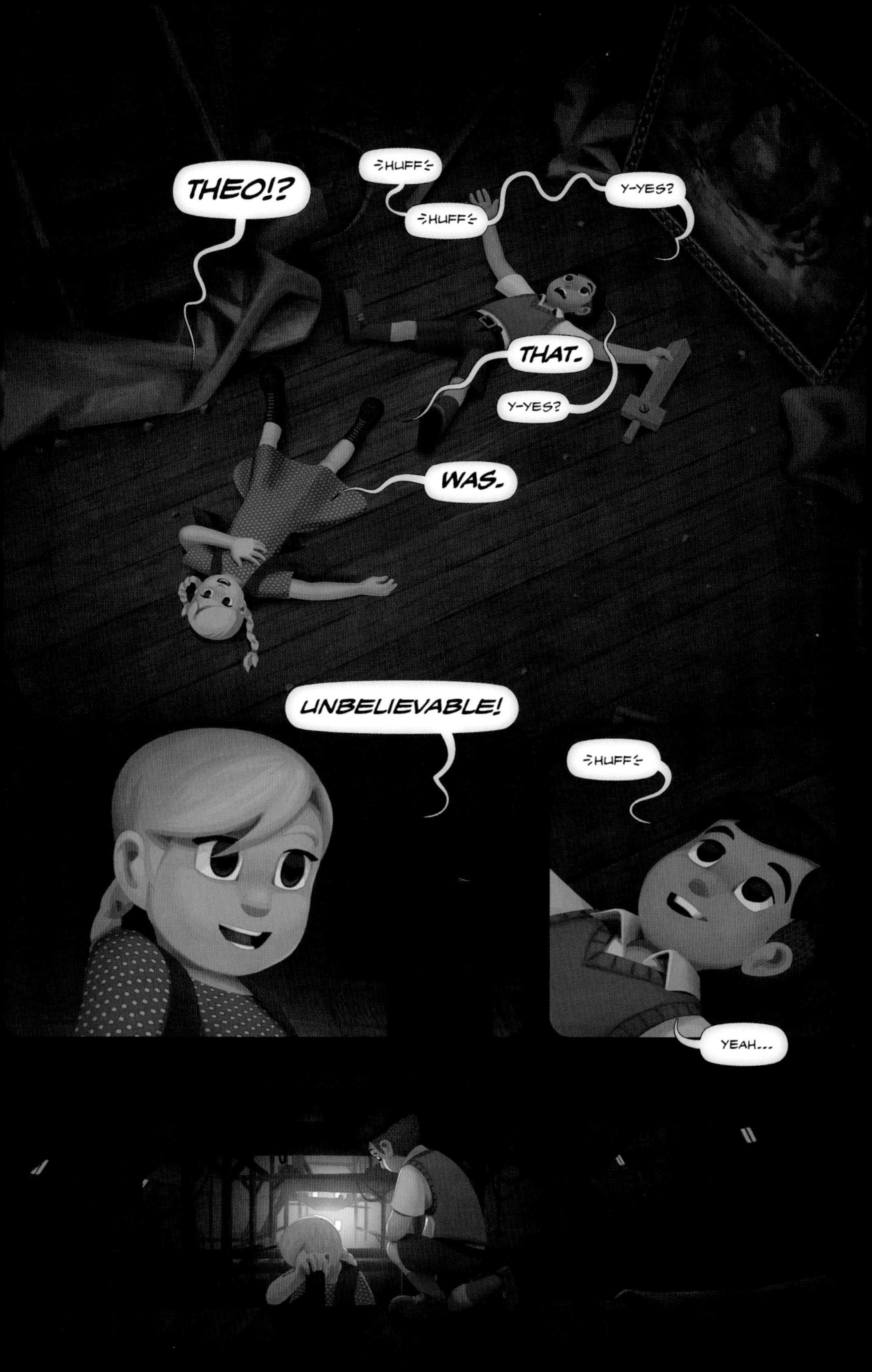
THEO!?
HUFF
HUFF
Y-YES?
THAT.
Y-YES?
WAS.
UNBELIEVABLE!
HUFF
YEAH...

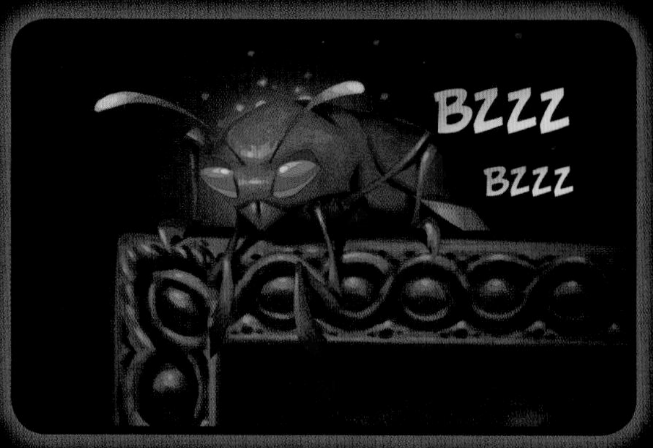
BZZZ
BZZZ
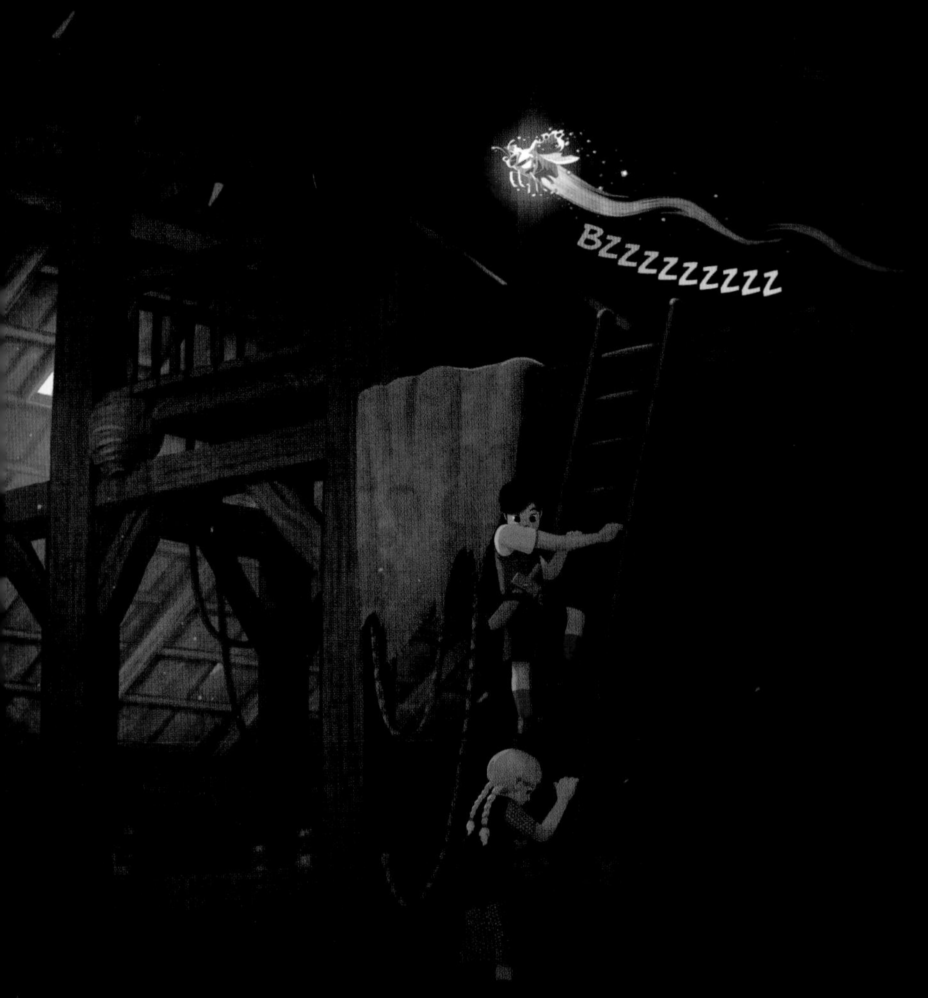
BZZZZZZZZZ

Artist Process: Working with 3-D models in *The Wormworld Saga* Prequel

LAURA

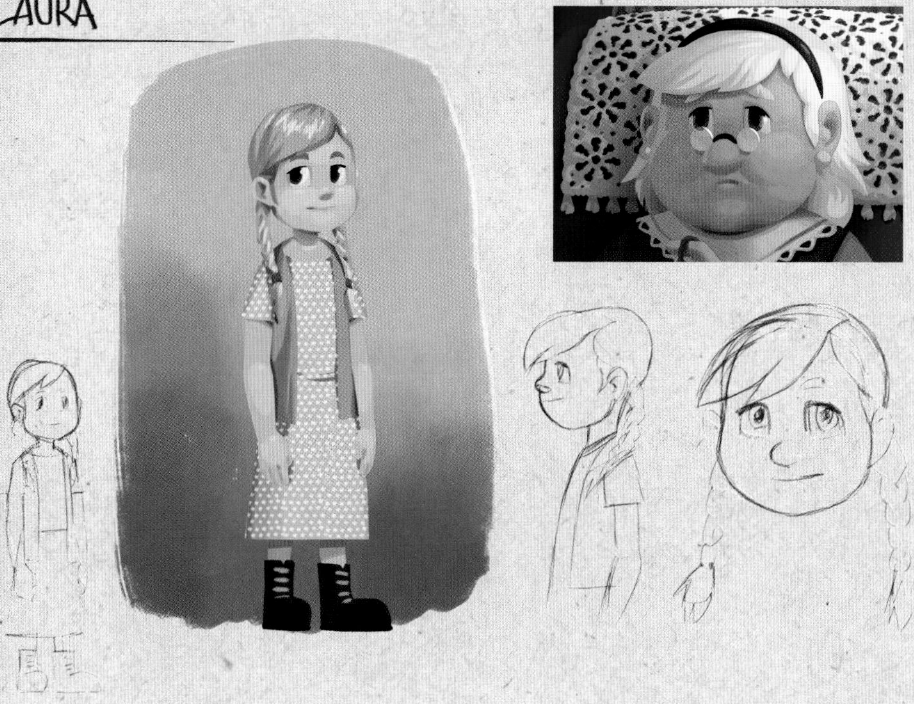

THEODOR

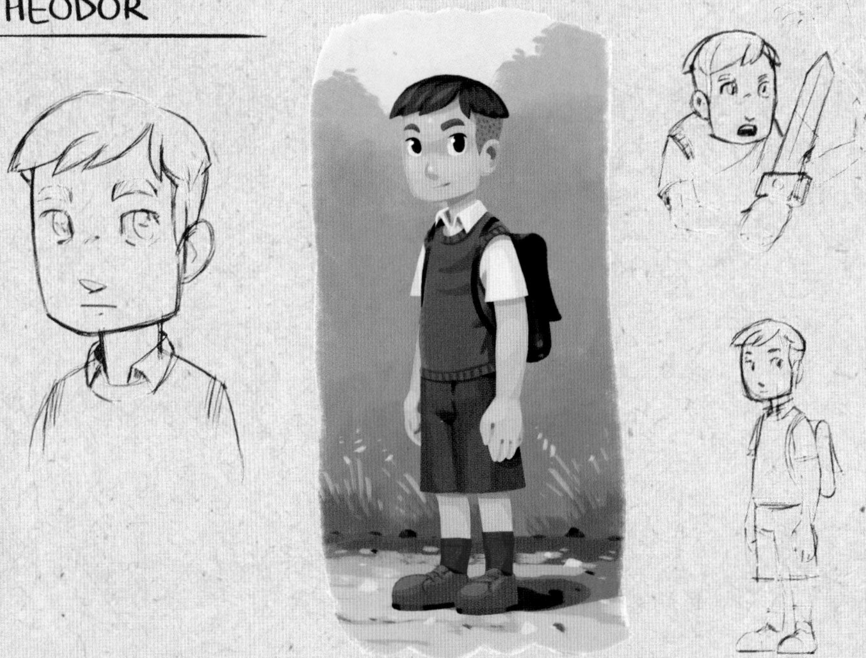

Concept sketches of Laura and Theo

I've made use of 3-D reference models throughout the production of *The Wormworld Saga*. In most cases, these were simple monochromatic models that only helped me to draw complicated structures in perspective. However, for the special prequel issue, I took the approach a step further. I created a detailed model of Theodor's father's studio and set up appropriate materials, so that I could experiment with different lighting situations. That way I could create direct visual reference for individual panel artworks. I used the same approach for all panels that include the "Shadow Lurker" Draconia. For these, I had prepared a completely posable 3-D model that helped me a great deal to create the complicated camera angles that I had planned for Laura and Theo's encounter with this dangerous creature.

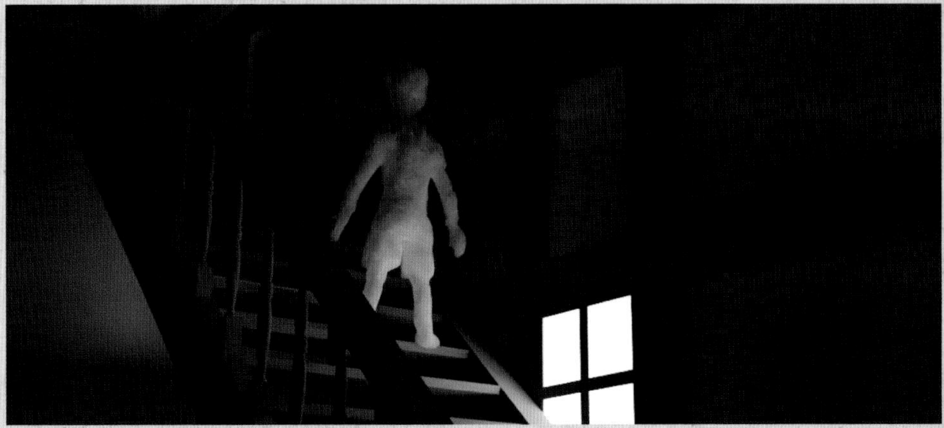

3-D-rendered reference for the first panel on the fourth page of the prequel issue

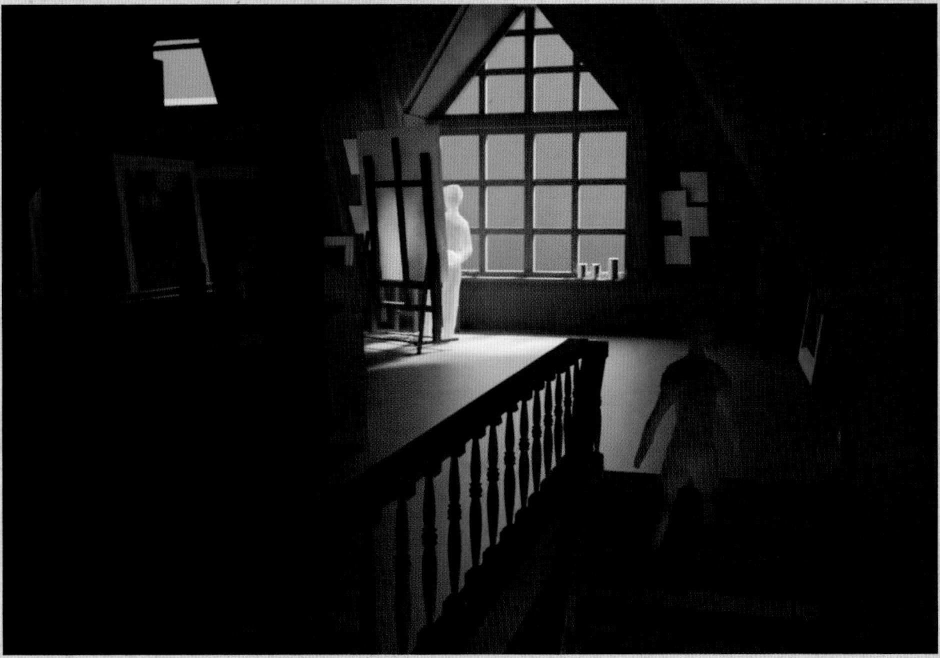

3-D-rendered reference for the fourth page of the prequel issue

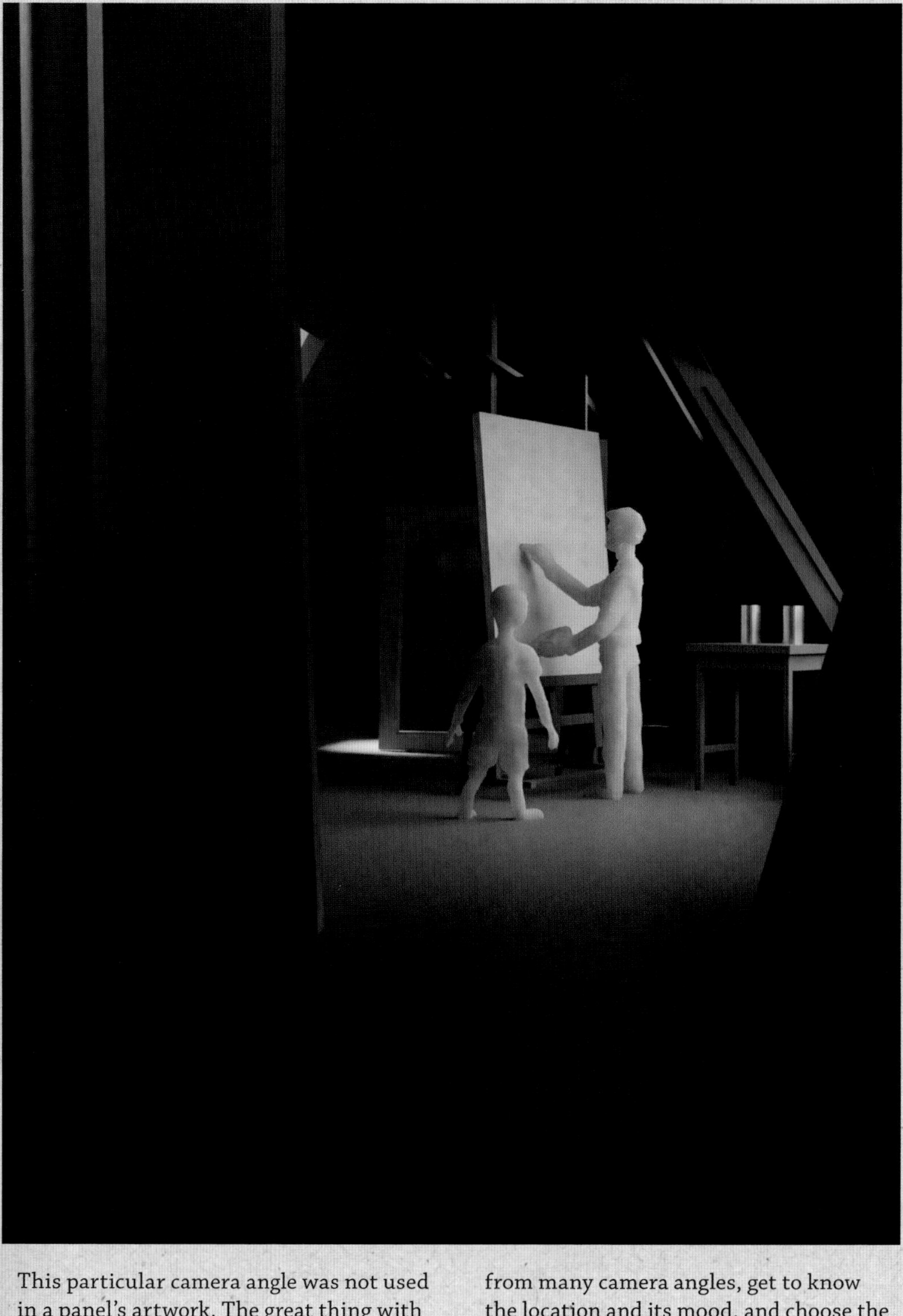

This particular camera angle was not used in a panel's artwork. The great thing with 3-D models is that you can explore a model from many camera angles, get to know the location and its mood, and choose the right shots for the story you want to tell.

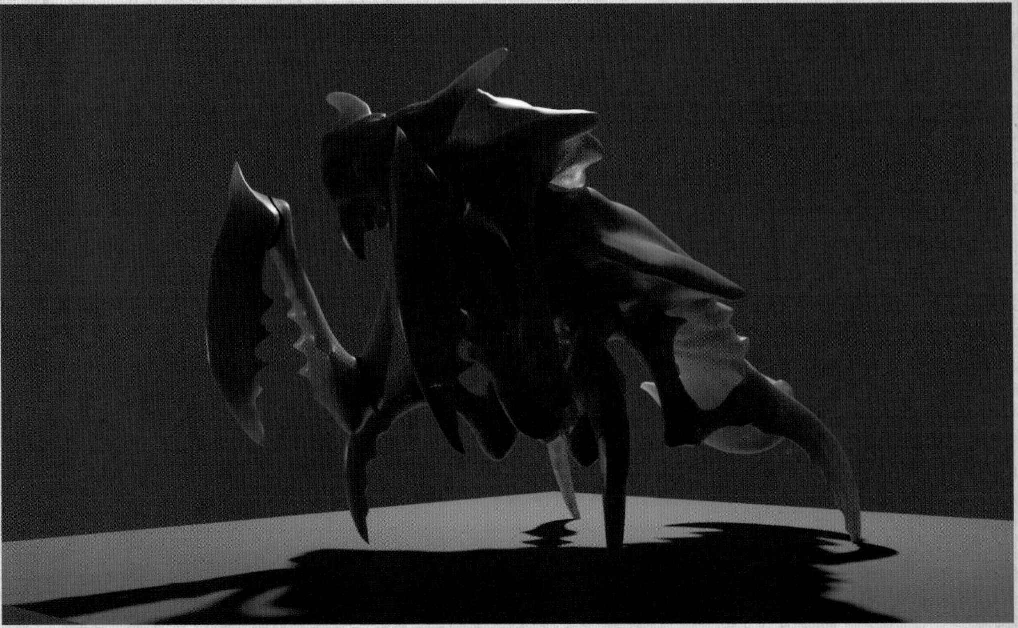
3-D model of the Shadow Lurker

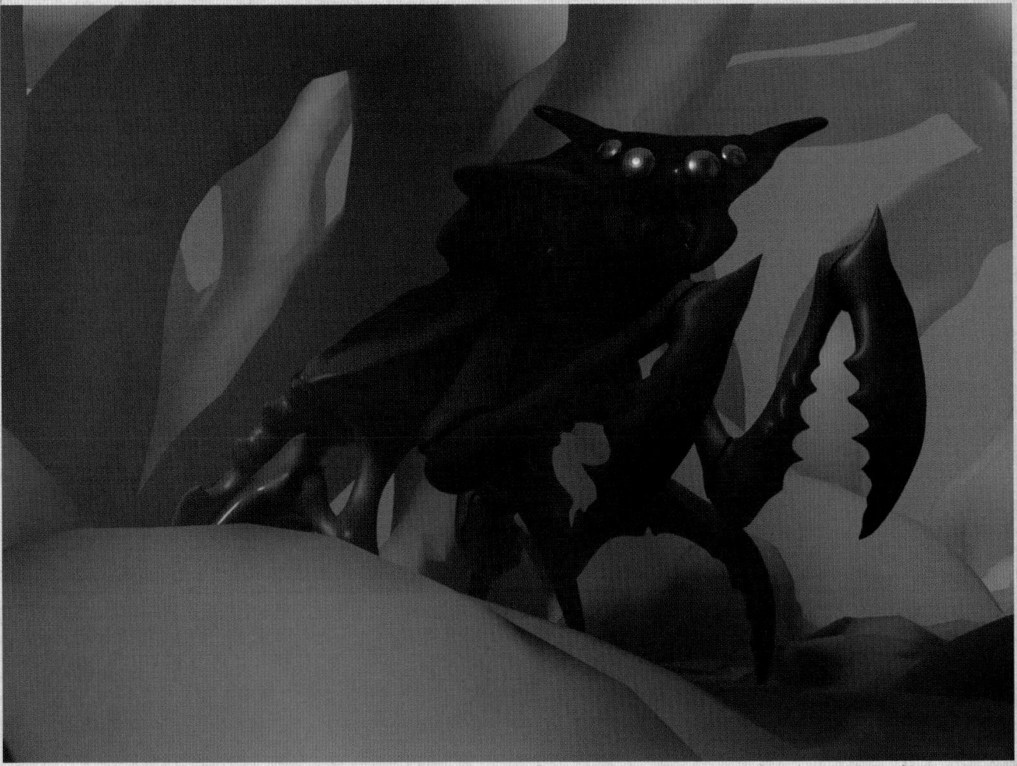
The dark colors of the Shadow Lurker's shell help the beast to ambush his prey.

Behind the Scenes of *The Wormworld Saga*

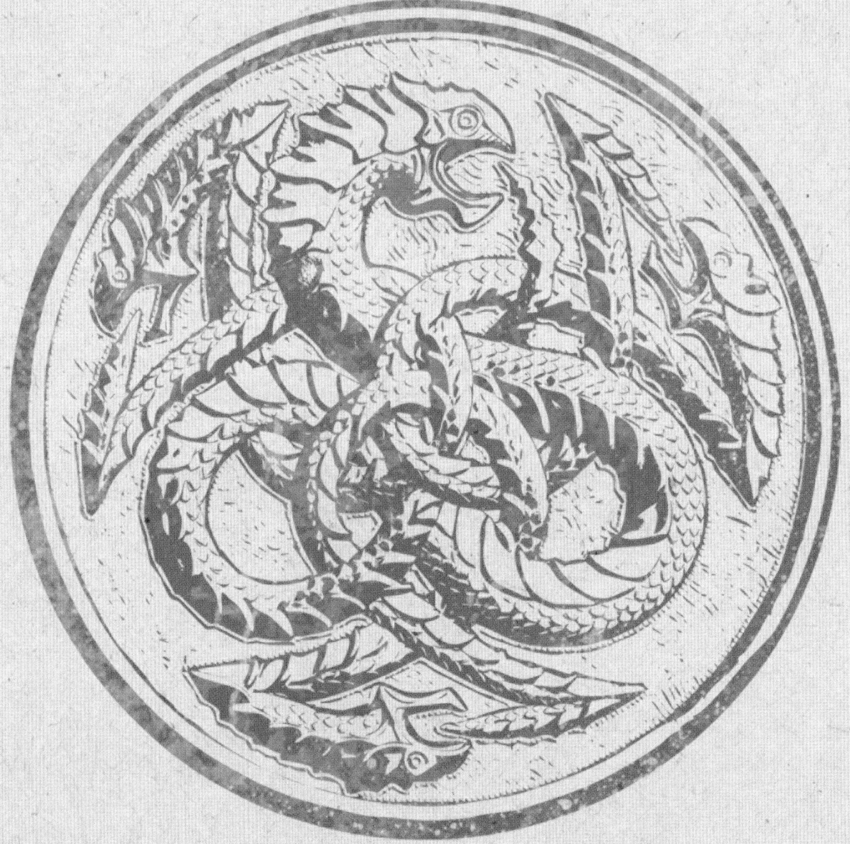

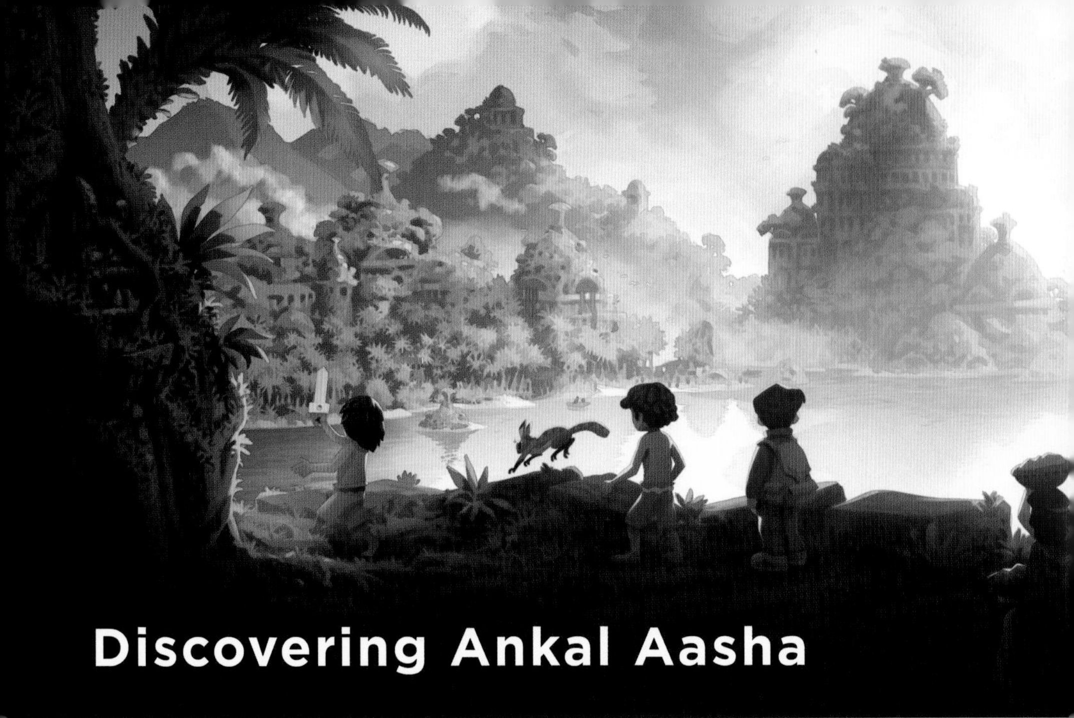

Discovering Ankal Aasha

Imagining New Worlds

Possibly the most enjoyable part of my work is the concept-art phase, which I tackle before starting any given chapter of *The Wormworld Saga* in earnest. During this phase, I explore the vistas that the story leads our heroes through. In the case of Ankal Aasha, I already had some vague images in my head for how it would look, but only after I started to render this sunken city did it actually come to life for me. My first step into the realm of Janaka Jiiva consisted of loose color studies that I painted to get a feeling for the light and colors of the place. I had to find out which shades of green

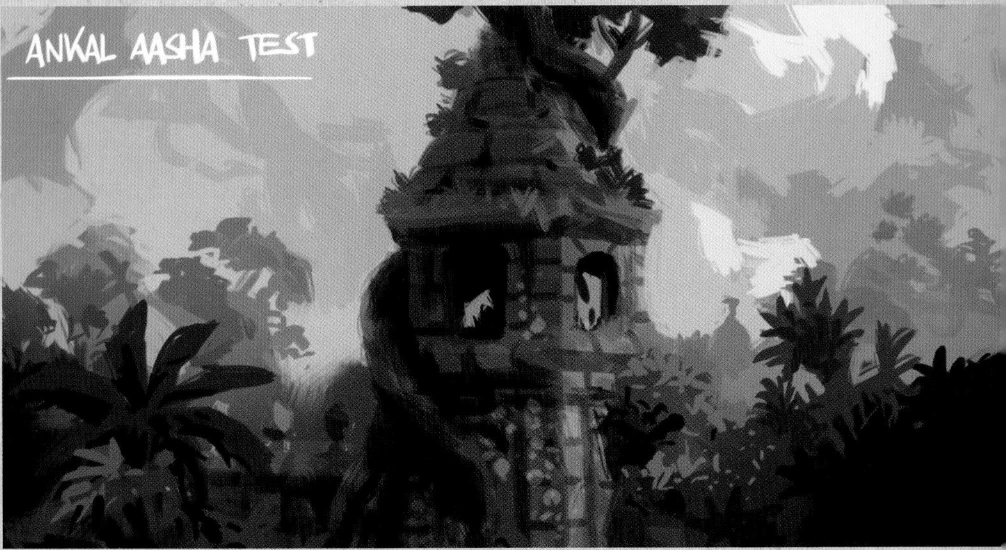
ANKAL AASHA TEST

Color study for Ankal Aasha. The grey of the ruins is broken with reds and yellows.

I should use on the vegetation and what colors to use to break the grays of the ruins.

After I found the right atmosphere and mood for the setting of the beginning of this book, I had to go into more detail and find out how exactly the ruins of Ankal Aasha would appear. The place has a history, and I had to consider this in the design of the city. I imagined the cityscape dominated by large domes and halls. The civilization that built the city in the ancient past was rich and had a highly developed architectural knowledge. The dominating design element of that culture was the rising silhouette of the god Unurtha in front of a semicircle. This element is found in many wall decorations and is also echoed in the spires that sit on top of the domes. My first architectural sketches also included arched lintels, but I discarded this later to come closer to the Khmer architecture of Angkor Wat in Cambodia, which strongly influenced my vision of Ankal Aasha. Other things that I had to design included the idol of Ankal Aasha and the room of Janaka Jiiva. For the latter, I built a simple 3-D model in which I could search for exciting camera perspectives and which also helped me to construct the many backgrounds. Each side of Janaka's room has a special feature. The south side, through which Jonas and Raya enter the room, has the huge relief of Unurtha above the entrance.

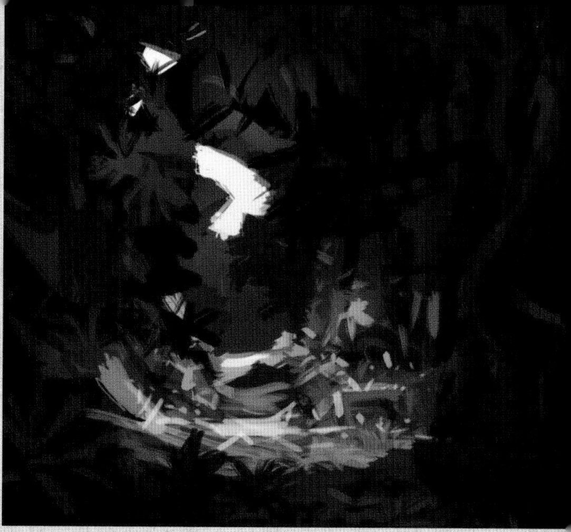

Another color study. An island of light introduces more yellowish greens into the jungle.

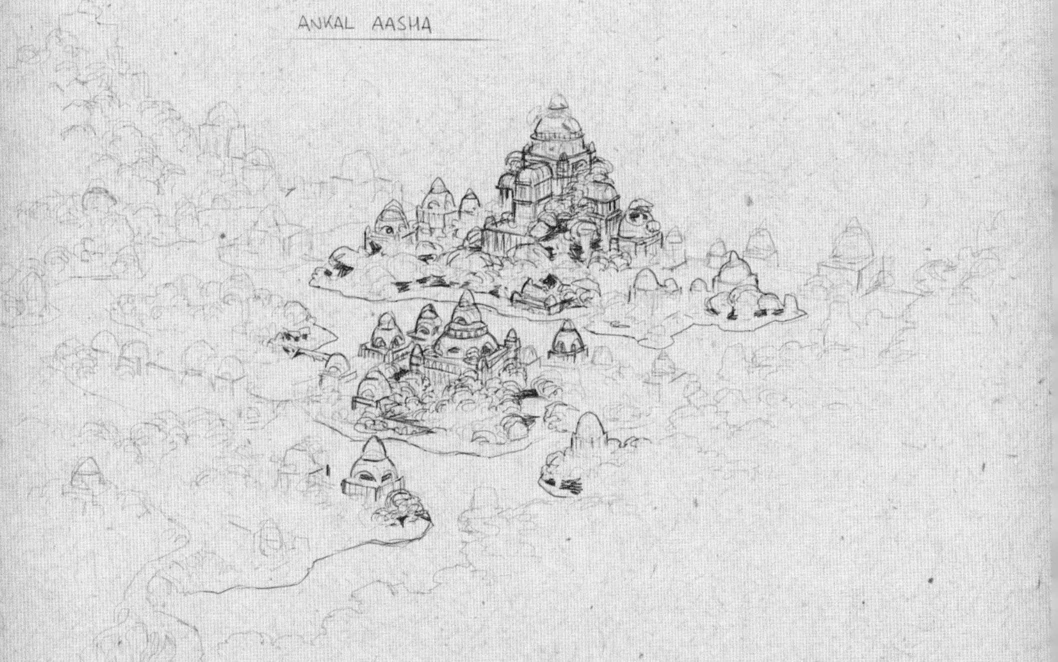
ANKAL AASHA

A first sketch of the city center of Ankal Aasha as seen from the distance

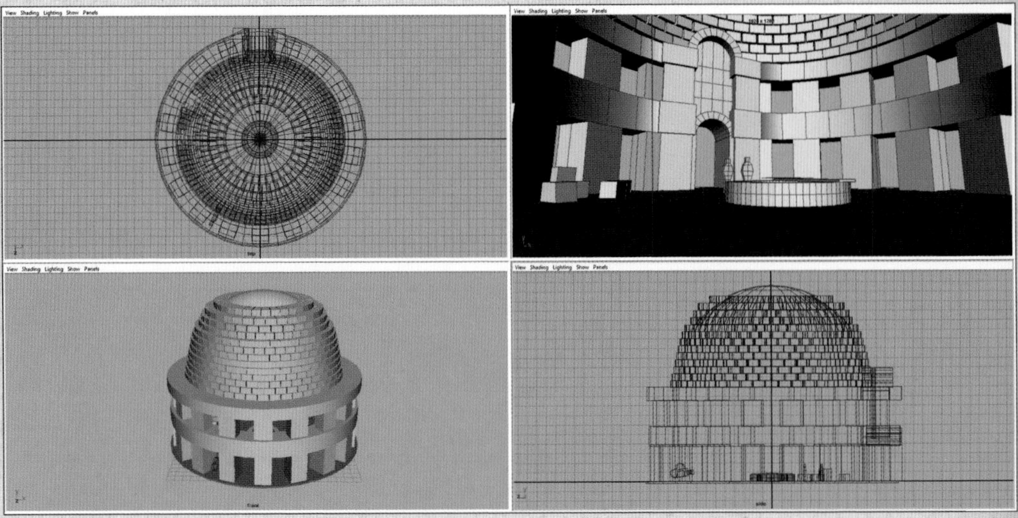

Several views of the 3-D model of Janaka’s room built in Maya

On the east side, we find Janaka's resting place, which faces the broken ceiling on the west side where thick vines are forcing their way into the room. The north side is where the sun shines through the windows and the drapery hangs from the ceiling. These different parts of the room are revealed throughout the beginning of this book. I also pondered creating a 3-D model for the idol but ultimately abandoned the idea. For the beginning of this book, it would just have been too much work to create a 3-D model.

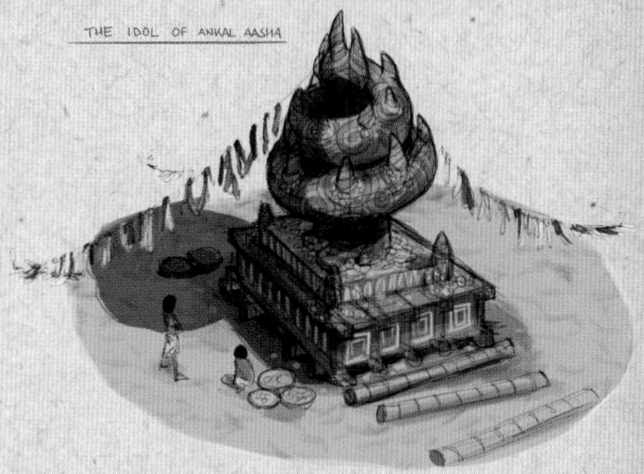
THE IDOL OF ANKAL AASHA

Concept drawing of the Ankal Aasha idol

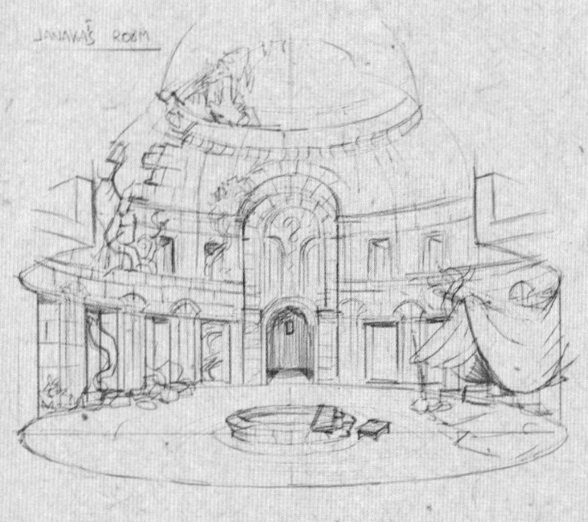
JANAKA'S ROOM

First rough sketch of Janaka’s room

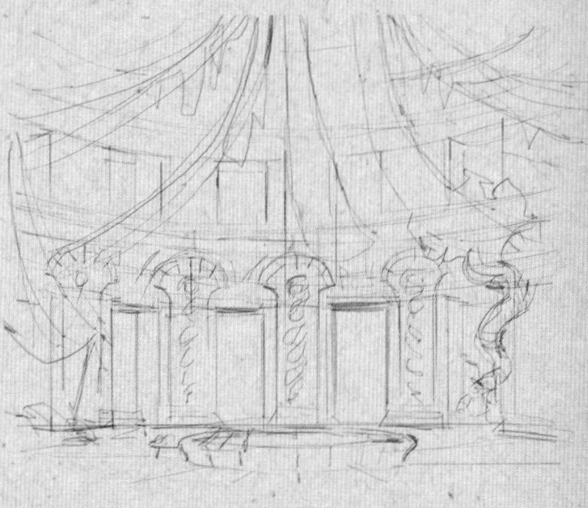

A more detailed sketch of Janaka’s room as seen from the north side

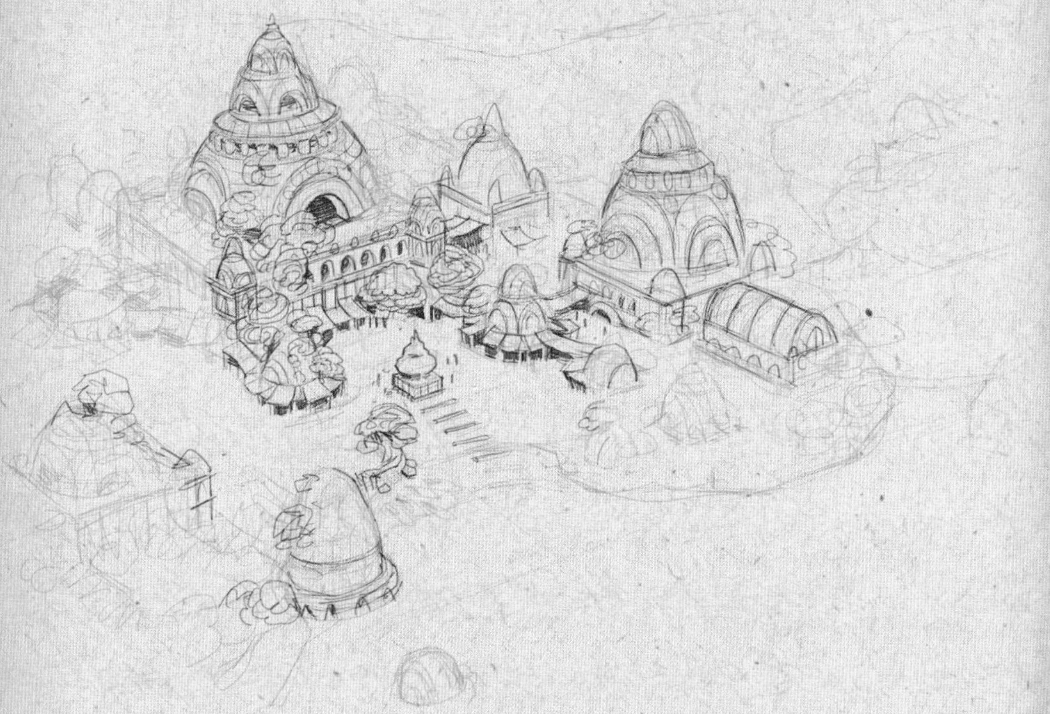
A view of the town square with the idol

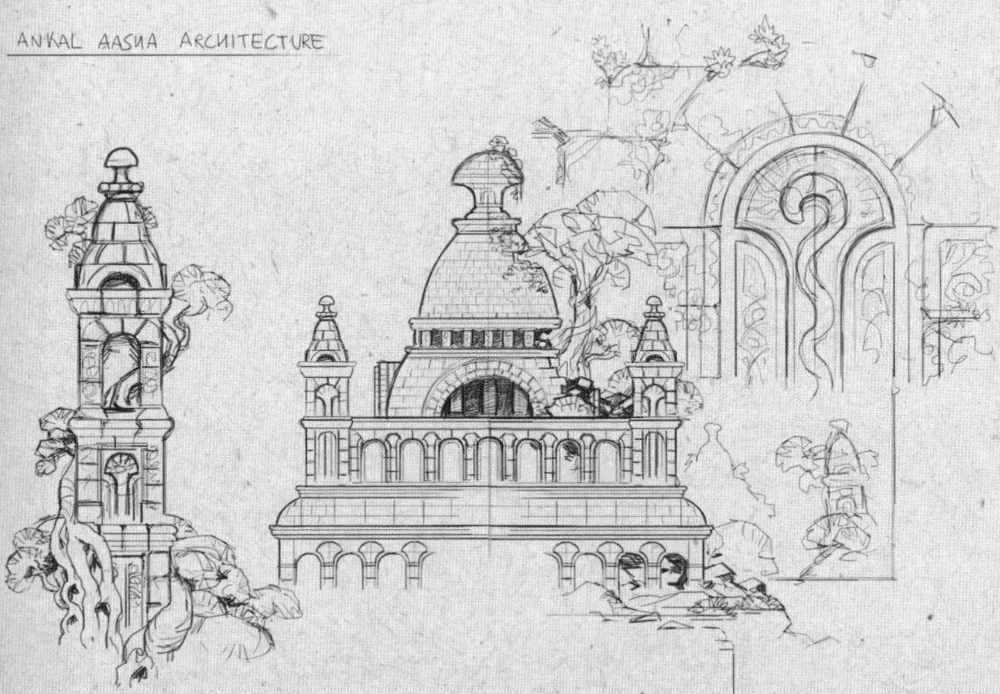
ANKAL AASHA ARCHITECTURE
Architectural details of the buildings. I later discarded the arched lintels and kept them straight.

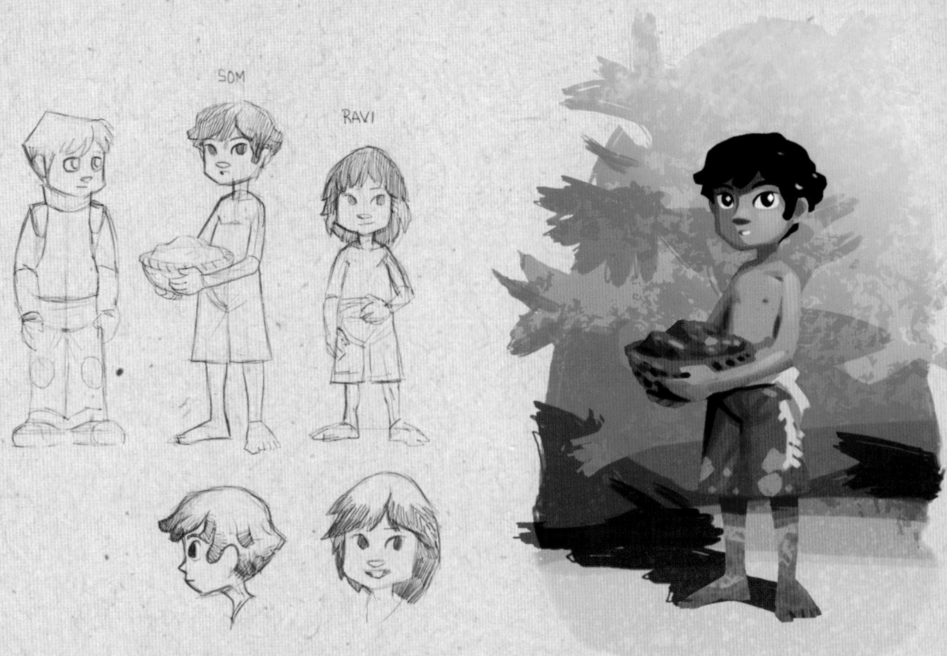
SOM
RAVI

Sketches of Ravi and Som

New Characters

"The Shelter of Hope" introduced some new characters and, of course, the majority of work went into the design of Janaka Jiiva. However, my secret favorites of the chapter are the brothers Ravi and Som, and I just loved to paint in every panel they appeared in. The name "Ravi" is inspired by the Indian sitar player Ravi Shankar whose music I often listened to during my work on this book. I researched that Ravi means "sun," and I found it appropriate to name his brother after another celestial body—Som means "moon." For Janaka Jiiva (which means "father of life"), I created a digital sculpture like I did for the other main characters. Again, I used it as a starting point to refine his look and to get a general feel for the different angles in which we might see his face.

Painting a Jungle

"The Shelter of Hope" takes place in the sunken city of Ankal Aasha, and that meant I had to paint a lot of jungle backgrounds. To keep a certain consistency between the panels, I developed a special workflow, which I used to paint most of the backgrounds. In the following example, I'm going to show you how exactly that worked.

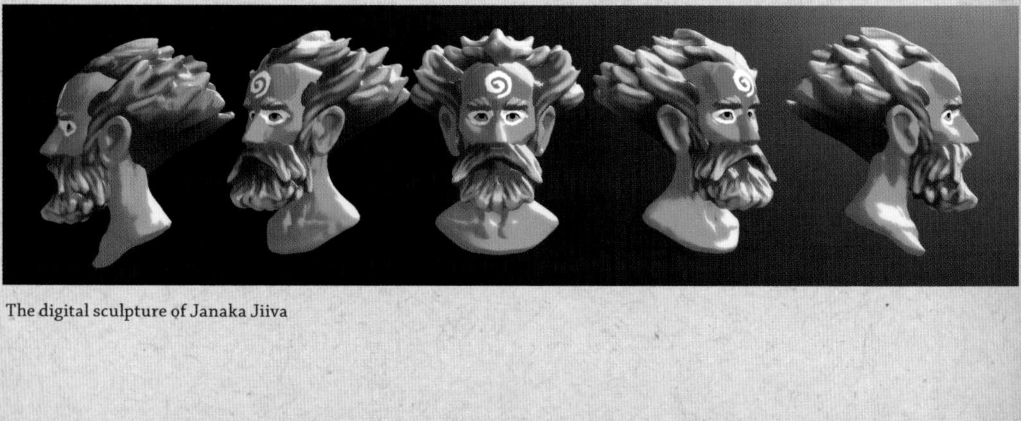

The digital sculpture of Janaka Jiiva

In the first step of the process, I would fill the background with a basic green color and then paint all the shadows of the image as a separate layer. A rough preliminary drawing would guide me on this step. In the next step (2), I would paint a second layer of even darker shadows inside the existing shadow layer. Then I would introduce the sky into the background (3), and then add several layers of haze on top of the background (4). After that I would add another layer that would only include color information for all the parts that are not foliage (5). What was created up to this point was a scene that looked like it was lit by a single diffuse light source. In the next step (6), I would duplicate the whole background and superimpose it over the image in a way that it brightens everything up, like it would look in direct sunlight. I would then use a mask on this layer to define the parts of the image that receive sunlight and those that do not. In the last step (7), I would add clouds to the sky and add haze between the different spatial layers of the background. The interesting thing about this workflow is that it moves very fast since I only work on a single aspect of the image at a time and can change the intensity of haze or the brightness of the light at any time in the process. If, for example, I'd want to later change the direction of the sunlight, I would only have to change a single layer and wouldn't have to repaint the whole background from scratch.

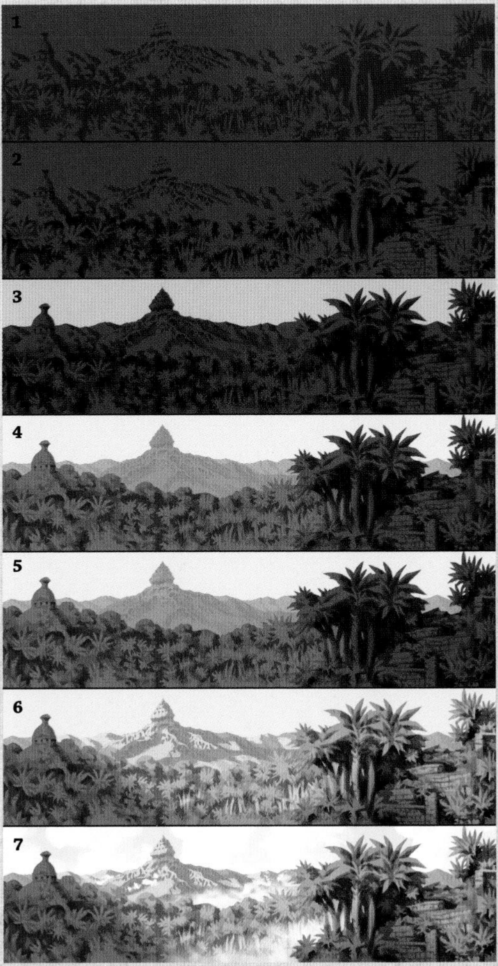

1
2
3
4
5
6
7

The different steps of my background painting workflow for the jungle scenery

The background from the example above in the final panel

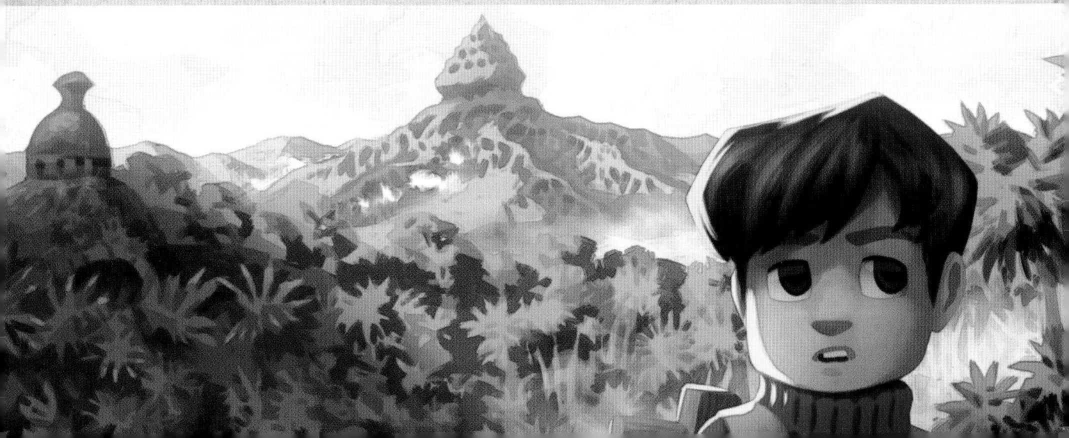

Delving Deeper into Ankal Aasha

One thing I was especially looking forward to in this book was fleshing out my vision of Ankal Aasha. The fact that the town center and Janaka's tower are situated right next to a waterfall—and that a huge part of the city is actually flooded by it—wasn't revealed in the preceding chapters. However, the waterfall and the ruined structures inside were the main feature of Ankal Aasha when I created the first visual designs as early as 2010. So the idea of the flooded city existed before the first chapter of *The Wormworld Saga* was even published.

I thought that it was a nice trick to reveal the waterfall as an eye-opener at the end of the Great Celebration. It lends a dramatic quality to the scene and serves as a symbol for the unexpected—things that blindside you when you're looking in the wrong direction. I actually would have loved to put more vistas of Ankal Aasha into the chapter, but then it would have exploded into a giant behemoth that I would never have been able to finish.

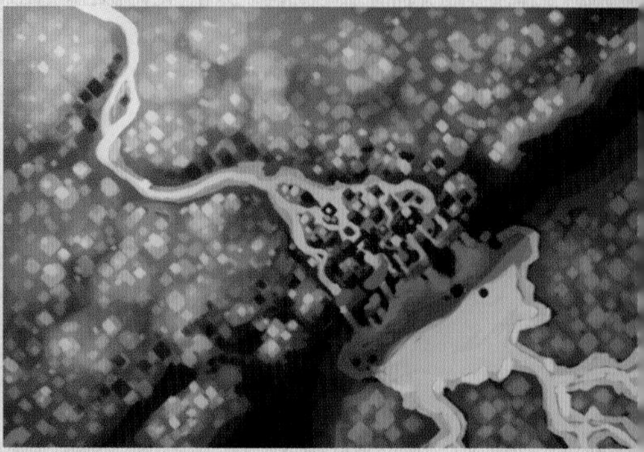

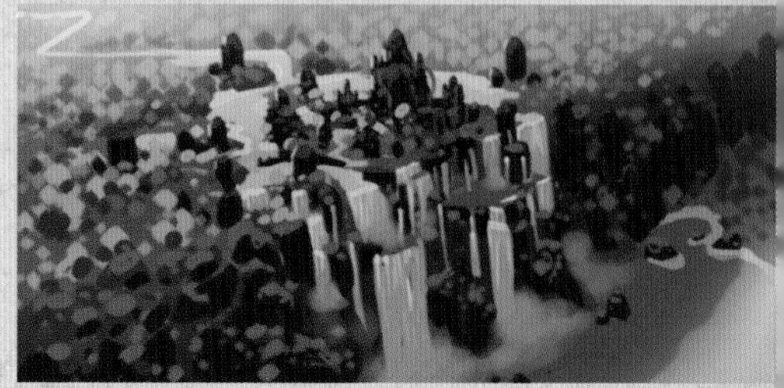

Aerial views of Ankal Aasha that show that the city was a lot smaller at first. Painted in 2010.

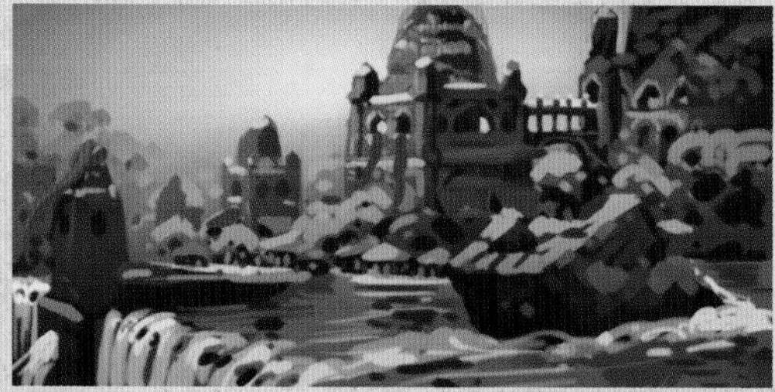

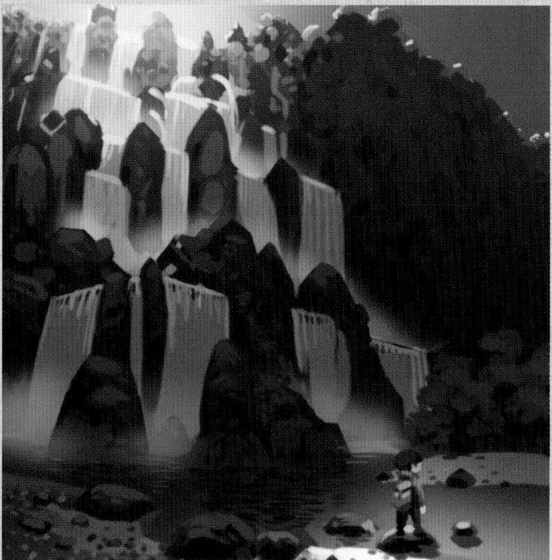

Two studies at eye level to get a feeling of the location. Painted in 2010.

Color Studies

There are basically two cases in which I will create a color study. The first is right at the beginning, when I've got nothing in my head but a very faint idea of a certain color combination or a particular composition that I can imagine as a panel of the graphic novel. This step typically comes even before I create the preliminary version of a chapter. Sometimes I use a gray scale version of some of these color studies and put them right into the preliminary version so that the process can be regarded as a pre-preliminary step. The second case in which I will create a color study is when I'm ready to paint a panel—the preliminary gray scale version being complete—but I haven't developed a color scheme yet. Developing a color scheme for an

entire scene means I have to define a set of colors that will be used throughout, to keep the look and feel of the scene consistent. For example, if Jonas's jumper has a certain color in one panel, it should have the same color in all the other panels unless the lighting changes during the scene. Since scenes often start with an establishing shot, I normally develop the color scheme for the entire scene in the first panel. However, sometimes the first panel of a new scene doesn't include all the colors of the scene (for example, in the scene after the Great Celebration where we only see a close-up of the sandy ground), and in these cases I either start my work on the scene with a different panel or I paint a color study that includes all colors of the scene. An example of the latter case would be the last scene of this book, for which I painted a color study that included all the colors of the scene (except for the colors of the characters).

Concept Design

The second chapter didn't introduce a lot of concept design work for me. Elements like the Ankal Aasha architecture and the idol

had already been designed. There are a lot of people in the second chapter, but none of them had the status of "real characters" and so they were all designed "on the fly." I had a lot of fun designing Raya's room, because, for that, I had to think about the ways the inhabitants of Ankal Aasha would have made themselves comfortable inside the ruins. I figured that the domes with their open arches on four sides weren't very cozy. So Raya closed three of the arches with rough masonry and little window openings and left only one arch open to access the balcony.

I really enjoyed designing the transport ship. My main inspiration was images from people traveling on the roofs of trains in India. The ship was introduced into the preliminary version quite late and, at first, it was just a background element in one panel to give some insight into the lifestyle of the people and the logistics of the Wormworld. However, when I saw the first sketches of it, I decided that it would be exciting to enter the ship and see more of it, so I decided that Jonas and Raya should continue their journey on the ship.

A set of color studies in which I developed scenes from the Great Celebration. The color scheme changed in the final artwork, but the basic compositions remained the same.

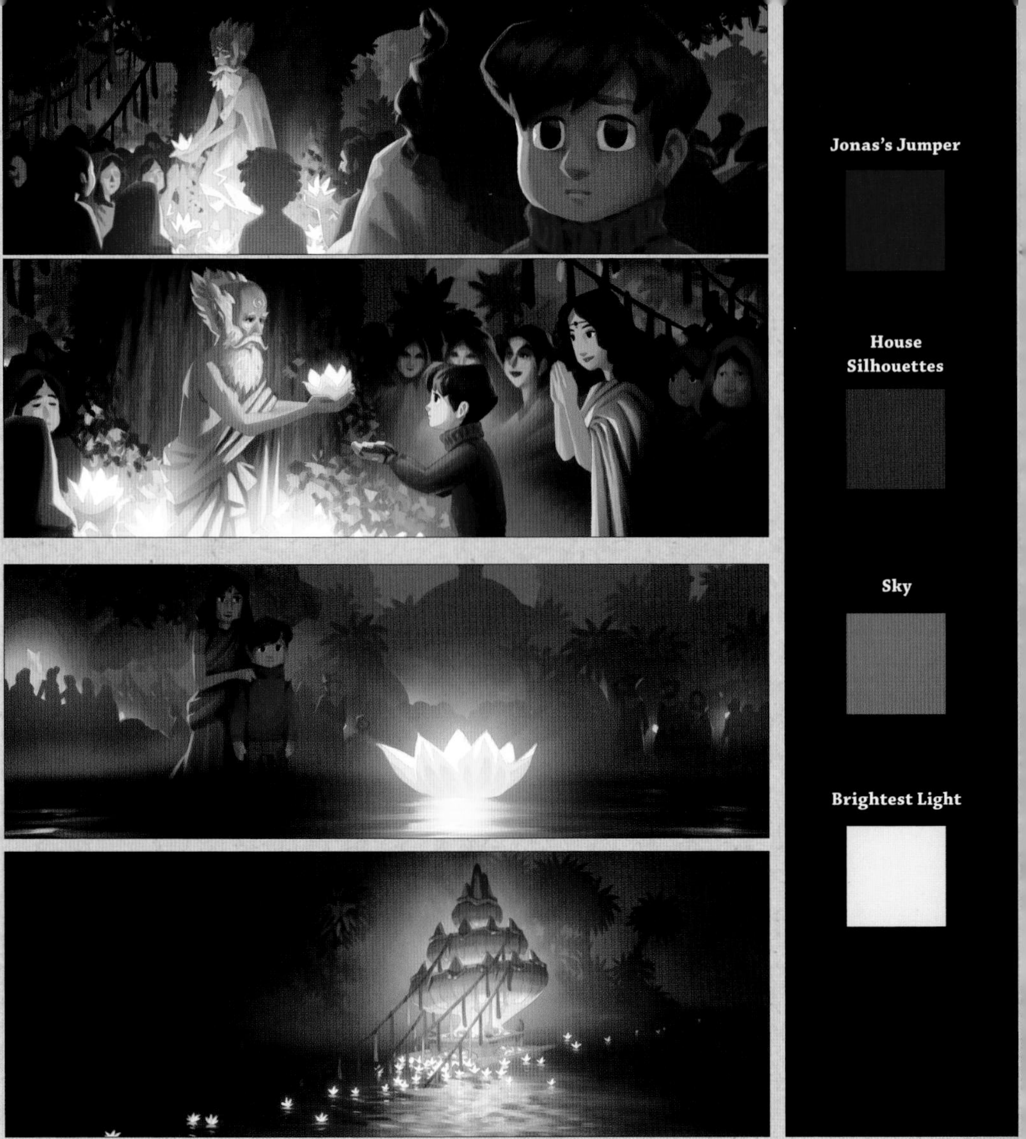
Jonas's Jumper
House Silhouettes
Sky
Brightest Light

This illustration shows some of the colors that make up the color scheme for the Great Celebration scene.

The encounter with the Scrat was originally planned to happen while Jonas and Raya were traveling in their small boat. The Scrat would have been a farmhand working near the river where Jonas would have seen him. When I decided to let Jonas and Raya board the transport ship, I simply changed the Scrat into a worker on the ship, and, that way, the encounter could be arranged much more effectively. I also used a little bit of digital sculpting for the second chapter. There were no new characters to sculpt but I had a particular problem in some of the panels in which Jonas and Raya were inside the boat. It wasn't trivial for me to imagine the proper camera angle to capture both Raya and Jonas inside the frame because Raya was standing and Jonas was sitting. That meant I had to raise the camera to look down. The perspective on this was tricky because I wasn't able to see where Raya's feet touched the ground, and, without that, it was hard to determine the right perspective for the boat. I solved the problem by building a rough digital sculpture of the two characters inside the boat and captured the framing of several shots inside the sculpting software.

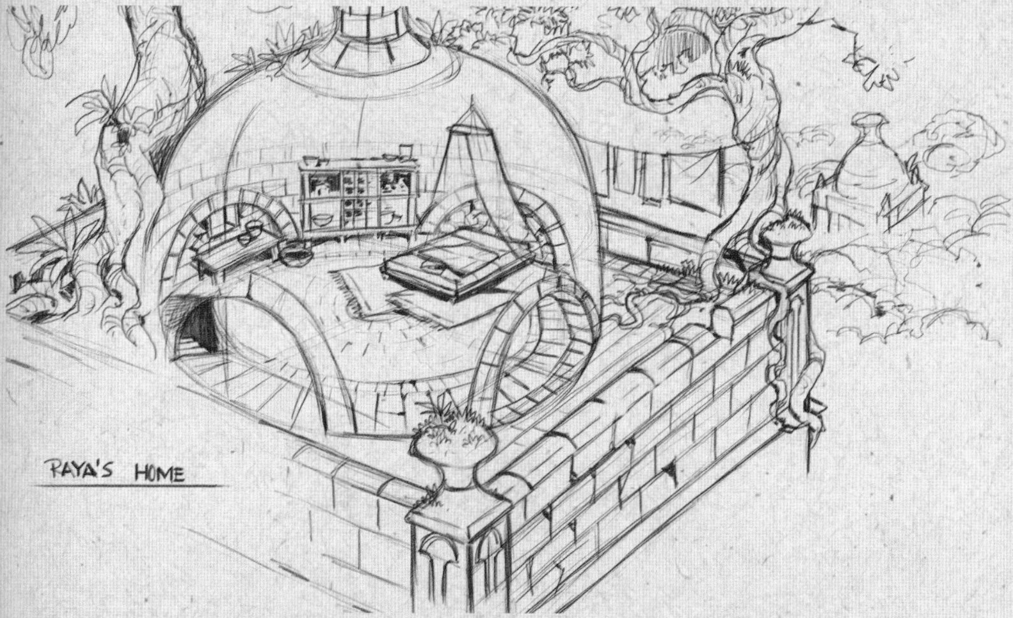
RAYA'S HOME

Sketches of Raya's home

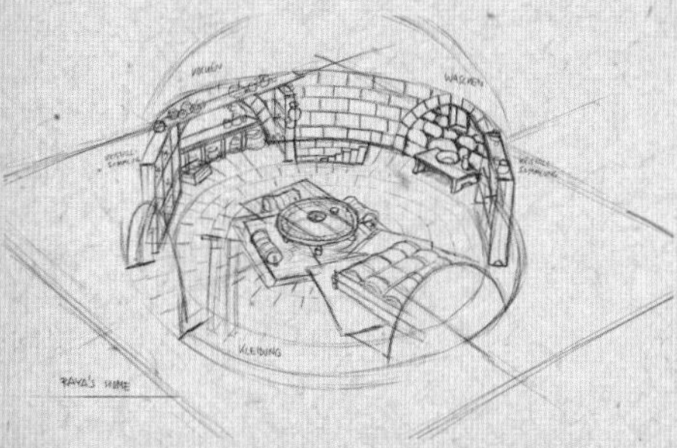

One of the panels in which I determined the right camera angle by posing a digital sculpting in ZBrush

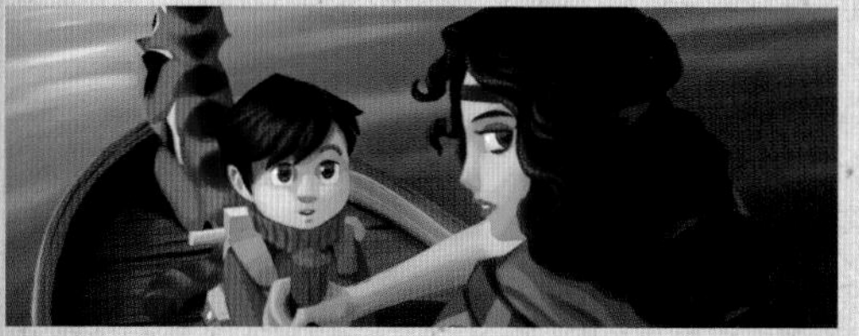

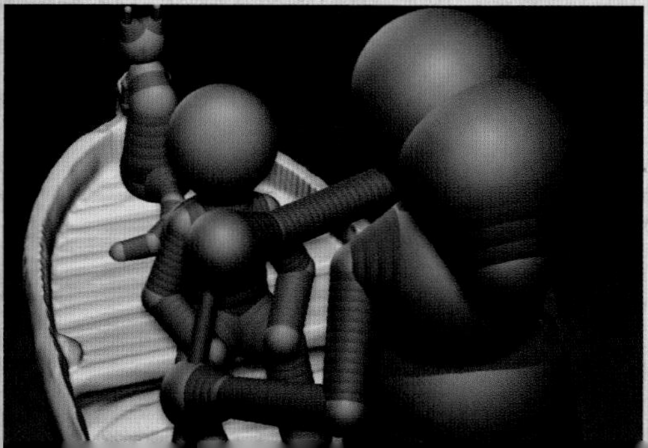

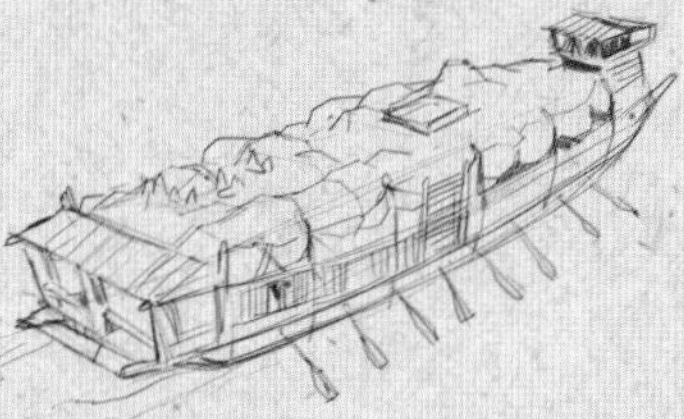

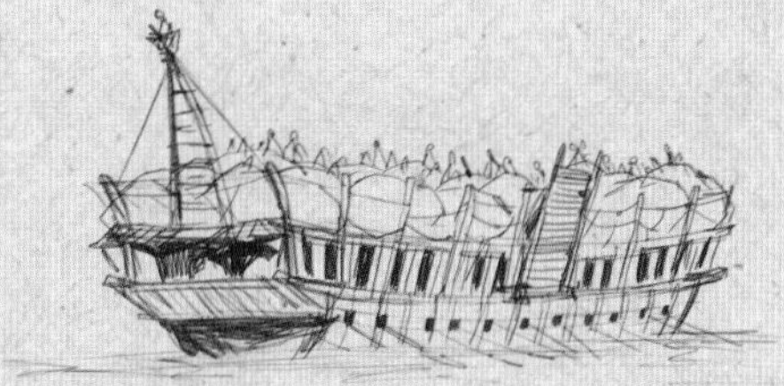

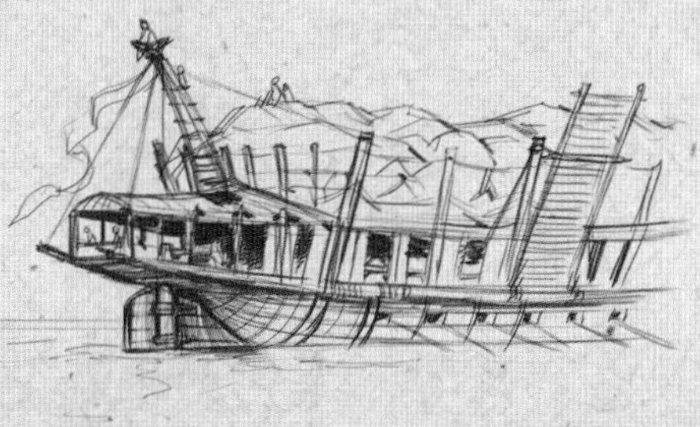

Sketches of the transport ship. I experimented a lot with the shape of the bridge.

A Timeline of the Wormworld

The Course of Things plays a central role in *The Wormworld Saga*. It actually shows the history of the Wormworld in the form of a spiraling timeline that starts at the outside of the ornament and ends at its center. It wasn't possible—let alone advisable from a storytelling standpoint—to elaborate on all the things that are depicted in Janaka's mandala inside this chapter. But here I have the opportunity to tell you a little bit more about Janaka's mysterious vision.

1 – The Age of Fire

The first age known to the people of the Wormworld was the Age of Fire when Unurtha ruled over the world.
The beginning of this age is lost to antiquity. It ends when the god of life and the gods of the elements—earth, water, and air—united against the fire god Unurtha to end his reign.

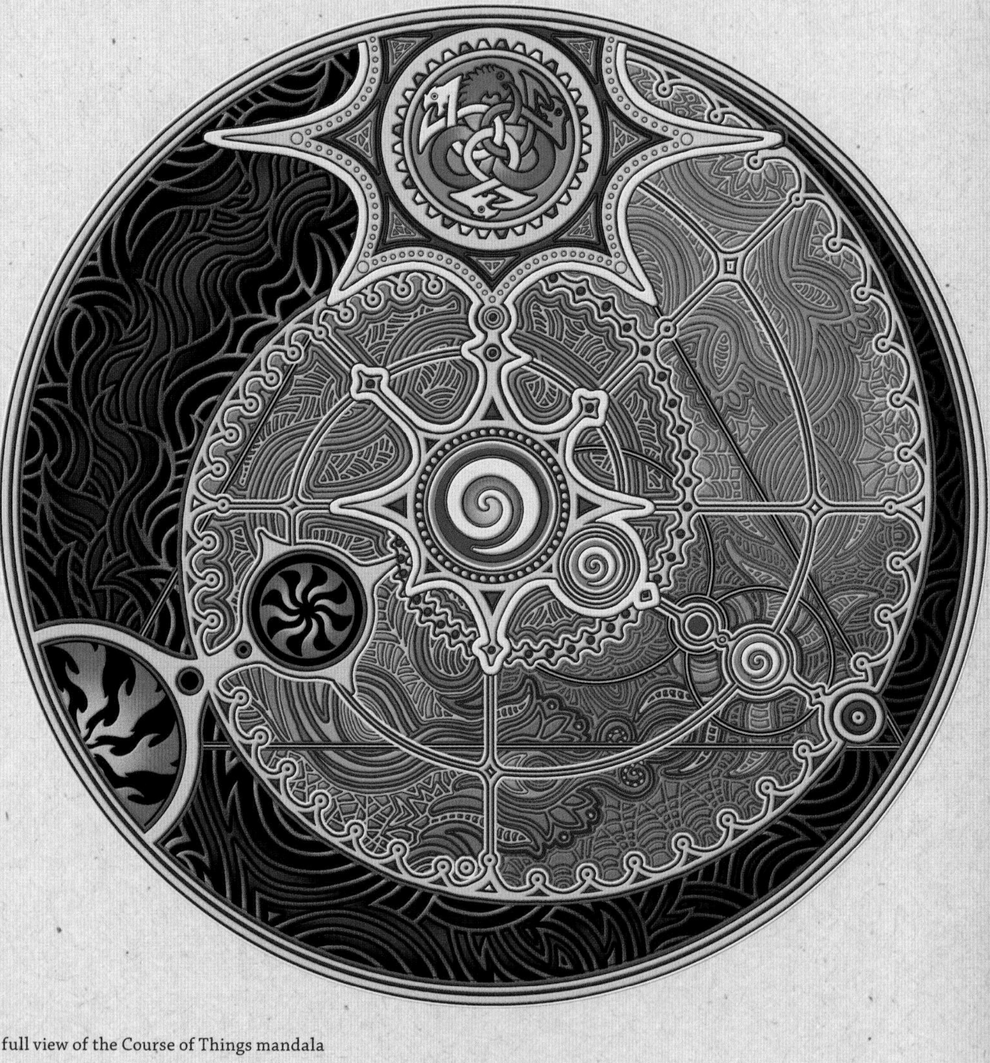

A full view of the Course of Things mandala

A rough color sketch of the Course of Things

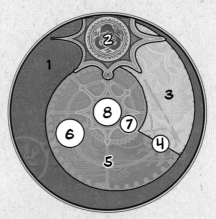

The order of the eras in the mandala

2 – The Fall of Unurtha

Unurtha was overwhelmed by the other gods and became imprisoned inside the Worm Mountain, which is also known as the Mountain of Kings. Jiiva, the god of life, endued the mountain with a magic seal, known as the Wormseal, to keep Unurtha in his prison. After the struggle, the gods were exhausted and had to rest.

3 – The Barren Age

During the struggle between Unurtha and the other gods, fire rained down from the sky. When Unurtha was at last defeated, all fires within the Wormworld ceased forever, and the settling smoke revealed a scorched world. What followed were difficult years for the people. Nature recovered slowly from Unurtha's devastating blow.

4 – The Germination of the World Root

When the major celestial bodies assumed a special order in which they were all aligned, Jiiva regained enough power to create the World Root. From that day on the World Root grew and the River of Life began to flow.

5 – The Age of the Central Kingdom

Life returned to the center of the Wormworld and the kingdoms of the mortals flourished. The King of the Center grew powerful and opposed the older kingdoms around him.

6 – The Faltering of the Wormseal

During the war between the King of the Center and the Desert Prince, the Wormseal was damaged and its magical power was diminished. Unurtha was not able to escape his prison, but he took this chance to send his dark minions into the world, with the mission to destroy the seal for good.

7 – The Champion of Life

When the celestial bodies aligned for a second time, Jiiva sent out a champion to fight against Unurtha's dark minions and to protect the Wormseal.

8 – The Day of Ressurection

Once Jiiva has fully recovered his strength, he will rise once again and herald the true era of life. Unurtha's power will be banned forever, and the people of the Wormworld will live in everlasting peace.

Daniel Lieske

Daniel Lieske was born in 1977 in Bad
Rothenfelde, a small town in Germany
situated at the edge of the Teutoburger
Forest. He began his career as a graphic novel
author at a young age by selling his early
comic creations in the schoolyard.

After school, he started to work in the
computer games industry where he learned
to draw and paint digitally. He developed his
skills for over ten years before he decided to
try his luck as an independent comic creator.

Today he lives with his wife, two sons,
and two cats in an old framework house
in Warendorf, a small town in northern
Germany.

The thought that his work is read and
appreciated all around the world still
dazzles him.